The 2020 COMMISSION REPORT

on the

NORTH KOREAN
NUCLEAR ATTACKS

Against

THE UNITED STATES

A SPECULATIVE NOVEL

The 2020 COMMISSION REPORT

on the

NORTH KOREAN

NUCLEAR ATTACKS

Against

THE UNITED STATES

A SPECULATIVE NOVEL

Dr JEFFREY LEWIS

WH
ALLEN

5 7 9 10 8 6

WH Allen, an imprint of Ebury Publishing,
20 Vauxhall Bridge Road,
London SW1V 2SA

WH Allen is part of the Penguin Random House group of companies
whose addresses can be found at global.penguinrandomhouse.com

Penguin
Random House
UK

First published in the United Kingdom by WH Allen in 2018

First published in the United States by
Houghton Mifflin Harcourt in 2018

www.penguin.co.uk

A CIP catalogue record for this book is available from the British
Library

ISBN 9780753553169

Printed and bound in Great Britain by Clays Ltd, Elcograf S.p.A.

Penguin Random House is committed to a sustainable future for our
business, our readers and our planet. This book is made from Forest
Stewardship Council® certified paper.

CONTENTS

PREFACE

THE EVENTS OF MARCH 2020 represent the greatest calamity in our nation's history. It is impossible for any of us to forget the scenes of horror and devastation, first in Korea and Japan, then in Hawaii, New York, northern Virginia, and south Florida. We present this final report and the recommendations that flow from it mindful that our nation is more divided than ever before, particularly over the question of responsibility for the chain of events that led to the first use of nuclear weapons in more than eight decades—and their first use against the United States of America.

Unlike any previous adversary in our history, North Korea waged a nuclear war against the United States and its allies. Although our forces prevailed, the scale of the destruction was unprecedented. We lost almost a million and a half of our fellow citizens that day.

As a result, Congress and the president established the Commission on the North Korean Nuclear Attacks Against the United States (Public Law 117-321), commonly called the 2020 Commission, "to find and report the relevant facts leading to the attacks using nuclear weapons made by Democratic People's Republic of Korea upon the United States and its allies on March 22–24, 2020." We, the members of this commission, established our offices at the Mount Weather Emergency Operations Center in rural Virginia so that our project could be co-located with the vast majority of government functions, which had to be relocated here to avoid interfering with reconstruction efforts in northern Virginia. We also established smaller satellite offices in Washington, DC; at Site R in rural Pennsylvania, where the Defense Department's National Military Command Center is currently located; and at the Emergency Operations Center in Albany, New York.

Our mandate was a broad one: to investigate how the nuclear war began, whether our emergency preparedness efforts were sufficient, and whether our government understood North Korean views about nuclear weapons and was adequately prepared for combating a nuclear adversary.

In hindsight, we can see that the crisis that brought us into nuclear conflict with North Korea was many years in the making. Examining the period leading up to the events of March 2020 is difficult, as the nuclear attacks against the United States have further deepened the partisan divisions in our country. For the most part, this commission has elected to focus on the events of the four days in March during which the attacks took place rather than to engage in the broader questions of the impact of US policy toward the Korean Peninsula since 1948.

We do not seek to assign blame for the tragic events of

March 2020, but merely to provide an impartial, thorough, independent, and nonpartisan account of the events leading to the calamity. Over the course of our investigation, we held twenty-two days of hearings and took public testimony from almost two hundred survivors in Hawaii, Florida, New York, and Virginia. We were given access to a substantial number of government documents, a portion of which were declassified for use in this report. We have also had the opportunity to interview former regime officials from the now-defunct North Korean government, as well as survivors from Seoul, Tokyo, Busan, and elsewhere. Their voices and others fill these pages, standing in for the millions of others who were forever silenced by the horrors of nuclear war.

We were asked many questions in the course of our work: What disagreement between South and North Korea was worth exposing American citizens to a nuclear attack? Were failures in diplomatic efforts over the years to blame for the crisis? Did our military and intelligence leaders take appropriate steps to respond to and prepare for the emerging threat of North Korea's nuclear and missile programs? Why did the missile defenses that were supposed to protect our homeland fail? And what more might the federal government, as well as states and municipalities, have done to improve our emergency preparedness?

We would be remiss, however, if we did not note the one question that, to our surprise, was asked far more frequently than any other at our public hearings and to which we cannot agree on an answer. The single question that we were asked most often was a deceptively simple one: Should the United States seek to reduce nuclear dangers and ultimately eliminate these weapons? While some commissioners believe that the devastation of the nuclear attacks showed the importance of taking additional steps to reduce nuclear dangers and ultimately eliminate these weapons, others believe that the events of March 2020 demonstrated the continuing need to prepare to fight and win nuclear wars against future foes. As reasonable people of goodwill can differ on such an undoubtedly important question, we offer no consensus recommendation on it.

Mount Weather Emergency Operations Center
Berryville, VA
May 1, 2023

1

THE SHOOTDOWN OF BX 411

THE SKIES OVER THE Korean Peninsula on March 21, 2020, were clear and blue. None of the 228 passengers who boarded Air Busan (BX) 411 at Gimhae International Airport in Busan, South Korea, had any reason to expect an eventful flight.

The boarding process was slow. Of the passengers on BX 411, 102 were schoolchildren—students from a Busan secondary school that sponsored an international exchange program with a sister school in Mongolia. Witnesses at the departure terminal at Gimhae Airport recalled the children as a gleeful and excited bunch. For most, this was the first time they had traveled outside of South Korea, and even for the lucky few who had, Mongolia was an unusual and exotic destination. They had shared their wonder and enthusiasm for the adventure in texts and photographs posted on social media channels like Snow, the Korean video messaging app, where they joked about sleeping in yurts and riding horses.

The crew worked hard to settle the students into their seats, but despite the slow boarding, the flight took off from Busan on time, at 11:10 AM. It was scheduled to land in Ulan Bator two hours later.

The flight plan that the crew of Air Busan Flight 411 filed was typical for the route from Busan to Ulan Bator. The aircraft would take off from Gimhae International Airport, heading northwest. Once the aircraft was at cruising altitude, it would turn west to follow the typical flight corridor over the Yellow Sea, through China, and on into Mongolia.

This flight path would bring the aircraft within 25 miles of North Korea—well within range of North Korea's most sophisticated air defense missiles. But that wasn't uncommon for commercial aircraft. US and South Korean military aircraft typically followed protocols near the demilitarized zone (DMZ) that helped avoid the possibility of making a tragic mistake. Passenger jets that followed their flight plan could expect to pass near North Korean airspace in safety. Air Busan had flown this same flight plan day after day, week after week, year after year, without incident.

A LOUD *CLUNK*

The trouble started shortly after Flight 411 leveled off at 34,000 feet. At 11:52 AM, the crew heard a loud *clunk* and all the navigation screens went dark. "Oh," said one of the pilots, loudly enough for her exclamation to be captured on the cockpit voice recorder. She attempted to transmit a Mayday call on the aircraft's very high frequency (VHF) radio, but the radio had no power. Air traffic control (ATC) did not receive the signal.

The technical malfunction that afflicted Flight 411 was a well-known bug found in the Airbus A320 model that Air Busan used for this route that day. In the years prior to 2020, the Federal Aviation Administration (FAA) in the United States and aviation regulators in Europe had observed that A320 sometimes suffered a loss of power in the cockpit. Indeed, the failure on board BX 411 looked very much like a series of previous incidents (none of which, it must be noted, resulted in any fatalities). For instance, on October 22, 2005, a British Airways A319 flight from London Heathrow Airport to Budapest, Hungary, suffered a similar problem: as the airplane climbed through 20,000 feet, five out of its six flight displays went blank and the autopilot disconnected. The VHF radio and intercom stopped working, and most of the lights went out in the cockpit. In January 2008, a United Airlines flight from Newark to Denver suffered a nearly identical failure.

Following the 2008 incident, the FAA issued a 2010 order that gave US airlines four years to deal with this issue by modifying any Airbus aircraft in their fleets. The FAA's European counterpart issued a similar regulation in 2009. South Korean regulators did not. Even if stronger regulations had been in place, however, they probably would not have saved BX 411. At least four such incidents had occurred in the United States *after* the FAA directive was issued in 2010.

Airbus strongly denied responsibility for the outcome of this particular incident. The company's director of flight operations explained that electrical failures are common in all makes of jet aircraft, and he noted that the Airbus 320 has backup systems in place to effectively address power loss in the cockpit. Airbus officials also noted that, although this problem has occurred frequently in the A320 model, there had not been a single fatality prior to the events of March 2020. "The loss of the BX 411 was the result of the actions of North Korean air defenses," a company spokesperson told investigators, "not the temporary power loss in the aircraft cockpit which for most systems lasted less than two minutes."

The company's statement is technically accurate. Judging by the timing of the next radio transmission from Flight 411 to South Korean air traffic control, the pilot and copilot of Air Busan Flight 411 were able to restore power to most affected systems in about two minutes. But a few other systems took longer. As in other such incidents, it took about six minutes for the pilot and copilot to bring all systems back on line, after which the aircraft was operating normally.

During this period, the aircraft was flying at 400 miles per hour. Over the course of those six minutes, it traveled more than 50 miles. As crucial minutes ticked away, the aircraft missed its turn west and continued on a northwest route, heading north past Seoul and toward the DMZ separating North and South Korea. When the pilot realized that the aircraft was rapidly approaching North Korean airspace, she radioed air traffic control and was told to turn the aircraft westward and follow a path out to the Yellow Sea. As in other cases of temporary electrical failures, the captain made the decision to continue toward her destination, expecting that her westward turn would bring her back onto the original flight path to Ulan Bator.

The captain, Chung Jae Eun, has been criticized for continuing the flight, but her decision was not unusual. Other commercial pilots had made similar decisions with no adverse outcomes, including the captain of the stricken Airbus A320 flying from London to Budapest in 2005, who completed that flight as planned despite the problems with the aircraft's flight displays, radio, cockpit lights, and other affected systems. While air traffic control had ordered Flight 411 to turn west to avoid North Korean airspace, controllers did not require Captain Chung to further alter her flight plan. Had another factor not intervened, the 228 passengers aboard BX 411 probably would have landed safely in Ulan Bator a few hours later.

RATTLING THE POTS AND PANS

But there *was* another factor—one that until now has remained largely classified. It was publicly known that the United States and South Korea were holding the annual FOAL EAGLE/ KEY RESOLVE military exercise. North Korea routinely objected to such exercises because the massing of an enormous number of forces in South Korea for the exercises was indistinguishable, from a North Korean point of view, from preparations for an invasion. The North Korean military was therefore on edge and alert to any provocation.

But unbeknownst to most political and military leaders, not to mention South Korea's civil aviation industry, in the months preceding the events of March 2020 the United States had initiated a covert program of air and naval probes as part of an extensive psychological operations campaign against the regime of North Korean dictator Kim Jong Un. In the final year of this commission's investigations, press reports have described a broad program of psychological operations (PSYOP) initiated by the Trump administration late in 2019, after the collapse of the diplomatic thaw that had begun with North Korea's participation in the Pyeongchang 2018 Olympic Winter Games. The commission has been asked specifically to investigate the role these operations may have played as a contributing factor in North Korea's shootdown of BX 411 and, more generally, the nuclear exchange that followed.

The commission was given access to a number of classified documents concerning these covert US programs, and we have also had the opportunity to conduct extensive interviews with former officials who served in the Trump administration. In doing so, our primary goal has been to understand the role these operations may have had in shaping the subsequent decisions made by Kim Jong Un. While many aspects of these programs remain classified, they have been broadly described in the press, and some key details have been declassified to allow the public to understand how these operations may have contributed to the shootdown of Air Busan Flight 411 and the chain of events that followed.

This campaign comprised various air and naval efforts, the most consequential of which appears to have been an operation undertaken by the US Air Force. Known internally within the US government as SCATHE JIGSAW, this operation used bomber flights to systematically probe North Korean air defenses. According to documents provided to the commission and interviews with participants, the United States conducted twelve bomber missions under SCATHE JIGSAW to collect data on North Korean air defense capabilities and convey US resolve to Kim Jong Un. These missions are summarized in Table 1.

TABLE 1. SCATHE JIGSAW BOMBER FLIGHTS

NUMBER	DATE	NUMBER OF AIRCRAFT	TYPE OF AIRCRAFT	ORIGIN
1	December 7, 2019	3	B-1B	Andersen AFB (Guam)
2	December 18, 2019	6	B-1B, B-2, B-52	Andersen AFB (Guam), Whiteman AFB (CONUS), Kadena AFB (Okinawa)
3	December 25, 2019	3	B-1B	Andersen AFB
4	January 8, 2020	1	B-2	Whiteman AFB
5	January 10, 2020	4	B-1B, B-2	Andersen AFB
6	January 24, 2020	2	B-1B	Andersen AFB
7	January 26, 2020	2	B-2	Whiteman AFB

| 8 | February 8, 2020 | 3 | B-2 | Whiteman AFB |

TABLE 1. SCATHE JIGSAW BOMBER FLIGHTS

9	February 18, 2020	4	B-1B	Andersen AFB
10	February 29, 2020	2	B-2	Whiteman AFB
11	March 6, 2020	1	B-1B	Andersen AFB
12	March 12, 2020	3	B-1B	Andersen AFB

Pentagon officials developed SCATHE JIGSAW on the basis of a Reagan-era program of psychological operations initiated to strengthen deterrence against Moscow. "It really got to the Soviets," is how one official explained the earlier program. "They had no idea what it all meant. Bombers would fly straight at Soviet airspace, forcing them to turn on their radars and put aircraft on alert. At the last minute, the bombers would peel off and fly home."

Similar psychological tactics, officials believed, would be effective against North Korea and, specifically, its young leader, Kim Jong Un. This conclusion reflected a broader consensus within the US intelligence community that Kim Jong Un was rational and could be deterred. American policy toward North Korea had been guided by this idea in the years leading up to the 2018 thaw, leading officials to propose aggressive measures to keep Kim in check. With the collapse of diplomatic efforts between the United States and North Korea, the president's advisers returned to proposals for forceful methods to address North Korea's growing nuclear and missile capabilities.

SCATHE JIGSAW was among the less aggressive proposals considered by the Trump administration for combating the challenge presented by North Korea. One faction, including former national security adviser John Bolton and speechwriter Stephen Miller, favored what some have called a "punch in the nose" or a "bloody nose"—a limited military strike to destroy a North Korean facility related to its missile program. (White House officials strenuously denied using either term. "The phrase has never, ever been uttered by anyone in the White House," said one former administration official involved in Asia policy.) The other faction feared that North Korea would respond to such a strike with disproportionate force, creating a dangerous dynamic that could lead to rapid and uncontrollable escalation between the two sides. These officials proposed a psychological operations campaign as a less volatile, less public option—one aimed at frightening Kim Jong Un without forcing him to retaliate.

The implications of this tactic do not seem to have been fully thought through by the officials who suggested it. According to one former Pentagon official, the original purpose behind the proposal for psychological operations was to dampen talk about a military strike within the White House. "You can't beat something with nothing," she explained. "The purpose of the psychological operations was to have a strong containment alternative to the military strike that Bolton kept pushing." The proposal garnered widespread support within the Trump administration after it became evident that the main alternative—the so-called punch in the nose—carried even greater risks.

The White House, in a National Security Council (NSC) meeting on November 18, 2019, directed the Air Force to develop a psychological operations campaign against North Korea that would include air probes near and along the North Korean border. The program that the Air Force developed consisted of frequent but irregularly timed bomber flights in which small numbers of American aircraft would fly directly at North Korean airspace, forcing North Korean units to turn on their radars and aircraft to go on alert. Administration officials pointed to a tweet sent by President Trump as confirming, in a general way, the initiation of psychological operations.

Donald J. Trump @tehDonaldJTrump
If China doesn't get little Rocket Man under control, we're going to start RATTLING THE POTS AND PANS.

After the tweet, officials inside the White House began calling the campaign "Pots and Pans." The term appears to have originated with Secretary of Defense James Mattis. "The idea was to take the Reagan plan," one official testified, "and to do the same thing to Kim Jong Un. Mattis said we should 'rattle our pots and pans' to frighten Kim and show the Chinese we mean business. The president just kind of tweeted that, verbatim."

It is important to note that there are differences between how the Pentagon and the White House saw SCATHE JIGSAW. In Air Force documents, the effort is described as a "ferret" mission to map North Korean radar sites and determine the readiness of North Korean air defense units. Such missions had been flown routinely during the early part of the Cold War, until they were suspended following a 1969 incident in which a US reconnaissance aircraft was shot down by North Korean MiG fighter jets.

The emails and text messages of White House officials suggest, however, that for them the more important goal of SCATHE JIGSAW was to unsettle Kim Jong Un and his military leaders. A secondary objective was to persuade leaders in Beijing that a failure to resolve the crisis on the Korean Peninsula might result in a military conflict. The guidance to the Air Force provided by the White House, under Bolton's signature, makes only passing reference to the military value of intelligence gained from such missions and describes the option nearly exclusively in terms of the impact it might have on Kim and other North Korean leaders. The guidance directs the Air Force to develop a plan to "deliver the message of war" to leaders in Pyongyang and Beijing and take steps to "win the battlefield of perception." A clearer statement of the purpose of this effort is written in the margins of a draft copy of the order, retained by Bolton: "PRESIDENT SAYS KNOCK SOME SENSE INTO THAT FAT CRAZY KID."

White House and Pentagon officials were unanimous in their belief that the psychological operations campaign against the Soviets had been successful in frightening Soviet leaders, who had subsequently acted far more cautiously, and that it would similarly prove a workable approach for the current standoff with North Korea. In advocating for this tactic, Secretary of Defense Mattis sided with those officials in the administration who believed the bomber flights to be less provocative than the "bloody nose" approach.

Yet this course of action also contained certain dangers that, by now, are obvious. Specifically, the White House was directly warned that previous psychological operations had resulted in the loss of both military and civilian aircraft and ships. A classified "memo to holders"—prepared by the Central Intelligence Agency (CIA) in response to a White House inquiry about the consequences of this possible course of action with regard to North Korea—noted that past efforts had carried significant risks:

```
WE ASSESS THAT A ROBUST PSYOP CAMPAIGN
CARRIES SOME RISK OF ESCALATION BASED ON PAST
EXPERIENCE WITH SUCH MISSIONS. NORTH KOREA
SEIZED A US INTELLIGENCE GATHERING VESSEL
IN 1968 AND SHOT DOWN A US RECONNAISSANCE
AIRCRAFT IN 1969. THE REAGAN-ERA EFFORT
TO PROBE SOVIET AIR DEFENSES WAS ALSO A
SIGNIFICANT FACTOR IN THE SOVIET SHOOTDOWN OF
KAL 007 IN 1983, WHICH TRIGGERED THE WORST
```

SUPERPOWER CONFRONTATION SINCE THE CUBAN
MISSILE CRISIS.

Perhaps because of this warning, the White House decided that the psychological operations campaign was best conducted in secret, and staff took unusual measures to guard against further leaks, such as the president's tweet. "The idea was to keep 'Pots and Pans' limited to a small circle," one of Bolton's aides explained. "Only the core staff at the White House and Mattis's people executing it would know about the program, along with the Chinese and North Koreans, of course." White House officials discussed whether to approach civil maritime and aviation authorities about altering air and sea routes, but decided not to do anything that might result in the public disclosure of SCATHE JIGSAW. Moreover, the Trump administration chose not to notify South Korean authorities about the full extent of the program, although the South Koreans understood generally that the additional flights through their airspace were part of a more aggressive American military posture.

"The whole point of the campaign was that it was supposed to be a secret," one adviser explained. "If you start approaching shipping companies and airlines, then it will be in the paper the next day and Kim will be forced to respond."

It is unclear how many senior officials knew about this program. There are references in the emails of half a dozen White House staff members, including National Security Adviser

Bolton. More ambiguous references appear in emails and text messages among a larger group that mention "Ivanka's new line of kitchenware," which one official claimed was a tongue-in-cheek reference to SCATHE JIGSAW. The program was sizable enough, and Trump's tweet drew enough attention, that many officials believed that word of it must have spread around the White House.

In the roughly four months that elapsed between the NSC meeting on November 18, 2019, and the BX 411 episode on March 21, 2020, the Air Force conducted a series of SCATHE JIGSAW sorties without incident. In general, the missions had the same profile, one similar to that of the Reagan-era program that inspired them. A small number of aircraft would directly approach North Korean airspace in a manner that appeared to be a bombing run against a location in North Korea that was considered high-value, usually either a military site or a leadership compound. This would force North Korean air defense units to turn on their radars and pilots to scramble to aircraft, as well as initiate a general alert that went up to the highest echelons of the North Korean command. At the last moment before entering North Korean airspace, the US aircraft would turn around and head home. The United States could, in this way, probe North Korea's air defenses for weaknesses, while also conveying to Kim Jong Un and his lieutenants that he was vulnerable to attack.

Trump administration officials were adamant that the bomber flights in SCATHE JIGSAW were an evolution of previous missions begun under Presidents George W. Bush and

Barack Obama. The US Air Force had established a "continuous bomber presence" mission at Andersen Air Force Base on Guam in 2004 during the Global War on Terror. The goal was to ensure that the United States always maintained a significant number of bomber aircraft capable of conducting exercises in Asia on short notice to demonstrate that the United States remained instantly willing and able to conduct bomber strikes anywhere in the region.

In particular, Trump administration officials made frequent references to former President Obama and former secretary of state Hillary Clinton. "You are blaming us," said one official, "but Obama did it all the time. He had dozens of bomber flights." Another claimed, "This was Hillary Clinton's brainchild."

In fact, the number of bomber flights around the Korean Peninsula remained relatively consistent through 2016. What changed following North Korea's January 2013 nuclear test was the public prominence given to routine bomber exercises. After North Korea's 2013 test, the Department of Defense developed a program to highlight ongoing training that might strengthen deterrence on the Korean Peninsula. This work fell to the Joint Information Operations Warfare Center (JIOWC) at Lackland Air Force Base near San Antonio, which is responsible for assisting US military commanders around the world with developing what JIOWC called an "integrated approach to information operations." JIOWC worked with US Forces Korea, US Pacific Command (PACOM), Air Force Global Strike Command, and US Strategic Command (STRATCOM) to develop an information operations strategy.

As a result, the United States began to publicize bomber flights following North Korean nuclear and missile tests. Pentagon officials highlighted a series of three flights involving B-1 and B-52 bombers in March 2013. Again, in 2016, the Obama administration publicized three more flights—one in January following the nuclear explosive test, and another two following the September 2016 nuclear explosion.

The number of bomber flights increased in number only after the Trump administration took office, with twelve publicly announced flights taking place in 2017. The number of flights fell during the thaw in 2018, before increasing to eighteen in 2019 as tensions returned. Moreover, the profile of these flights changed. Starting in 2017, operations were in some cases conducted at night and much farther north than US aircraft had operated in decades. (Prior to 2017, US aircraft tended to stay south of the DMZ rather than flying north into the international airspace between the Korean Peninsula and Japan.) These activities occurred within full view of North Korean radars.

Moreover, the mission profile of the bomber flights in the SCATHE JIGSAW air probes differed considerably from even the more aggressive bomber missions begun during 2017. The more aggressive flight plans reflected a sense that the United States needed to make an impression upon North Korea's leadership. "There had been so many bomber flights already,"

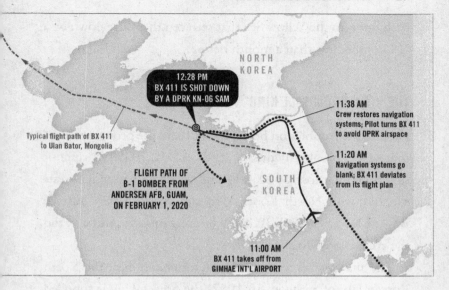

one administration official explained. "We wanted something new that would get [Kim Jong Un's] attention."

In most SCATHE JIGSAW missions, the bomber would fly toward North Korea, turning around at the last moment before entering North Korean airspace. In a smaller number of cases, bombers would fly along the *edge* of North Korea's airspace, dipping in and out of radar contact. The eleventh mission, on March 6, 2020, was one of these. A US bomber from Guam flew northward over South Korea. As the bomber approached the DMZ, the pilot banked to the west, flying out over the Yellow Sea, along the very edge of North Korea's airspace.

It was Air Busan's bad luck that, on March 21, 2020, its crew, working to restore power to the ailing electrical systems, banked hard to avoid flying into North Korea, then followed a path out into the Yellow Sea that retraced the route flown by a US bomber less than a month before.

THE VIEW FROM TALL KING

Despite the troubles on board BX 411 and the provocative nature of US bomber flights under SCATHE JIGSAW, responsibility for the loss of BX 411 and all of its passengers rests squarely with North Korea. Why did North Korea mistake BX 411 for a SCATHE JIGSAW bomber mission, and why did the crew choose to shoot it down?

The answer may rest atop a high mountain, near the North Korean city of Sariwon. In 1987, the Soviet Union supplied the Democratic People's Republic of Korea (DPRK) with two batteries of SA-5 Gammon long-range surface-to-air missiles (SAMs). Each of these batteries came equipped with a P14 TALL KING radar. It was these two radars—one atop the mountain near Sariwon and the other situated to the east, near Wonsan—that provided the primary means by which North Korea detected aircraft approaching its airspace. Communications intercepts made available by the Department of Defense indicate that it was the TALL KING radar that first saw BX 411 approaching North Korea.

The view from the TALL KING radar was limited. What the radar operators saw was a blip on a screen—in this case, an aircraft flying without a transponder and traveling along a path that resembled that of a previous bomber flight.

Communications intercepts show that the TALL KING radar near Sariwon detected BX 411 just as the electrical problems began. At around 11:50 AM, the commander of the SA-5 missile unit placed a call to the sector commander to report a strange apparition on the TALL KING screen.

SA-5 UNIT: Track 37, unknown.

SA-5 UNIT: Bearing 3-3-0, north.

SECTOR COMMANDER: Can you identify it?

SA-5 UNIT: Transponder off. Looks like another American bomber.

SECTOR COMMANDER: Okay. I'll send it up.

The detection was noted and passed up the chain of command. Communications intercepts show that the sector commander promptly contacted the Korean People's Army (KPA) Air and Anti-Air Force, headquartered in Chunghwa. For SCATHE JIGSAW flights, the protocol in place required the duty officer at Chunghwa to put the sector commander in direct communication with the commander of the Air Force. But at this moment, shortly before noon on March 21, the commander was not available, so one of his subordinates took the telephone call instead.

SECTOR COMMANDER: Tell the boss we have another one.

ANTI-AIR COMMAND: He's asleep.

SECTOR COMMANDER: It's the morning. You might want to wake him up.

ANTI-AIR COMMAND: He had , . . a meeting. It went late. He took a pill.

SECTOR COMMANDER: Okay.

ANTI-AIR COMMAND: Don't shoot unless it comes into our airspace.

SECTOR COMMANDER: Okay, we'll shoot if it comes in our airspace.

The order handed down to the SA-5 unit from Chunghwa reflected standing orders to shoot down foreign aircraft that entered DPRK without permission. In 1994, when a US helicopter strayed into DPRK airspace, the North Koreans shot it down. Until now, none of the US bomber missions had crossed this threshold—but clearly Kim's air commanders were on alert for such an incursion.

As the aircraft turned westward, the SA-5 unit handed tracking of the target over to another missile unit, this one deployed near the city of Ongjin. The crew of this unit was inexperienced. They had been deployed with a brand-new system, which the North Koreans called the Pongae-5 surface-to-air missile. One member of the crew, Roh Pyong-ui, was captured as a POW and subsequently debriefed. "It was the first time we had seen such a target in real life," Roh said. "It looked just like training."

Within the US intelligence community, the Pongae-5 SAM was known as the KN-06. North Korea had begun development on it in 2009, but that effort was plagued with problems, as were the attempts to construct the missile's accompanying radar and engagement software. When North Korea announced mass production of the KN-06 in May 2017 — "to be deployed all over the country like forests" — North Korean state media openly referenced the "defects" that had slowed its development.

As a consequence of the delays in the missile system's development, the KN-06 unit that now took over the tracking of BX 411 had only begun training with the new system in February 2020, just after the lunar new year. This training was cut short following the eleventh and penultimate SCATHE JIGSAW bomber flight on March 6, at which point military authorities rushed the KN-06 unit to Ongjin.

The deployment of the unit seems to have been part of a general repositioning of North Korean air defenses using a limited number of KN-06 batteries. Following the initiation of SCATHE JIGSAW, North Korea probably repositioned the units to prevent their locations from being compromised by air probes. A minority within the US intelligence community believed that North Korea was positioning KN-06 units to improve the chances of shooting down an American aircraft.

But in either case, the pressure on the inexperienced crew of the KN-06 unit near Ongjin explains why they behaved as they did in the crucial minutes that followed their acquisition of the unidentified target. The sector commander made contact with the unit, passing along identifying information about the target and reiterating the standing order to shoot down any American aircraft that crossed into North Korean airspace.

Communications intercepts show that the call, by radio, was hurried and brief:

SECTOR COMMANDER: American bomber coming into your sector, heading 275 degrees.

KN-06 UNIT: Okay, shoot it?

SECTOR COMMANDER: If you see it cross, shoot it.

KN-06 UNIT: Okay, if we see it, we will shoot it.

SECTOR COMMANDER: If it crosses. Don't lose it.

KN-06 UNIT: Okay. We won't.

The original Korean transcript leaves some doubt about whether the KN-06 crew understood that the order was a reiteration of a standing order to shoot aircraft that entered DPRK airspace without permission, or whether the crew believed that it was being told by the sector commander that BX 411 had *already* violated North Korean airspace and should be shot down if an opportunity presented itself. What *is* certain is that the KN-06 had a FLAP LID tracking and engagement radar that provided little information to the missile's operators about what they were targeting. Thus, the KN-06 crew continued operating under the assumption that Air Busan Flight 411 was a bomber—rather than a jetliner with a payload of schoolchildren.

Neither can there be any doubt about what happened next. The missile unit at Ongjin tracked BX 411 out over the Yellow Sea. At 12:28 AM, the unit fired two surface-to-air missiles at its target. The first missile struck the Airbus A320 near the tail section, tearing the fuselage in two and sending the aircraft into the sea.

It remains unclear why the KN-06 crew concluded that the BX 411 had crossed into North Korean airspace and then chose to down the aircraft. Roh Pyong-ui, in his interrogation, insisted both that the aircraft had violated North Korean airspace and that it was a military aircraft sent as a provocation by the Trump administration. "We received an order that an American bomber was violating our airspace," Roh told his interrogator. "For us, that is everything. It means we need to shoot it down." Roh was asked repeatedly whether his crew made the determination itself that the aircraft had crossed into North Korean airspace or whether he understood the sector commander to have made that judgment. Each time, without answering the question, Roh insisted that the aircraft had violated North Korean airspace.

Roh also insisted that the aircraft was an American bomber or another type of military aircraft, despite being shown evidence that the aircraft was a civilian airliner. "That means nothing," he responded when interrogators told him the aircraft was a civilian Airbus 320. "It is easy to turn a civilian type of plane into one for military use. We did it all the time."

While it is impossible to understand what the North Korean crew was thinking, it is clear in retrospect that they were primed to see a bomber. The crew had specifically been moved to this location in the expectation of an American bomber flight; the crew was then told that the aircraft was a bomber; and in fact the aircraft was retracing, however inadvertently, the flight path expected for an American bomber. In the confusion, it seems the crew felt pressured not to let the aircraft get away.

A final factor may also have shaped the crew's perception. North Korean military commanders worried that their radars were not detecting all US bomber flights. In some cases, North Korean radars did not detect bomber flights that were later reported in the press. In other cases, the North Koreans saw the aircraft only at the last moment and responded sluggishly. Captured documents indicate that the top leadership placed enormous pressure on air defense units to detect overflights and to be prepared to use force in the event of an incursion into DPRK airspace. It was in this context that Kim Jong Un and others reaffirmed that any American aircraft that strayed into DPRK airspace was to be shot down. The heads of the KPA Air and Anti-Air Force, as well as local air defense commanders, felt incredible pressure to demonstrate extraordinary levels of readiness.

Reporting indicates that some local commanders, in response to this extraordinary pressure from the top, offered bounties to air defense crews—bonuses promised both to crews that detected enemy aircraft approaching DPRK airspace and to any unit that shot down a US aircraft for violating it. Other prisoners confirmed that units were promised additional pay or rations for detecting or shooting down US aircraft, although the description of what was offered varies considerably.

Roh, too, claimed that his crew was offered a bonus. "Those who sat in chairs and stared at screens received double salary for seeing an airplane!" he complained to his interrogators. "At the time, monthly pay was 3,000 won. So I was expecting at least 6,000 for shooting down the American bomber. But the war started. I never got my bonus."

2

SOUTH KOREA HITS BACK

AS SOON AS BX 411 disappeared from South Korean air traffic control radars at 12:28 PM, it was clear that the aircraft had crashed. Crashes are tragic, but they do happen. There was no reason for South Korea's civilian air traffic controllers to suspect that the loss of the aircraft was anything other than an accident. The air traffic controllers initiated the standard procedures for responding to a civil aviation accident and notified their superiors. The message that an aircraft had been lost moved swiftly up and out to various government agencies.

South Korean military authorities, meanwhile, had initiated standard procedures of their own. They had detected the missile launch and explosion. These officials also began notifying their superiors and sending their message up and out. These two messages—that a civil airliner had been lost and that North Korea had shot it down—began racing through South Korea's government, winding their way up and up the chain of command and ultimately reaching the office of the South Korean president himself.

THE BLUE HOUSE

The President of South Korea lived in an elegant palace with the lilting name Cheong Wa Dae, which is literally translated as the Pavilion of Blue Tiles—a reference to the azure tiles of its distinctive, traditional Korean roof. In English, however, South Koreans simply called it "the Blue House." This name was easier to remember and pronounce for the American military officers and diplomats who arrived in-country knowing little or nothing about Korea and speaking only a few words of the language. But like many things in Korea, this simple name obscured a fundamentally different reality.

The White House, for example, is a single building in which the president's key advisers are close at hand. The chief of staff, national security adviser, and essential White House staff cram themselves into tiny offices that have no redeeming feature except proximity to the Oval Office—and in the toughest moments, the Situation Room. In Washington, proximity is what matters.

The Blue House had little in common with the White House. It wasn't even a *house*. There was a house, to be sure, but Cheong Wa Dae was a complex of buildings, spread across a kind of campus. Key staff members, including the president's chief of staff, had workspaces in a series of contemporary office buildings that looked nothing like the traditional main building that sheltered the president's office under those beautiful blue tiles. The president's residence was in yet another building, a short walk away. In the event of an emergency, the president's aides had to converge on the main building, where they would gather in the Crisis Room that sat beneath it. To do so, they had to walk ten minutes or more across the palace grounds, passing through two gates and a guard post, before entering the main building and descending into the small bunker beneath.

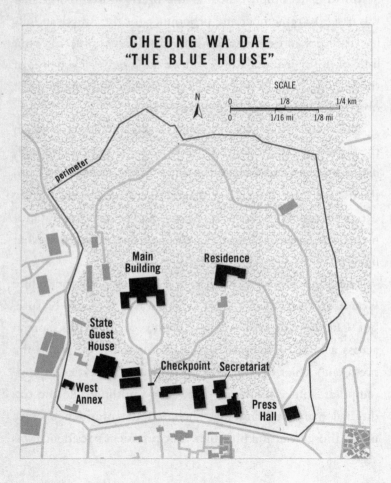

South Korean officials had long complained that this layout made it take far too long for officials to gather in an emergency. As Kwon Hyuck-ki, former chief secretary to the president of South Korea, said, "It is retrogression of sorts that the president's office exists as a small *Cheong Wa Dae* within *Cheong Wa Dae*." In 2010, after North Korea began shelling a South Korean island, it took some twenty minutes for the key national security staff to assemble in the bunker.

South Korean president Moon Jae-in, too, had complained about the luxurious palace that housed his predecessors —including Park Chung Hee, the dictator who had jailed a young Moon for participating in a student protest. One of Moon's campaign pledges had been to relocate his office and other functions to a government facility about a mile south of Cheong Wa Dae. But even after the move to the Central Government Complex was largely completed in early 2020, the Cheong Wa Dae complex retained two very important government functions: it remained the president's residence, and it continued to house the underground Crisis Room, known simply as "the bunker."

Early in the afternoon of Saturday, March 21, President Moon was at his residence, thinking about ships, not aircraft. He was looking over remarks that he would deliver a few days later at a shipyard—where he would announce progress on a public corporation that would aid South Korea's struggling shipbuilding industry—when the message arrived.

At 12:35, Im Jong-seok, Moon's chief of staff, knocked on the door and told Moon that a South Korean airliner en route from Busan to Ulan Bator had disappeared from radar screens over the Yellow Sea and was presumed lost. Moon asked Im to convene his security council. A few minutes later, Im returned with a second message. The South Korean military had detected a surface-to-air missile launch from North Korea that was believed to be the cause of the loss of the aircraft. At this point, Moon went immediately to the underground Crisis Room.

Moon sat at the head of an empty table, waiting for his national security team to arrive. As he waited, he appeared to grow anxious and then irritated at the delay. "He wasn't the sort of man who fidgeted," recalled Im. "This was the first time I saw him tapping his pen on the table. That's the memory of him that stays with me, him sitting in that room, just waiting."

Weighing on Moon were the political dangers of appearing indecisive. "I am sure the *Sewol* was in his mind," Im explained, "because he made a bitter comment about 'seven hours.'" "Seven hours" referred to the long period of inaction on the part of the South Korean government that followed the sinking in 2014 of the South Korean ferry MV *Sewol*. Then-president Park Geun Hye had waited most of the day before convening an emergency meeting of her security advisers, a delay that permanently turned public opinion against her. Many of her political opponents, including Moon, had demanded to know what became of the "seven missing hours" when the passengers of the *Sewol*, most of them students, were drowning. Park's aides had not offered a convincing explanation, allowing wild rumors to spread. She had been in an assignation with an aide, one tabloid claimed, while another reported that she was having plastic surgery.

Park was eventually impeached for corruption and sentenced to twenty-four years in prison. But Moon and his aides believed that the public anger toward Park had its roots in the *Sewol* disaster. They had seen evidence of her malfeasance firsthand: upon taking office, Moon's staff found a cache of documents that showed that Park's aides had lied about when she was notified about the disaster. They turned the documents over to investigators and filed a complaint with the Seoul prosecutor's office. Moon's surviving aides all believe that he was determined not to repeat Park's mistakes. "Moon was so hard on Park over her failure with the *Sewol*," Im recalled. "He was not going to open himself up to the same criticism."

This crisis was precisely what Moon had tried to avoid. The president had thought that North Korea's participation in the 2018 Winter Olympics in Pyeongchang, South Korea, might offer the chance to fundamentally change the relationship between the two countries. President Moon had been an unapologetic advocate for reviving the "Sunshine Policy" of South Korea's first progressive president, Kim Dae Jung. The idea was simple: hostility toward North Korea would only make Kim Jong Un cling to his nuclear weapons, the same way a cold wind might make a man draw a heavy winter coat around him. If you want the man to take off the coat, the warm sunshine is far more effective.

It was inevitable that the new version of the policy would be nicknamed "Moonshine." The term was a pun on the president's name, of course, but it also conveyed a certain weary skepticism about the enterprise. It wasn't an indictment of diplomacy *per se,* so much as a weary acceptance that all of the policies tried to date, both hard and soft, had failed to deliver a Korean Peninsula free from nuclear danger. It is only with hindsight, perhaps, that the brief and intense period of summit diplomacy that followed the 2018 Olympics seems like a heroic effort to avert a catastrophe.

In the end, however, it had come to nothing. For Moon and his advisers, persuading Kim Jong Un to abandon his nuclear weapons would take time. Reduce tension, get a peace agreement, and Kim would eliminate his nuclear arms just as a man would take off his coat in the hot sun. But President Trump wanted Kim to give up his nuclear weapons right away —permanent, irreversible, and verifiable disarmament, without delay and, in any event, no later than the end of the president's first term. Kim had suspended nuclear and missile tests in the hope that summits with Moon and Trump marked the beginning of a new relationship between North Korea and the rest of the world. Those around Trump, though, continued to insist upon what Bolton called a "Libya-style" disarmament agreement. The notion that Kim would surrender his weapons as Muammar Gaddafi had, only to suffer a grisly death at the hands of opposition forces supported by American airpower, was a nonstarter. More than a few White House staffers believed that was precisely why Bolton, who was generally thought to oppose the negotiations, kept bringing it up. Kim ordered his scientists and engineers to resume missile and nuclear tests in order to make the point as clear as possible: North Korea was, and would remain, a nuclear power.

The implosion of negotiations between the United States and North Korea put unbearable pressure on Moon Jae-in. Moonshine simply could not work without a simultaneous improvement in relations between Pyongyang and Washington. The issues were simply too closely intertwined. "Neither South-North relations nor US-North relations will go far if the other fails," explained South Korean diplomat Suh Hoon following the short-lived thaw. "They are like two wheels on a wagon that must roll together." Without a deal between Trump and Kim, and with North Korea resuming its nuclear and missile testing, the wheels came off.

Once North Korea resumed missile and nuclear tests, support for Moon's efforts collapsed. Jokes about the Moonshine policy had a sharper edge to them. The political center in South Korea had shifted, and Moon was forced to shift with it. "Dialogue is impossible in a situation like this," Moon lamented in one interview. "International sanctions and pressure will further tighten to force North Korea to choose no other option but to step forward on the path to genuine dialogue."

It is hard to recall that, at the time, Moon's decision to step back from his policy of engagement was widely lauded as a return to realism rather than the collapse of the last real diplomatic effort to head off a crisis. This sense that Moon was adopting a pragmatic policy was particularly strong among national security experts in Washington, many of whom believed that the Moonshine policy was dangerously naive. Some suggested that Moon had been "mugged by reality" and would now adopt a more traditional approach.

But according to those who knew Moon, he was still seeking a path toward dialogue with North Korea even until the very end. What was no longer clear to him was how to get to that path from the bunker in which he was now sitting.

"FIXED WILL"

It was cold enough on March 21 that there was still snow on the ground in Seoul. Perhaps because of the inclement weather, Moon's aides trickled in slowly, and he was not able to convene the meeting until 1:00 PM—some twenty-five minutes after he had been notified of the downing of Flight BX 411 and more than thirty minutes after the aircraft had been lost. By this time, Moon was upset and let the others know it, according to a memorandum of the meeting. He wanted to know what had happened and what was being done to look for survivors.

Moon's actions that day are essential to understanding why events unfolded as they did. There are some discrepancies between the memorandum summarizing the meeting and the recollections of Moon's surviving aides. The memorandum records that the first few minutes were dedicated to simply explaining what had happened—the flight itself, the problems in the cockpit, the detection of the missile launch.

"Moon had been given fragments of information while waiting for the meeting to start," Im Jong-seok explained, "and we didn't take time to go back over what we thought he knew. This was maybe a mistake, but it was very stressful, very upsetting." Moon seemed focused on the emergency response, asking about search-and-rescue operations, apparently in the hope that the aircraft had been damaged but somehow survived a water landing. Moon's aides appear to have been reluctant to explain that there was no realistic hope of survivors. "I remember when the navy chief, Admiral Um [Hyun-seong], finally told President Moon that he didn't think any of the kids had survived," one aide recalled. "President Moon flinched at the word 'kids.' I could see on his face that he hadn't known the plane was full of students."

At 1:11 PM, North Korean state media released a statement confirming that the state's missile forces had deliberately shot down the aircraft, which it called a bomber. A military aide brought a printout of the statement into the meeting room.

IT IS THE HEROIC [NORTH] KOREAN PEOPLE'S ARMY'S METTLE TO MERCILESSLY PUNISH ANY PROVOKERS WHO HURT THE DIGNITY OF THE DEMOCRATIC PEOPLE'S REPUBLIC OF KOREA, NO MATTER WHERE THEY ARE. AT ABOUT 11:45 ON MARCH 21, A US BOMBER INTRUDED DEEP INTO THE

SKY ABOVE KANGRYONG COUNTY, SOUTH HWANGHAE
PROVINCE OF THE DPRK, BEYOND THE MILITARY
DEMARCATION LINE IN THE WESTERN SECTOR OF THE
FRONT. A SURFACE-TO-AIR MISSILE UNIT OF THE
KPA ANTI-AIR FORCE SHOT DOWN THE AIRCRAFT
WITH A SINGLE SHOT, DISPLAYING ITS FIXED WILL
TO SHOW NO MERCY TO THE AGGRESSORS.

The few surviving meeting attendees all remember that
the statement changed the tone of their deliberations immediately. "I remember when the military aide brought in the
North Korean statement," said one survivor. "He handed it
to the president, which was a very strange thing to do and,
in fact, a breach of protocol." "He should have handed it to
me," Im Jong-seok recalled. "The president read the paper,
and then he put it down. And then he turned the paper over,
like he didn't want to look at it. That was when he asked for
options."

"That message changed the meeting," recalled Kang Kyung-
wha, a career diplomat then serving as South Korea's foreign
minister. "Moon wanted to know what his military options
were, to hurt Kim Jong Un. I don't know why, but up to that
point I had only thought about this as an accident, and about
trying to rescue the survivors. After that, we realized there
weren't going to be any survivors. We only talked about kill
chains."

"I don't know, in my mind, I always remember it as two
different meetings, maybe even on different days," recalled

Chung Eui-yong, South Korea's national security adviser at the time. "Are you sure it was just one meeting? I guess things changed after the statement. We stopped talking about a rescue and started talking about revenge. It was a strange meeting in that way."

THE KILL CHAIN

When President Moon Jae-in asked for military options, Air Force general Jeong Kyeong-doo, chairman of South Korea's Joint Chiefs of Staff, was ready. Ever since his confirmation hearing in August 2017, General Jeong had taken a very tough line on responding to what he called North Korea's relentless "strategic and tactical provocations." Asked during his confirmation hearing whether President Moon should set red lines with North Korea, his answer had given the impression of a man far more hawkish than the president: "President Moon seems to have meant that we ought to be doing everything we can to prevent a crisis situation in which we find ourselves at a dead end."

In the Crisis Room, according to the memorandum of the meeting, General Jeong used that same word — "dead end."

The military plan that General Jeong presented to President Moon during the emergency meeting on March 21 should not have come as a surprise. It had been developed a decade earlier, after a terrible year in which North Korea had engaged in a pair of high-profile provocations. In March 2010, a North Korean submarine used a torpedo to sink a South

Korean naval corvette, the ROKS *Cheonan,* tearing the ship in half and sending forty-six South Korean sailors to a watery grave. (North Korea, of course, denied responsibility.) Then, in November, North Korea unleashed an artillery bombardment against Yeonpyeong Island, killing four South Koreans and injuring twenty-two more.

South Korea's president at that time, Lee Myung Bak, had been enraged by the attack and ordered a retaliation against North Korea, but was frustrated by American officials who restrained him. Lee wanted a big and bold response, but military officials pushed him to consult with the United States, which retained wartime control over South Korea's military forces. The Americans pressured Lee to scale back his plans for a retaliation. "South Korea's original plans for retaliation were, we thought, disproportionately aggressive," wrote Secretary of Defense Robert Gates. "We were worried the exchanges could escalate dangerously." South Korea's eventual response was anemic: satellite images later showed that its retaliation had done little or no damage to the North Koreans.

In the wake of this crisis, Lee pushed for South Korea to develop its own plans and capabilities to retaliate against North Korea in the event of a serious provocation such as a nuclear attack. These plans still required consultation with the United States, but Lee hoped that his successors would have more options to respond boldly to future aggressions by the North.

It was these capabilities that General Jeong presented to President Moon in the Crisis Room as a "three-axis" response to the downing of Flight 411. The military option featured a plan of attack, intelligence and strike capabilities to execute that plan, and missile defenses to limit the damage North Korea could do in retaliation.

The plan of attack presented by General Jeong was called "Korea Massive Punishment and Retaliation" and had been publicly described in some detail after 2016. It described an effort to "decapitate" North Korea's government and military by using hundreds of long-range missiles and special forces to kill North Korea's leadership, including Kim Jong Un. The plan named seventy-two distinct targets, including leadership targets in Pyongyang, military headquarters, and sites linked to North Korea's nuclear and missile programs. The goal, according to one former Ministry of Defense official, was "wiping a certain section of Pyongyang completely off the map." Pyongyang, a second official explained, would "be reduced to ashes."

After presenting President Moon with the option of killing North Korea's senior leaders, General Jeong explained that the plan would be carried out using what he called the "kill chain": a series of military capabilities designed to detect and locate North Korea's leaders and military forces linked to precision-strike capabilities to kill them. These capabilities included aircraft, long-range ballistic and cruise missiles, and a regimental-sized special forces team called SPARTAN 3000 that could be inserted into North Korea within twenty-four hours. General Jeong also offered a brief description of South Korea's missile defense program, called Korea Air and Missile Defense (KAMD).

"Massive punishment, kill chains, KAMD—I don't like things explained with military jargon," Chief of Staff Im Jong-seok recalled. "But when General Jeong put it in plain words, I wasn't sure it was an improvement."

President Moon questioned General Jeong about the size of the strike and the number of targets. "President Moon was really surprised at how long the list of targets was," Im recalled. "But General Jeong explained that the plan was based on an American operation against Saddam." In 1998, the United States conducted Operation Desert Fox against Saddam Hussein's Iraq, striking ninety-seven targets over four days, including three presidential palaces and the headquarters of the Iraqi Ba'ath Party. The two plans bore a striking similarity to each other.

According to survivors who had been present at the meeting, President Moon explained to General Jeong that he did not want to start a general war, but that he did want to find a small number of targets whose destruction would punish Kim Jong Un for the downing of BX 411. President Moon also suggested using only long-range missiles for this retaliatory attack. There was no reason, he said, to ask the special forces team to carry out a suicide mission or to put pilots at risk. Besides, it was important to hold something back to give Kim Jong Un something to think about. A small strike would shake Kim's confidence, while the possibility of a larger strike to follow would box him in. "The general idea was to start with one or two targets," Im explained. "Kim would know we were holding back the rest of the plan if he tried to escalate."

President Moon looked over the list of targets. He asked about the first entry on the list of leadership targets, labeled L-01. It named the main Kim family compound on the outskirts of Pyongyang. Some of General Jeong's military officers were uncomfortable with the idea of targeting Kim's family home, but appeared reluctant to say so. "No one said, 'I think this is too dangerous,'" Im explained, "but General Kim Yongwoo, the chief of the Army, and Admiral Um both said, 'The Americans won't like that.'"

General Kim suggested that, instead of hitting the Kim family compound, the missile strike should destroy the headquarters of North Korea's Air Force, which was located in Chunghwa and commanded the air defense troops who shot down the aircraft. Chunghwa was a small military town about eleven miles south of Pyongyang. The Air Force headquarters there was a large compound with an office building and a pair of statues of Kim Il Sung and Kim Jong Un. These could be struck with little chance of civilian casualties. Admiral Um pointed out that North Korea's Air Force bore responsibility for the mistake and that targeting it was a proportionate response.

"Moon got very angry," Im explained. "He asked, 'What's a proportionate response for more than one hundred schoolchildren? I don't think there is such a thing.'" Moon then turned the meeting back to Kim Jong Un's residence. "I think Kim Jong Un must bear some responsibility too. He can't always get away with things," Moon finally said.

The South Korean president instructed General Jeong to

hit both targets—to use a limited number of long-range missiles to strike both the Air Force headquarters and L-01, the Kim family compound outside Pyongyang.

Foreign Minister Kang made one last effort to take L-01 out of the strike package, raising the idea of consulting with the United States. But Moon turned the discussion aside by stating that this was his responsibility. Im recalled that Moon's response to Kang's suggestion that they contact Washington was ambiguous. "What he actually said was, 'I'll take responsibility.' That might have meant that he would personally consult with the Americans, or it might have meant that he would be responsible for not consulting them."

Moon then asked to speak directly to the commander of South Korea's Army Missile Command. The subject, Im realized, was no longer up for discussion.

ROK ARMY MISSILE COMMAND

Prior to the events of March 2020, very few people were aware that South Korea maintained an elite military unit armed with long-range ballistic and cruise missiles. Once in a while, a South Korean leader might attend a missile test. But the military units assigned to launch these weapons in wartime were shrouded in secrecy. The South Korean press might allude to the fact that the Republic of Korea (ROK) Army had long-range missiles of its own, but the idea that there were about one hundred such missiles deployed to a half-dozen operational bases scattered across the country was almost never directly acknowledged.

US and South Korean officials did, of course, visit the headquarters of the ROK Army Missile Command in Eumseong County from time to time. Even so, the South Korean military emplaced security measures to conceal the location of this unit, and its precise location was never mentioned in South Korean press reports. When VIPs visited, the location was never described. The main headquarters was also obscured with digital trees in the apps Naver and Daum, South Korea's versions of Google Maps. Army Missile Command's soldiers were even required to remove their unit patches, fixed to their sleeves with Velcro, before any photograph could be taken.

On March 21, Major General Lee Jin-won was sitting in his office at the main Army Missile Command outpost when, at 1:42 PM, his secure phone rang. It was President Moon's staff, informing him that the president wanted to speak with him and that he would soon be in charge of launching a counterstrike. As soon as the call ended, Major General Lee gathered his aides and went into the underground bunker behind the main administrative building.

Photographs from that day show that Major General Lee wasn't wearing his patch. According to officers under his command, the unit was preparing for yet another VIP visit in a few weeks. The unit was regarded as a "spit-and-polish" unit, although this was largely a function of seemingly endless VIP visits that constantly disrupted training and wreaked havoc on any effort to establish a regular schedule. As Lee walked into his command bunker, the only evidence that he commanded an arsenal of long-range missiles was his dark blue baseball cap with an interlocking A-M-C. The cap was a security violation, but only a very well informed outsider would know what those letters stood for. Most South Koreans did not.

According to transcripts provided by the South Korean Army, in the short teleconference that followed, President Moon directed General Lee to develop a plan to strike L-01, the Kim family compound, as well as the North Korean Air Force headquarters in Chunghwa, with the minimum number of missiles. Moon left it to Major General Lee to determine which units would carry out the strike. All he asked was that the number of missiles be kept to the minimum necessary. He did not want Kim Jong Un to think this was the start of a war.

Major General Lee asked President Moon about his obligation to notify his American counterpart. "General Lee hesitated about taking military action," explained Lee's assistant. "He said the plan required him to consult with the Americans. President Moon said that he would take responsibility to inform the Americans. [Major General Lee] seemed uncertain for a moment, but ultimately agreed to follow the order."

A significant question is why Major General Lee followed President Moon's directive to disregard established procedures for consultation and ordered South Korean units to launch without informing US Forces Korea, as dictated in contingency plans that had been agreed between Seoul and Washington. The answers offered by officers from the Army

Missile Command vary: some blamed Washington, and others observed that in a serious crisis the interests of even close allies may differ. All agreed, however, that the Americans had been slow to recognize that South Koreans no longer saw themselves as junior partners in the defense of their own country and its citizens.

South Koreans of all political stripes had long been irked that, in the event of another war, they would have to surrender control of the country's military forces to the Americans —the same arrangement that had existed during the Korean War so many decades ago. The humiliation of this arrangement was driven home in November 2017, when South Korean forces had not even been allowed to return fire as North Korea fired heavy weapons across the DMZ to stop the defection of a North Korean soldier. Moon had expressed his frustration with these constraints. "The issues on the rules of engagement . . . should be discussed, although it is under the [United Nations Command's] control," President Moon publicly said. "The people would generally think of a rule of engagement as something that permits our soldiers to at least fire warning shots if a bullet from the North Korean is fired at us."

On March 21, those frustrations helped drive the crisis forward. The military officials who opposed the strike tried to do so by suggesting that they consult with the Americans. And those who supported the strike wanted to avoid telling the Americans and deal with the consequences later.

Crucially, the officer responsible for actually carrying out the counterattack found himself much closer in his views to the latter camp. Major General Lee saw the choice starkly: following the consultation procedures outlined in the contingency plan would simply result in American pressure to do nothing. "The Americans were just going to tell us no, and we knew that," his assistant explained. "They said no in 2010. They dragged their feet when we asked for wartime control of our own forces. They came up with reasons why we couldn't use our rules of engagement in the DMZ. It was always 'no,' or 'maybe later,' or 'be reasonable.' Think of all those dead kids. What's a reasonable response to that?"

Moreover, in the end, President Moon was Major General Lee's commander. Whatever ties of professional respect bound Lee to his American counterparts, he was a Korean officer, not an American one. "I think sometimes you know there are rules, but this is still your country," explained his deputy. "Those students were Korean. President Moon was our commander. We followed his order."

Major General Lee selected two units to conduct the attack, one based in central Korea near Wonju and the other on the far western edge of Baengnyeong Island. He ordered his staff to prepare an attack plan that would be ready to execute within about six hours — at 8:00 PM. This launch time would enable the missile launch units to conduct their launch preparations under the cover of darkness — and also give the president a chance to change his mind.

President Moon had no intention of changing his mind. Nor did he have any intention of informing the Americans, let alone asking for permission. When Moon learned that the attack would be ready at 8:00 PM, he asked his aides to schedule an address to the nation from the press hall, known as the Chunchugwan, located on the Blue House grounds. He also instructed them to not take any calls from the Americans. "[Moon] thought American officials might try to restrain us," Chief of Staff Im explained. "Trump could learn about the strike the same way that everyone else did—when it was announced on television."

Moon's remarks that night were brief enough. He stated simply that North Korea had shot down a civilian airliner, one filled largely with children. He said that the attack "crossed all lines of human decency" and described North Korea's claim that the aircraft was on a reconnaissance mission as a "pathetic lie." He expressed his profound grief over the loss of so many innocent lives, over the pain their families were suffering, and over the senselessness of North Korea's crime. And then he announced that military operations had begun:

"As I speak, Republic of Korea armed forces are responding to this cruel and unjust act. Our grief at this moment knows no bounds. But our response does, as it has been carefully limited to those responsible for perpetrating this horrible crime. The armed forces also stand ready to expand our operations if North Korea persists in attacking our citizens."

When his remarks were finished and the television cameras were turned off, Moon walked back down to the Crisis Room and asked his staff to place a call to the White House. Now that the strike was under way, Moon wanted his national security adviser to smooth things over. At this point, Moon and his advisers were mainly worried about the American reaction, not the North Korean one. They worried that the Trump administration would be angry about not having been consulted, but they also assumed that US leaders would fall into line now that the counterstrike, a limited operation, was a *fait accompli*. None of Moon's surviving aides appear to have believed that the strike would escalate into a general war. The targets had been carefully selected, the number of missiles was small, and Moon's speech had made clear that he was holding the full strike in reserve.

"We were so worried that the Americans might try to stop us," Im explained, "that it never occurred to us they might make things worse. I don't even use Twitter."

THE FIRE MISSION

Launching a ballistic missile strike is not as easy as simply pressing a button.

Each missile is carried by a massive truck. Those trucks are parked within massive earthen bunkers with a curious shape. They are called "drive-through" bunkers because they have an entrance on one side and an exit on the other so that the massive vehicle can drive in one side and out the other without having to turn around.

The bunkers in South Korea had the same distinctive shape as the ones that the United States built in Europe during the Cold War. The American bunkers, abandoned at the end of the Cold War, now sit empty—although one of the locations was used as a set for a *Star Wars* movie. A space ship sat in the same spot once occupied by a ground-launched cruise missile armed with a 100-kiloton nuclear warhead.

The bunkers in South Korea, by contrast, were neither abandoned nor empty.

After the teleconference between President Moon and the Army Missile Command, Major General Lee placed two missile units on alert, one located near the South Korean city of Wonju, the other sitting on the far edge of Baengnyeong Island. Both units received the same order: to fire three ballistic missiles at targets in North Korea, for a total of six missiles. The crews waited through the day until the sun set—first over Wonju and then, nine minutes later, at 6:52 PM, over Baengnyeong Island.

The order, called a "fire mission assignment," contained three kinds of information. It told the crew where to go (the "fire point"), specified when the unit should launch (the "method of control"), and then told the crew where to go after the launch.

The crews did not have to go far to reach their fire points. Major General Lee's order specified that the trucks should park on a series of pre-surveyed concrete pads just outside the massive earthen bunkers and launch their missiles from there.

The orders also gave the missile crew instructions as to the method of control. A missile commander can give a crew the freedom to "fire when ready," but in this case Major General

Lee told both the crew and the commander to launch "at my command." That would give him one last opportunity to call off the strike before the missiles were airborne.

Finally, Major General Lee ordered the units to move to new positions several miles from each base once they had completed their fire missions. While his surviving aides all testified that they did not expect North Korea to retaliate, this final precaution makes sense in light of the fact that North Korea almost certainly knew the location of many of South Korea's missile bases; prudence dictated that the launch vehicles move to safety and reload. "If things did get out of control," Lee's deputy explained, "we wanted to be prepared." Had Major General Lee not given this final order, it is unlikely that the commission would have had the opportunity to interview the launch crews.

One by one, each truck drove out into the night and parked on a concrete square. Each vehicle was aligned along a heading specified in the fire order, pointing toward Pyongyang or Chunghwa. Each crew parked its vehicle in the darkness, with no lights, set the brake, and then extended the hydraulic jacks that would lift the vehicle just off its tires and ensure that it was perfectly horizontal.

Once the trucks were in place, the crews turned on their fire control systems. They did not have to type in the target coordinates themselves. Once the fire control computer was turned on, it automatically downloaded the target locations sent by radio and began to compute a firing solution—essentially aiming the missile. The computer also checked to ensure that the vehicle was level and aligned correctly, adjusting for any deviation that might otherwise put the missile off course, even by a few meters.

When the trucks' computers had completed their firing solutions, the display inside one of the vehicles provided a different message than the others. It read:

INCORRECT HEADING MOVE VEHICLE

The vehicle had been aligned incorrectly, forcing the crew to stop what they were doing and repark the vehicle, a process that took several tense minutes. "I was really embarrassed," recalled the driver of the vehicle that had been misaligned. "I felt very ashamed that I was holding up the entire mission." Eventually, all the vehicles were correctly aligned and a firing solution had been found for each missile.

As the computer in each vehicle found a firing solution, the display inside the cab alerted the crew. One by one, in each of the vehicles, a crew member pressed a key marked LAY that confirmed to the unit commander that the vehicle was in the correct position. The computer completed the aiming process by telling the truck to raise the canister containing the missile into a vertical position. Soon, all three canisters were pointing upward into the night sky at Wonju. On Baengnyeong Island, three more did the same.

Inside the trucks, each crew followed the same checklist, completing each step by touching a key marked XMIT, or "transmit." This key would send a confirmation back to Army

Missile Command, allowing Major General Lee to follow along as the crew prepared to launch. Once the canister was vertical, the display read READY TO FIRE. The crew member touched XMIT. The display read ARM MISSILE. A crew member lifted a small cover on the control panel, flipped the arming switch, then touched XMIT again. The display read READY TO COMPLY. A crew member hit XMIT for a final time, and then they waited.

When the moment arrived, Major General Lee appears not to have hesitated. His order to fire arrived promptly on the display at 8:00 PM: FIRE MISSILE.

Within seconds, the ballistic missiles went streaking into the sky, one after the other. South Korea's retaliation was, as President Moon had said, limited. There were now six missiles, no more, no less, heading toward North Korea.

3

HURRICANE DONALD

BY THE TIME DUSK settled over the Korean Peninsula on Saturday evening, the government of the United States had been on high alert for hours. As soon as the North Korean missile unit at Ongjin fired at Air Busan Flight 411, the launch had been detected by an American satellite. In that moment, a complex system within the US government had sprung into action, working to inform the nation's leaders, including President Donald Trump, that the crisis on the Korean Peninsula had taken a dangerous turn. The same spy satellites and other classified intelligence systems that had detected the two surface-to-air missiles fired at BX 411 at 12:28 PM also registered the explosion that destroyed the aircraft minutes thereafter.

We now know that, although every one of these events was detected, assessed, and promptly passed up the chain of command, the overall system did not work as intended. The process broke down; information failed to reach the very top. The president was not informed that North Korea shot down BX 411 for more than six hours, and ultimately only learned about the event the following morning when he saw television reports. Nor did President Trump know at the time of his first public remarks on the events on the Korean Peninsula that South Korea had responded to the shootdown of Flight 411 with a limited missile strike against targets in North Korea.

This mismanagement of information within the Trump White House squandered several crucial hours during which American leaders might have otherwise managed the escalating crisis. This bureaucratic breakdown also resulted in confused messaging from the White House that, as we now know, dramatically increased the danger confronting the United States and helped to precipitate the cataclysm that followed.

The central problem, as has become clear in the course of this commission's investigations, arose from the peculiarities relating to both process and place. It is impossible to grasp the reasons for the breakdown of the Trump administration's executive functions without understanding both the process that was in place to provide the president with information and the unusual features of its implementation that arose from the fact that, as the crisis unfolded, the president was not in Washington, but in Palm Beach.

THE MAR-A-LAGO CLUB

Mar-a-Lago proved a challenging location for President Trump to manage an international crisis. There is some irony in this, given that Mar-a-Lago's original resident intended it for essentially this role. Although the property was built as a private residence in 1929, its owner, Marjorie Merriweather

Post, had arranged for Mar-a-Lago to be transferred to the federal government for use as a "Winter White House" after her death. Although the US government held the title to the property from 1973 to 1981, the high cost of maintenance resulted in the government returning the property to her heirs. Donald Trump purchased it in 1985. With Trump's election as president in 2016, Mrs. Post's vision had in one sense come to pass.

But Mar-a-Lago was a very unusual presidential residence. Donald Trump, in the mid-1990s, reinvented Mar-a-Lago as a private club with fifty-eight guest rooms. At the same time, he maintained a private residence in the former "owner's house" at the south end of the main building. As a result, Mar-a-Lago served as both a private members' club and a private residence for the president, two functions that were often in obvious tension.

That tension was an early headache for the Secret Service. The agency had to provide for the security of the president, but it also had to accommodate the club's fundamental business as a luxury resort for wealthy members, many of whom complained about the introduction of basic security screening measures. The club management fielded numerous complaints over the first year of the Trump administration about the imposition of such measures from members, some of whom began referring to presidential visits as "Hurricane Donald."

The result was an uneasy compromise between protecting the president and protecting the club's business model. Many workable solutions were found. For instance, the Secret Service determined that a service entrance off Southern Boulevard could provide the president with access to his residence, allowing him to slip in and out of the club with a bit more discretion, although it did not ease the security requirements on club members.

Yet such solutions created problems of their own. President Trump's use of the Southern Boulevard service entrance required that he traverse a walkway that connected the main building to another in which weddings were held. (Sometimes surprised wedding-goers even had an unscheduled appearance by the president.) The use of the Southern Boulevard entrance also created significant traffic delays, particularly on the Southern Boulevard Bridge, which is one of the roadways connecting the barrier island of Palm Beach to the Florida mainland.

In addition to security measures, the president needed facilities to handle classified information. Fortunately, Mrs. Post, a vigorous advocate of civil defense, had built numerous fallout shelters at all her residences, including three shelters at Mar-a-Lago underneath the main building. Over the years, these shelters had been repurposed to serve as storage and, for a time, as an office for Trump's butler. After Trump's election, one of the fallout shelters was converted to a secure compartmentalized information facility (SCIF) for handling classified information. This facility—which staff sometimes called the "cone of silence" in jest—could only be accessed from the main building. While the basement facility was better than the

PALM BEACH AREA

FLORIDA

The Colony
Palm Beach

ATLANTIC
OCEAN

Palm Beach
International Airport

Southern
Avenue
Bridge

Hilton Palm
Beach

Mar-a-Lago

Bunker

Trump International
Golf Club

N

SCALE

0   2   4 km

0   1   2 mi

terrace for holding classified briefings, club members could tell that a classified briefing was about to commence by the procession of staff in off-the-rack suits making their way down into the basement.

There were other ways in which Mar-a-Lago was simply not suitable as a presidential residence, particularly in regard to the large staff that had to travel with the president. For example, Mar-a-Lago offered a limited number of rooms, and its high rack rate substantially exceeded the General Services Administration (GSA) per diem of $195. As a result, the president's senior staff, including his chief of staff, rarely stayed at Mar-a-Lago itself. Instead, senior staff booked rooms at the nearest hotel, Colony Palm Beach. The Colony is about ten minutes north of Mar-a-Lago by car. It does not have facilities to handle classified information.

Other staff stayed at the Hilton Palm Beach Airport, which is located in West Palm Beach on the mainland, a fifteen-minute drive west over the Southern Boulevard Bridge. This hotel, which is less expensive than either Mar-a-Lago or the Colony, offered staff easy access to the airport and to the Trump International Golf Club in West Palm Beach — roughly five miles across Lake Worth Lagoon from Mar-a-Lago — but also kept them separated from Trump by a minimum of a quarter-hour's travel.

The layout of President Trump's properties in Palm Beach scattered his staff around Palm Beach. In a time of crisis, Trump and his senior staff were spread across three different locations, with the president himself on an island — both literally and figuratively.

EXECUTIVE TIME

Jack Francis was President Trump's fourth chief of staff. It was not an easy job. Reince Priebus had lasted only six months, John Kelly a little over a year, and then Dan Scavino for another year after Kelly's departure. Francis had more in common with Kelly than Priebus or Scavino. Like Kelly, Francis was a retired Marine four-star general. And like Kelly, he made it his mission to manage a chaotic White House. As Francis saw it, any chief of staff would behave in exactly the same way. Indeed, one of Francis's first priorities after taking over as chief of staff from Scavino was putting an end to the power struggles that had plagued the Trump administration and imposing some control over who the president saw and how he received information.

In this task, Francis worked closely with Keith Kellogg, a retired Army three-star general who became Trump's fourth national security adviser following Michael Flynn, H. R. Mc-Master, and John Bolton. Kellogg, who had previously served in the same role for the vice president, had no idea how long he would be around, but he was determined to help Francis keep things together for as long as he could. That was a tall order, as the myriad scandals and investigations swirling around the president and key members of his staff created a constant sense of crisis within the White House.

Mostly Francis and Kellogg focused on keeping the president's legal woes from overwhelming everything else. They also worked to keep various international crises, like the threat posed by North Korea's growing nuclear and missile programs, from spiraling out of control. But Francis and Kellogg also knew they needed to tread carefully. After all, it had been North Korea that did in their predecessors. In fact, it had been the issue of negotiations with North Korea that had led Trump to show their predecessors the door.

During the brief thaw in relations in 2018, Donald Trump had relied heavily on Mike Pompeo to do the legwork in ad-

vance of his summit with Kim Jong Un. Pompeo's role began
while he was still the director of the CIA and continued after
he replaced Rex Tillerson as the secretary of state. Pompeo
had a reputation at CIA for giving Trump a steady stream of
rosy intelligence assessments about the impact of sanctions on
North Korea. "Pompeo kept feeding Trump assessments that
US military threats will force Kim to bow to US demands for
nuclear disarmament," one former White House official said.
Some officials felt that Pompeo's characterizations went far beyond what the CIA analysts actually believed and were in fact
an effort to flatter Trump. It was Pompeo who traveled to
Pyongyang to meet with Kim Jong Un. And it was Pompeo
who took the blame when it became clear that Kim Jong Un
had no intention of abandoning his nuclear weapons.

But, according to aides, the president also blamed Bolton.
Trump never enjoyed sharing the spotlight with the combative
Bolton, who often seemed to give the impression that he was
calling the shots. The president came to think that Bolton had
undermined him.

Trump blamed his entire national security team for the failed
effort to negotiate with Kim's regime. This deep dissatisfaction
underlays one of the strangest moments in American political
history: the president of the United States firing practically his
entire national security team with a single tweet:

Donald J. Trump @tehDonaldJTrump
I wanted a Summit! But Little Rocketman won't de-nuke!
No more Mr. nice guys! Thank you to Mike Pompeo,

John Bolton and John Kelly for your service! Tomorrow
we announce a GREAT new national security team!
Going to the mattress! I need a war time consillary!*
#MAGA

After the "Twitter Massacre," as it came to be known, only
Secretary of Defense James Mattis remained on the president's
national security team, which otherwise had to be entirely re-
built. In short order, Trump chose Francis and Kellogg to pick
up the pieces.

As chief of staff, Francis attempted to impose a semblance
of order around the life of a man who, prior to being elected
president, was used to having large blocks of unstructured
time. The president would rise around 5:30 AM and start the
day by watching news on television. The White House typically
scheduled a block of "executive time" from 8:00 AM to 11:00
AM. Official schedules listed that time as occurring in the Oval
Office, but in fact staff at the time indicated that, while he was
staying at the White House, Trump often "spends that time
in his [executive] residence, watching TV, making phone calls
and tweeting." Trump would not appear in the Oval Office
until his first scheduled meeting of the day, which was typically
his intelligence briefing at 11:00 AM.

Early on, Francis revived one of John Kelly's pet projects

---

* According to a follow-up statement released by the White House,
"consillary" is "an accepted anglicization of the Italian term *consigliere*"
and is "commonly used by real Americans who don't learn Italian at
fancy Swiss boarding schools."

—an effort to encourage the president to spend more time in the Oval Office rather than the executive residence, located between the East and West Wings of the White House. Francis attempted to schedule regular meetings with family and close advisers of the president to establish a routine. On a typical day, Trump would have meetings with Kellogg, his daughter Ivanka and son-in-law Jared Kushner, his legal team, and Kellyanne Conway, who was then serving as the president's counselor. Trump typically took an hour-long lunch at 12:30, followed by another block of either "executive time" or "policy time." The president's day typically ended around 4:15, at which point he was most likely to return to his residence. Dinner was usually served at 5:30.

Staff members had long been concerned about Trump's time outside of the Oval Office, even when he was staying at the White House. "Once he goes upstairs [to the residence], there's no managing him," one administration insider said. It was also clear that staff were concerned about flows of information, including social media and television. And yet, the president was the president. "But if he wants to watch [television], it's not like we can say, 'Oh, the TV doesn't work,'" a staffer remarked. Recognizing this problem, Francis sought to improve the overall quality of information available to the president, but he accepted that there would always be some things he could not control.

The president's insistence on spending time at Mar-a-Lago made Francis's job much harder, increasing the amount of unstructured time available to the president while physically isolating him from staff who might otherwise keep him engaged and focused. But Trump viewed his time at Mar-a-Lago as an escape from the pressures of the White House—and from Francis. The president rarely scheduled formal meetings during this time, opting instead to play golf.

While he was staying at Mar-a-Lago, it was also unusual for President Trump to receive a routine intelligence briefing, which would have required him to go down into the SCIF in the basement fallout shelter. Some aides suggested that this was because the president was uncomfortable walking down stairs, although others disputed that claim as "absurd" and indicated that Trump would go down to the SCIF when necessary.

In addition to isolating the president from his key staff, Trump's time in Palm Beach placed him in close and often unpredictable contact with club members. In one case, a golf club member invited a *New York Times* reporter as a guest and then introduced the reporter to Trump—who then agreed to give a thirty-minute, on-the-record interview without a single aide present.

Francis understood the challenges posed by Mar-a-Lago, but he also understood that the president needed time away from the demands of serving as president and his mounting legal problems. As a result, the chief of staff did little to control Trump's time at Mar-a-Lago beyond encouraging him to avoid the dining room. In retrospect, the chief of staff's hands-off approach at Mar-a-Lago appears to have made it all the more attractive to the president as a home-away-from-home.

On the afternoon of Friday, March 20, Trump arrived at Mar-a-Lago alone. First Lady Melania Trump and their son, Barron, were in New York, at Trump Tower.

When Trump spoke briefly with Francis at 5:06 PM, the chief of staff encouraged the president to skip the dining room and take dinner in his room.

Francis was looking forward to a relatively uneventful Saturday. As usual during the president's trips to Mar-a-Lago, no formal intelligence briefing was slated for March 21. The only item on Trump's schedule was a round of golf with his old friend Robert Kraft, owner of the New England Patriots.

TEE TIME

The crash of an airliner in South Korea had been reported in the American press shortly after the loss of Flight 411 at 11:28 PM Eastern Daylight Time on Friday. But it was not public knowledge that the aircraft had been shot down until the Korean Central News Agency (KCNA), the official news outlet of Kim Jong Un's government, issued its statement more than an hour later, at 1:11 PM on Saturday in Seoul—just after midnight in Palm Beach.

After the North Korean announcement, Francis conferred with Kellogg about whether they should inform the president. It was unclear if Trump was still awake. They briefly discussed calling the residence at Mar-a-Lago. "I remember Jack looked at me and then looked down at his phone," Kellogg recalled to this commission's investigators, "and then he said, 'We'll know pretty shortly if he's still awake.'" They both checked Twitter, but saw no new updates to Trump's Twitter feed. The newest tweet was still an angry lambasting of John Bolton's new memoir.

If Trump had gone to bed, Francis concluded, it would be a mistake to wake him. The president would need to be well rested and alert for the coming day of intense discussions with the South Koreans, Japanese, and other world leaders as they attempted to contain the crisis in East Asia.

Kellogg looked at the schedule and suggested that they let Kraft know that the president might be unable to keep their tee time. Francis disagreed. "We're going to have to be very careful not to disrupt his normal routine," the chief of staff recalled telling Kellogg. "This is dangerous business, and we need to keep him calm and focused." They worried about the appearance of Trump playing golf during the crisis, but in the end they decided it would be easier to manage the fallout from the press than the fallout from the president.

Kellogg asked Francis what time they should inform President Trump of the North Korean attack. Francis said that they should allow him to continue with his normal routine, as he would on any normal day—that is, to awake around 5:30, turn on the news, and start making telephone calls. Invariably, his first call would be to Francis, who could then ask the president to come down into the SCIF for a briefing. The plan was simply to let the president sleep and try to treat the day as normally as possible, not interfering with his routine. "We saw it on foreign trips all the time," Francis told investigators later. "When you disrupted his schedule, he got really cranky."

In the meantime, Francis and Kellogg decided to move to the SCIF at Mar-a-Lago and begin a long, sleepless night of attempting to get ahead of the emerging crisis. Kellogg went there immediately so as to place a call to his South Korea counterpart, Chung Eui-yong. Chung's office said that he was in a meeting and would call Kellogg back.

Francis, on the other hand, did not go immediately down into the SCIF with Kellogg. Instead, he first stopped by the rooms of the military aides traveling with the president. Among their other duties, these five mid-ranking officers took turns carrying the president's Emergency Satchel — the bag, also known as the "football," that contained the communications information that would allow the president to order a nuclear strike.

Francis spoke with each of the aides in turn. Later, he would insist that he was careful not to say anything that might be seen as disloyal or questioning the president's competence. Instead, he simply informed the officers that the next few days were going to be stressful and that, if the president should ask any of them to do anything unusual, they should check with the chief of staff first.

LONG NIGHT IN TURTLE BAY

While President Trump slept and Francis and Kellogg readied for the day ahead, the staff of the State Department Operations

Center—the hub that maintains around-the-clock communications for American diplomats—was busy with preparations
of its own. Soon, one of the country's top ambassadors would
be working feverishly as well.

The "Ops Center" contacted Nikki Haley, at the time the
US ambassador to the United Nations, at 11:22 PM on March
20 to inform her that a South Korean airliner had crashed
and later to inform her that North Korea had taken credit for
shooting it down. This call began an intense, nightlong period
of diplomatic maneuvering by Ambassador Haley. Her diplomatic efforts, conducted in isolation from those of the White
House, have come under scrutiny from critics who believe that
the chaotic and uncoordinated response by the Trump administration may have allowed the crisis to careen out of control.

When the Ops Center called, Haley had been asleep in her
apartment at United Nations Plaza, a residence leased by the
Department of State. Haley rarely worked late. Instead, she
had made a special effort to maintain a semblance of a normal
family life, keeping regular hours, attending her son's basket-
ball games, and making time to see family.

Haley's political ambitions, however, had often interrupted
her family's peace. Her campaign adviser when she ran for
governor of South Carolina, Will Folks, later alleged that he'd
had an affair with Haley during the campaign. She denied the
rumors, but many people both in and outside of the US government believed Folks, particularly after he published text
messages and phone logs between himself and Ms. Haley. Of
particular interest was a list of late-night phone calls, including

one that began at 2:24 AM and ended 146 minutes later. Haley was adamant that the lengthy calls were work-related. Folks was, after all, her campaign manager.

Once in office, even uglier rumors about Haley began to spread, owing in no small part to a thinly veiled allegation in a 2018 book, *Fire and Fury* by journalist Michael Wolff, that Haley was the object of the "special attention" of President Trump. The rumors were not true, and Haley found them disgusting and sexist. Even Folks had said he found them impossible to believe. And yet Haley felt compelled to deny them publicly.

"The worst part," according to a foreign service officer who worked in Haley's office, "is that she had to know Trump was the one telling people." Trump had famously posed as his own publicist to spread rumors to gossip columnists about supposed affairs he'd had with a number of well-known women — including Carla Bruni, the first lady of France, who had been compelled to come forward to deny Trump's boasts. Aides thought that Haley would have been a fool not to realize that it was Trump himself who was boasting to his friends about what she had done to stay in his good graces, both to boost his fragile ego and to diminish her standing.

As a result of this backbiting, Haley was careful not to do anything that would breathe life into the rumors about the nature of her relationship with President Trump. "Short of a nuclear war," the foreign service officer explained, "Nikki Haley was not calling Donald Trump after hours."

Nor did Haley, after learning of the North Korean attack

on BX 411, attempt to contact John Sullivan, the acting US secretary of state. Trump, despite his tweet promising a new national security team, had failed to nominate a replacement for ousted secretary of state Mike Pompeo, leaving Sullivan in his second stint as acting secretary.

According to Haley, she did not attempt to contact Acting Secretary of State Sullivan on the night of March 20 because he was traveling. She was "not sure where John [Sullivan] was or what time it was there," she later told commission investigators, and she did not want to expend valuable time trying to track him down. Others, however, have pointed to a general sense within Haley's office that Sullivan's staff was either nonresponsive or unhelpful. Some aides felt that Sullivan remained loyal to ousted secretary of state Rex Tillerson and was openly hostile to Haley, seeing her as ambitious and devious.

The lack of coordination within the State Department was in large part a function of the vast number of senior positions that remained unfilled during the Trump administration—including the top job. The State Department's Policy Planning Office, which was normally charged with developing long-term strategy, had instead assumed control over day-to-day operations that should have been conducted by assistant secretaries—officials who did not exist because they had never been nominated, let alone confirmed. Even under Tillerson and Pompeo, decision-making would often grind to a halt owing to lack of staffing. "The State Department was like a ghost ship," one foreign service officer explained.

Still, Sullivan was well liked within the State Department and generally seen as pragmatic and effective. His popularity, however, worked against him with Trump, who saw him as a holdover from Tillerson's time as secretary of state. Sullivan's relationship with the president made whatever support he enjoyed from State Department staffers irrelevant and, possibly, counterproductive. "She's no idiot," this foreign service officer said of Haley. "Trump thought Sullivan was a swamp guy. He hated those guys so much that the fact that she went around [Sullivan] and humiliated him would be a plus."

Rather than contacting Sullivan, Haley called her deputy in Washington, Jon Lerner. Lerner had been appointed with no foreign policy experience—he was a political strategist who handled analytics on both of Haley's campaigns for governor. To the extent that Lerner had a foreign policy outlook, he harbored a general anti-communism that, by his own description, had extended into a broad distrust of regimes that he saw as anti-American. Haley called him "Lemon" because of his dour demeanor.

In the course of their late-night phone call, Haley and Lerner settled on a strategy to use the shootdown, and North Korea's belligerent response, to drive a deep and permanent wedge between China and North Korea. And so Haley's second call after Lerner was to the Chinese mission and its ambassador, Ma Zhaoxu.

If Haley's political career had rewarded her for her obvious passion, Ma's had taught him to keep his composure. Ma had first won notoriety as a college student in China when that country was slowly opening to the outside world. Improbably, he had been named best speaker in an international debate competition in 1985. In the 1980s, to Chinese people, who were generally unable to even travel outside the country, the sight of a slim Chinese student beating foreigners in debates was a source of real pride and brought him a kind of celebrity. (Ma still met people on the street in China who remembered him from the 1980s.) From there, Ma rose steadily through the ranks of the Chinese foreign ministry, eventually serving as its spokesperson. Where many of his predecessors had been prickly, Ma had a way of appearing completely unruffled, remaining calm in the face of hostile questions. When asked about Liu Xiaobo, the Nobel Prize–winning author imprisoned by the Chinese authorities, Ma calmly asserted that "there are no dissidents in China." Ma was never defensive as the press spokesman. His appointment as ambassador to the UN was intended to signal China's confidence in its suddenly very important place in the world.

Ambassador Haley's effort to make the shootdown a turning point in relations between Beijing and Pyongyang fell flat. She implored Ma to think about the schoolchildren on Flight BX 411, but he was unruffled. Ma merely noted that the loss of life was regrettable, but that there had been many regrettable aviation accidents over the years. Haley even tried a veiled threat, warning that this was the sort of event that might very well prompt a military response from the United States. Ma said that this, too, would be regrettable—one senseless tragedy begetting another. He remained utterly unmoved.

In retrospect, it seems unlikely that any Chinese diplomat —whether possessed of Ma's talents or not—would have allowed himself to be drawn into colluding with the United States against his own foreign ministry. "I have no idea what Haley was thinking," admitted a former State Department official. "She had to realize that Ma wasn't going for a walk in the woods with her." Instead, Ma suggested that Haley speak with the North Koreans directly, offering to host the meeting in his office.

Ma's proposal appears to have caught Ambassador Haley by surprise. The United States did not have diplomatic relations with North Korea. Within North Korea, Sweden was the "protecting power" for US interests, serving as an embassy by proxy. In the United States, North Korea had a mission at the United Nations, a line of communication that diplomats sometimes called "the New York channel." Now Ma was suggesting that Haley activate this channel.

Haley was unsure how to respond. She ended the call, telling Ma she would call back.

The ambassador and Lerner conferred again by phone about whether to take the meeting offered by Ma. Lerner was strongly against it: using the New York channel would reward North Korea for the shootdown, he argued, and holding the meeting at the Chinese offices would convey weakness on the part of the Americans. They decided that they needed to give the Chinese time to worry—for the possibility of a military response to set in. Some of Haley's aides have said that her political ambitions clouded her judgment about what she might achieve. Haley and Lerner dispute this strenuously. Meeting with the North Koreans would, in their view, have sent the wrong signal.

Haley called Ma back at 2:42 AM and said that, without a formal apology from North Korea, no meeting would be possible. Ma said that he regretted her decision, and that he would miss her presence in the morning. This was when Haley became aware that the State Department had agreed to meet with North Korea's representatives without informing her.

THE NEW YORK CHANNEL

Although Haley did not know "where John [Sullivan] was or what time it was there," the Ops Center did. At the same time that one watch officer at the communications hub had contacted Haley, another had reached Sullivan as he was traveling abroad. The officer had quickly informed the acting secretary of state about North Korea's attack on BX 411.

Sullivan, after thinking about it for a few minutes, settled on an unusually aggressive step: he asked the Ops Center to call the North Korean ambassador in New York immediately.

While the State Department's uncoordinated attempts to manage the emerging crisis have come under considerable criticism, we feel obliged to note that, by all accounts, the State Department Operations Center functioned efficiently through the night of March 20. This commendable performance is in keeping with the center's record of fast and effective management of communications between diplomats.

Several historical examples can help to contextualize the center's performance on March 20 and throughout the turmoil that followed.

For instance, Hillary Clinton has often told a story—which she repeated for the benefit of this commission—about being patched through to a visiting ambassador during her tenure as secretary of state from 2009 to 2013. Only later would she learn that, at the time she had asked to be put in touch with him, the ambassador did not have his cell phone, his staff knew he was out to dinner but not where, and the hotel concierge did not know which of three restaurants he had recommended the ambassador had chosen, if any. The Ops Center called all three, texted a picture of the ambassador to each manager, and found him. The Ops Center tracked down the ambassador so quickly that Clinton wasn't even aware there had been a problem. Similarly, at one point during her own service as secretary of state from 1997 to 2001, Madeleine Albright needed to reach a diplomat who was out of contact at a football game. The Ops Center arranged to have the scoreboard flash a message for him to find a pay phone.

Compared to these challenges, Sullivan's order that the watch officer find Ja Song Nam, the North Korean ambassador, was a snap. Ja was asleep in bed. He had not been told about the emerging crisis. North Korea did not have an Ops Center.

Sullivan knew the State Department had used the New York channel before. He had watched it being used in 2017 to negotiate the release of Otto Warmbier, an American student whom North Korea had detained in North Korea on trumped-up charges. Warmbier had been terribly mistreated in North Korea: when North Korea returned him to the United States, he was in a coma and would die a few weeks later. (The Warmbier family subsequently emerged as favorites of Haley, who felt that the family's grief and ongoing lawsuit helped illustrate the fundamentally evil nature of the North Korean regime.)

Sullivan's intended use of the New York channel was less humanitarian than pragmatic. He saw the moment not simply as an opportunity to punish North Korea for killing innocent civilians, many of them children, but more importantly as a chance to further isolate the Kim regime. He was not the only senior State Department official with this hardheaded sensibility: during Tillerson's tenure, one of his aides, Brian Hook, had written a memo suggesting that human rights were useful largely as a means to "pressure, compete with, and outmaneuver" US adversaries. While many of Tillerson's aides had departed with Tillerson, Hook had stayed on, even traveling with Pompeo to Pyongyang. Now, in consultation with Hook, Sullivan came to see the shootdown of BX 411 less as a crime to be avenged than as an opportunity to pressure, compete with, and outmaneuver Kim Jong Un.

The loss of life was tragic, Sullivan reasoned, but North Korea had backed itself into a corner. He calculated that the resulting pressure on North Korea would offer him his best chance at negotiating an end to North Korea's nuclear and missile programs. "John thought he would offer North Korea a way out," according to Hook, "but he wanted that way out to be a loss for Kim and a victory for us."

Connected by the Ops Center to the North Korean ambassador, Sullivan explained that Sydney Seiler, the newly appointed US special representative for North Korea policy, would be on the 3:15 AM Amtrak out of Washington, arriving in Penn Station at 6:40 AM. Would the North Koreans take a meeting with him?

Ja agreed to meet with Seiler. After a brief discussion, the North Korean diplomat also agreed to ask the Chinese to host the meeting, although Sullivan secured his assurance that it would be a bilateral affair between the two representatives. "The Chinese just bring the donuts," explained Hook later. No one notified Haley or Lerner.

THE CHURCH LADY

President Trump chafed under the order imposed by Francis. Indeed, the president called his chief of staff the "Church Lady"—an insult that he had initially used against Kelly, but which he applied to Francis with even more regularity. In truth, however, Francis was less severe than this nickname implies. He knew he could not change the president. He simply had to try to steer Trump as best he could.

Among his many measures to impose order on the White House, one thing Francis did not try to do was to prevent the president from using Twitter or other social media—even though Twitter remained a constant source of information that Francis and Kellogg believed was often misleading or false and too often tempted the president to make ill-considered remarks that would disrupt days or sometimes weeks of his staff's careful preparations.

Francis and Kellogg had worked hard to persuade other governments not to take the president's tweets too seriously. Francis's predecessor Kelly had once told reporters, "Believe it or not, I do not follow the tweets," and Francis made a point of repeating that statement as often as possible. This was part of a strategy to downplay the importance of these often inflammatory, but technically official presidential statements.

In fact, Francis did attempt to impose some order on what the president tweeted. He asked for the same thing Kelly had asked for—to be informed of what Trump planned to tweet before he did so—and tried to discourage the president from using Twitter to make major policy announcements. Even so, Francis told colleagues, he knew there would always be late-night or early-morning tweets that he did not see. His overall goal was simply "pushing the tweets in the right direction."

But even such mild attempts to direct the president's Twitter habit had proven difficult, especially when it came to Trump's remarks about foreign leaders. In particular, his social-media bullying of Kim Jong Un had reached a new nadir following the collapse of the diplomatic thaw with North Korea in 2018. Of all the people President Trump blamed for the failure of negotiations with the Kim regime—and Pompeo, Kelly, and Bolton received their share of his animus—the person Trump held most responsible was Kim himself.

Of course, Trump could not fire the leader of North Korea with a tweet. But he could express his disappointment that their negotiations had come to naught. Thus, the collapse of the 2018 diplomatic effort was followed by a string of aggressive, baiting tweets that were impressively personal in nature.

> **Donald J. Trump** @tehDonaldJTrump
> That SHORT and FAT kid in North Korea is all talk and no action. He is doing nothing to de-nuke. Great opportunity missed. Too bad!

> **Donald J. Trump** @tehDonaldJTrump
> I have offered Rocketman a wonderful deal. De-nuke now and things will be much better! Or not. Maybe I should push my big Button! IT WORKS!

> **Donald J. Trump** @tehDonaldJTrump
> Little Rocketman has totally misrepresented denuke plan we offered. Deals can't get made when there is no trust! Fat kid blew it and will be sorry. Sad!

> **Donald J. Trump** @tehDonaldJTrump
> De-nuke issue is made increasingly difficult by the fact that Little Rocketman is too weak to stand up to his generals!

Even more noteworthy than these broadsides was a series of tweets directed at Kim's sister, Kim Yo Jong. This Twitter-storm appeared shortly after a *Fox News* segment on the collapse of US–North Korean negotiations and the possible role of Kim Yo Jong, all underneath a chyron reading, "NORTH KOREA'S IVANKA?"

> **Donald J. Trump** @tehDonaldJTrump
> Rocketman's sister IS NOT North Korea's IVANKA.
> Ivanka is 6 feet tall. She's got the best body.
> Rocketman's sister is flat as a board!

> **Donald J. Trump** @tehDonaldJTrump
> Some people say the problem is Little Rocktman's sister.
> They think she's a 10 but she's a TOTAL ZERO.

> **Donald J. Trump** @tehDonaldJTrump
> Lightweight sister of Kim, a total ZERO, "begged"
> President Moon-SHINE to get me me to come to
> Pyongyang (and probably would do anything get me
> there). No THANKS!

At the time of these tweets, few in the United States regarded them as remarkable. Most Americans saw Trump's remarks as simply the latest in a long line of inflammatory but politically inconsequential statements coming out of the White House, no different than the president's occasional online feuds with Oprah Winfrey or Rosie O'Donnell. But in North Korea the tweets about Kim Yo Jong were seen as something altogether different.

THE NARROW STAIRS

At about 5:40 AM on the morning of March 21, the president awoke in his residence at Mar-a-Lago. He turned on the television but showered before finally sitting down before the screen.

Fox & Friends aired at 6:00 AM, about an hour before Moon was to begin his address. (In fact, Moon's address one hour later would not be carried on any major American television stations because it was in Korean.) Instead, *Fox & Friends*, like other morning news programs, led with a general report on the shootdown of Flight 411.

Trump immediately called Francis. "What the hell is going on?"

"A South Korean civilian airliner was shot down," the chief of staff remembered explaining to the president. "It may have been North Korea. We are in the lobby and can meet you in the Situation Room for a full briefing."

"Okay. I have a . . ."

Francis said that Trump spent a moment searching for the right word.

"I have a . . . an *appointment* with Bob."

Francis explained to the commission that his goal was to keep the president calm and focused. "The briefing won't take long, sir. We can schedule our work today around the tee time with Mr. Kraft. We can talk about it downstairs, sir."

"Downstairs. Okay. Little Rocket Man won't be around much longer if he keeps this up, huh?"

"No, sir, he's really made a big mistake. See you downstairs."

Trump put his phone down and got dressed. Because he was still planning to play eighteen holes with Bob Kraft, he picked out his typical golfing outfit of khakis, a white polo shirt, and a red hat. He put his phone in his pocket and then headed out toward the main lobby, where he could take a staircase down into the Situation Room.

When President Trump reached the steep, narrow stairs, he hesitated. A club member in the lobby saw him stop, then feel for his phone in his pocket.

Trump looked down the stairs, winding down into the basement. He often complained that he never got reception down there. The member saw the president do one last thing before going down. Trump took out his phone and tapped out a short tweet. Then he hit SEND and began, ever so carefully, to walk down the stairs, one step at a time.

In the car on the way over to Mar-a-Lago, Francis's phone buzzed, letting him know that the president had sent a tweet. Keith Kellogg was in the car.

"When General Francis read the tweet," the national security adviser recalled later, "he put his head in his hands. I asked him what happened. He just said, 'Clean up, aisle Trump.'"

4

THE NOISE OF RUMORS

THE SIX SOUTH KOREAN missiles took about eleven minutes to reach their destinations in North Korea. At roughly 8:15 PM local time—7:15 AM in New York, long after President Trump had departed the basement at Mar-a-Lago—each missile slammed into its target, one after the other.

The South Korean missiles destroyed two buildings—the headquarters of the North Korean Air Force in Chunghwa and a villa at the primary Kim family leadership compound in Pyongyang. The exact number of fatalities is not known—nor will it ever likely be known, given the events that followed—but it seems that the loss of human life was minimal and confined to Air Force personnel and members of Kim Jong Un's household staff.

With the strikes, South Korea's President Moon Jae-in intended to send an unmistakable message of anger to North Korea's leaders. He had wanted to make clear that he would not simply look the other way as they murdered so many innocents. But while it was born of anger, in the grand scheme of things the strike was a mere gesture. Moon had chosen to use only six long-range ballistic missiles against just two buildings because he wanted to avoid a war, not start one. A smaller strike would punish Kim Jong Un, Moon had concluded, but not at the cost of a wider war that might kill hundreds of thousands, if not millions, of people.

Moon was, we now know, dead wrong.

"AN OPPRESSIVE SILENCE"

The headquarters of North Korea's Air Force was a large office building in an exurb of Pyongyang called Chunghwa. The main building was surrounded by smaller buildings. In front of the main building were a pair of statues—gleaming bronze likenesses of Kim Jong Un's father and grandfather.

The three missiles that struck the main building at the Air Force headquarters left gaping wounds in the four-story structure. After a few seconds, it shuddered and then collapsed, burying everyone who was inside.

The South Korean military had not anticipated the total collapse of the main headquarters building. Although each Hyumoo-2 ballistic missile carried one ton of conventional high explosives, a modern steel-and-concrete structure can take a tremendous amount of punishment. But perhaps not if that steel and concrete are North Korean: according to defectors, construction workers in North Korea routinely failed to follow safety regulations, ignoring building codes and diluting cement mixtures with dangerous amounts of sand. Poorly constructed North Korean buildings had collapsed under far less strain than a missile strike. In May 2014, a residential tower in Pyongyang suddenly fell to the ground, its foundation totally disintegrating under the weight of the building.

When the structure of the Air Force office building slumped down on itself, the collapse severed Kim Jong Un's link to North Korea's air defense forces. As North Korea's leader struggled to make sense of the strike, it would be some time before he was able to communicate with anyone in Chunghwa. Military personnel on site, as well as local civilians who heard the explosions and the sound of the building collapse, immediately began attempting to dig out survivors still trapped in the rubble. "When the building fell down, it was total chaos," according to one survivor. "We just ran to the rubble and started digging people out with our hands. Soon, more senior officers arrived to direct our work, ordering some of us to move the statues and others to go into the bunker."

According to accounts provided by prisoners of war, after several minutes of frantic digging, some troops were ordered to stop and instead evacuate the two monumental statues to safety. The adoration of objects representing members of the Kim family was a peculiar feature of the cult of personality that prevailed in North Korea at the time. No distinction was made between Kim and a likeness of him. This may be hard for those who are not North Korean to understand. In 2013, a traffic warden was awarded the title of "Hero of the Republic" for protecting the leader in an "unexpected situation." Dissidents immediately speculated that she had foiled an assassination attempt, perhaps one disguised as a traffic accident. In fact, she had merely extinguished a trash fire next to a poster with an image of Kim Jong Un. The threat to the image was, in North Korea, synonymous with a threat to the man.

And so, amid the confusion at Chunghwa, airmen brought out a mobile crane to move the two statues to safety. They carefully lifted the statue of Kim Jong Il off its pedestal and placed it lying down, on its back, on a truck bed. They then hooked the crane to the statue of his father, Kim Il Sung, which was sunk in the mud where it had toppled during the strike. They hoisted it up and then laid it down next to the statue of Kim Il Sung in the truck bed. One soldier, later captured as a POW, told his interrogators that as the two statues were driven to the underground storage site, Kim Il Sung's outstretched hand, damaged in the fall, appeared to wave to the soldiers still working frantically to rescue their comrades buried in the rubble.

Only once the statues had been moved to safety did the surviving commander send staff into the nearby underground bunker outfitted to serve as an alternate command center in the event of an attack—but the surviving personnel were not able to set up operations inside it and reconnect with Pyongyang for more than an hour. Some of this delay was due to the confusion and shock in the immediate aftermath of the building collapse as the search for survivors was organized and the statutes evacuated. But most of the time was lost to simple procedural steps; it took time to staff and activate the alternate facility. Much as some readers might like to think otherwise, this problem was not exclusive to North Korea. After smoke began pouring into the National Military Command Center (NMCC) beneath the Pentagon on September 11, 2001, the US Department of Defense took more than an hour to activate its alternate command center at Site R in rural Pennsylvania.

The scene at the Kim family residence was similarly chaotic. Kim's lakeside villa was badly damaged in the strike, suffering direct hits by two of the three South Korean missiles. The explosions that ripped through the building killed a number of cooks, maids, and other household staff. Others were deafened by the explosion, knocked down by the blast, and pelted with debris. Still, the building remained standing, and the survivors who could do so stumbled out into the night. "After the blast, I couldn't hear, and I could only breathe with a tremendous amount of pain," one recounted. "Walking out of the building, there was an unbearable, oppressive silence."

Neither Kim Jong Un nor any important members of his family were at the residence. Nor had anyone in South Korea expected them to be. Members of the Kim family were, after all, routinely spread across a vast web of palaces that stretched throughout North Korea: an enormous complex near the Chinese border at Samjiyon, for example, or an oceanside palace near Wonsan, or a lakefront compound near Kusong. Kim Jong Un had an entire administrative office dedicated to the upkeep of his estates and the management of their staff. When Kim took up piloting small airplanes, he had runways added at no fewer than five of his primary residences.

Despite South Korea's designation of the Kim family residence outside Pyongyang as L-01 ("leadership target one"),

President Moon and his aides had selected this site for attack not because North Korea's dictator was likely to be there, but because he was likely not to be. At the same time, they chose it because it symbolized Kim just as much as any poster or statue.

The flesh-and-blood Kim vastly preferred being outside Pyongyang, either at the beach in Wonsan or in the mountains near Kusong. And because its leader was a dictator, the entire country bent to accommodate these and all of his other whims as well. North Korea's Strategic Rocket Force even mothballed its main missile testing site in the country's far, freezing north in order to shift test launches of long-range missiles—always big events under Kim Jong Un—to friendlier terrain where Kim might view them in comfort. Kim had watched one missile launch from atop a ski resort near Wonsan. Another launch was conducted from a lakeshore shared with his retreat in Kusong.

Of course, discomfort could not be entirely eliminated for the supreme leader. At the moment he was informed of the explosions around Pyongyang, for example, Kim was standing in an unheated warehouse near Kusong, watching a crew prepare a long-range missile for a test the next day.

The United States was completing an annual war game hosted with South Korea, and an enormous number of forces were massed in South Korea for the exercises. From a North Korean point of view, the presence of so many enemy forces was indistinguishable from preparations for an invasion, and so North Korea always placed its own armed forces on alert for the duration of the exercises. Indeed, in recent years North Korea had begun staging missile launches to show that two could play at war. "Every year, you practiced invading us," Jo Yong Won, a close aide to Kim, explained to his interrogators. "So every year, we practiced repelling your invasion with our nukes. It was balanced, like the Taeguk," he added, referring to the national Korean icon that resembled the yin and yang. This ancient symbol represented interdependence and complementarity — principles that, in retrospect, were vital to the tenuous peace that had been maintained on the Korean Peninsula until this fateful moment.

THE THIRD CHANNEL

The missile test whose preparations Kim Jong Un was observing on the night of March 21 was to be part of North Korea's response to the annual American war games. A long-range missile launch, it was intended to simulate a nuclear attack against Guam. During the war game, American bombers had taken off from Guam, flown to a South Korean bombing range, and simulated a strike on the North. It was now North Korea's turn to simulate striking Guam, demonstrating the ability to destroy those bombers with nuclear weapons before they could even take off.

In the warehouse near Kusong, Kim was watching a group of soldiers bolting a dummy warhead to a long-range missile when Choe Ryong Hae, his most important aide, whispered in his ear that there were reports of explosions in Pyongyang. Choe suggested that they immediately seek shelter. Kim agreed.

A small party was traveling with Kim—Choe, a handful of important missile engineers, and Kim's sister, Kim Yo Jong. They immediately walked out of the warehouse and then into the basement of a nearby building. A table and chairs were brought in so that Kim could sit down while his aides tried to figure out what was happening in Pyongyang.

In the basement, Kim and his aides discovered that their cell phones were not working. They were largely cut off from any communication with Pyongyang.

Despite the common impression of North Korea before the war as a "hermit kingdom" cut off from the outside world, there were in fact more than three million cell-phone users in North Korea by 2015, largely located in and around Pyongyang. These users relied on a single state telecommunications network that was provided by a North Korean joint venture with an Egyptian firm called Orascom. The North Korean cellular network was called Koryolink.

Koryolink was a single cell-phone network that offered three separate services—one service for local North Koreans, a second service for foreigners, and a third service for government officials that was encrypted. This "third channel" was in fact the primary method used by senior leaders to communicate with one another because it was the only encrypted communications channel that North Korean leaders believed was secure from American and South Korean eavesdropping. According to Ahmed El-Noamany, an Egyptian national who served as technical director of the network from 2011 to 2013, only high-ranking officials had SIM cards that could access the third channel. North Korea relied on this channel, El-Noamany explained, because sanctions had prevented North Korea from building its own secure military communications system.

The "third channel" was not immune to disruption, however. As soon as people in and around Pyongyang saw and heard the explosions at the Kim family compound there, rumors began to spread. Cell-phone users in Pyongyang began calling and texting one another, quickly generating a mass call event that overloaded the telecommunications system. Because all three channels—domestic, foreign, and governmental—relied on the same physical network, as the calls flooded Koryolink the third channel became largely unavailable to North Korea's leaders. Apart from sporadic text messages and calls, cell communication all but ground to a halt.

Kim Jong Un appears to have become extremely unsettled while sitting in the basement in Kusong with little or no cell-phone service. He was not accustomed to the spartan accommodations of the makeshift shelter. He was in the dark, literally and figuratively. "The supreme leader was very uneasy. He really did not like being underground or uncomfortable," explained Kim's aide Jo Yong Won. "The easiest way to see if he was unhappy was to watch how much he smoked. It was hard to breathe in that little room, with him smoking so much. But of course no one dared ask him to stop."

For Kim Jong Un and his aides, the sudden inability to

communicate with Pyongyang appeared to be no coincidence. "We assumed it was an American cyber-attack," Jo said, then added, "wouldn't you?"

"PLOTTING BASTARDS"

With the spotty cell-phone service in the Kusong shelter, Kim Jong Un had only intermittent and unreliable updates about the situation in Pyongyang. The absence of a steady stream of reliable information led Kim Jong Un to jump to a number of conclusions based on his strongly held beliefs about the United States and South Korea. Understanding these views is essential to understanding the decisions that Kim now made.

During the extensive military operation to stabilize the shattered, post-conflict Korean Peninsula, US and United Nations forces captured thousands of hours of secret recordings of meetings, phone calls, and conferences that detailed the decision-making process of the North Korean leadership in March 2020. It is unclear whether the participants knew they were being recorded, although surviving regime functionaries said that eavesdropping and surveillance were so pervasive that they expected monitoring to be the norm. Others said that the recording reflected a culture of documentation. Although aides were always photographed taking notes, apparently many recordings also were made by personnel who wanted a record of Kim's decisions so that they could track the implementation of his edicts. Until this material became available, the United States had only a few minutes of clandestinely taped conversations of Kim Il Sung and Kim Jong Il—and nothing from the era of Kim Jong Un—on which to base its assessment of North Korea's decision-making.

The image of Kim Jong Un that emerges in these transcripts is that of a leader who, much like Saddam Hussein, was highly intelligent but also frequently ill-informed about the United States and the outside world. Kim was, to borrow a phrase used to describe Saddam, a "curious mix of shrewdness and nonsense." It was this mix of shrewdness and nonsense that, in the basement at Kusong, filled in the gaps and connected the dribs and drabs of information that were trickling in.

Above all else, Kim believed that the United States in general and Donald Trump specifically were embarked on an active campaign to assassinate him. Moreover, Kim believed that the United States was conspiring with China to replace him with another more compliant member of his extended family. Kim frequently referred to Americans in the transcripts as 불쾌한 새끼—which translates roughly as "plotting bastards."

The tapes make clear that, over the past years, Kim's concerns about his personal safety led him to see plots and conspiracies lurking everywhere. And Kim acted on these concerns repeatedly, purging officials whom he believed to be disloyal. In 2013, a young Kim Jong Un concluded that his uncle, Jang Song Taek, was working with China to establish a kind of regency over him. Kim acted decisively, ordering security forces to publicly drag his uncle out of a meeting. Images of Jang being led away from the meeting and then appearing, badly beaten, before a North Korean court were published along with an announcement that Jang had been executed for treason. Kim then ordered a purge of dozens of Jang's lieutenants. There were often grisly stories about how the aides had been executed, involving anti-aircraft machine guns and starving dogs. The North Koreans simply said that Jang had been shot.

Kim also ordered the murder of his half-brother Kim Jong Nam, a plan that took years to execute but was eventually implemented successfully in April 2017, when North Korean agents rubbed a nerve agent in his face at the Kuala Lumpur airport. Even after Kim Jong Nam's murder, North Korean agents continued to make attempts on the lives of his children. Even by the standards of dictators, Kim was particularly motivated to eliminate threats from within his family, a tendency that some of the people close to him attributed to his mother's background. "She was born in Japan, and her father worked for [the Japanese] during the war," one former aide explained. "Just mentioning that . . ." The transcript notes that the aide finished the sentence with a gesture, drawing his hand across his throat like a knife.

The picture of Kim that emerges from these tapes is consistent with prewar intelligence assessments, although it is deeper and more complex. Intelligence assessments correctly judged that Kim was a "rational actor" motivated by clear, long-term goals that revolved around ensuring regime survival—that is, his own survival. Speaking about Kim's behavior prior to the war, Yong Suk Lee, deputy assistant director of the CIA's Korea Mission Center, said succinctly: "There's a clarity of purpose in what Kim Jong Un has done."

What the tapes and interview reveal, however, is that Kim's clarity of purpose was not always matched with a clarity about the reality of the United States or South Korea. Kim was driven by a sense that plots against his life, both real and imagined, were constantly being hatched in Washington, Seoul, and Beijing. Sometimes these suspicions became public. In October 2017, for example, North Korea alleged that it had discovered a plot to assassinate Kim Jong Un that it claimed was carried out by the Central Intelligence Agency and South Korea's National Intelligence Service.

Statements by American leaders stoked Kim's fears. While campaigning for the American presidency in early 2016, for instance, Donald Trump had suggested that his administration would "get China to make that guy disappear in one form or another very quickly." (The Office of the Director of National Intelligence [DNI] declined to make available documents relating to prewar intelligence operations within North Korea, although DNI did provide the commission with a letter strongly denying that there had been "any US-directed effort to assassinate Kim Jong Un" prior to the events of March 2020.) Trump's aggressive stance on Kim was frequently on display in his tweets about the North Korean dictator.

The North Koreans had initially dismissed Trump's angrier missives on Twitter. But Kim had, according to aides, expected that Washington's talk of regime change would end once he obtained nuclear-armed missiles that could strike the United States. This assumption was rooted in history: China tested its first nuclear weapon in 1964, and within a few years Richard Nixon had opened relations with the People's Republic. Kim had believed that the 2018 diplomatic thaw, brief though it was, proved that North Korea's nuclear and missile capabilities left the United States with no choice but to accept him, just as it had accepted Mao's China.

Once negotiations collapsed, however, Trump's tweets took on a more ominous quality for the North Koreans. Far more than the bomber flights or military exercises, it was the slow accretion of personal attacks on Kim and his family that led the dictator to conclude that Trump could not deal with North Korea as an equal, as one nuclear power to another. And in particular, Trump's personal attacks on Kim's sister following the collapse of negotiations had disturbed Kim Jong Un deeply. North Korean propaganda, even at its most hateful and vitriolic, had never once mentioned the American president's daughter or his family members.

From Kim Jong Un's perspective, the meaning of Trump's tweets—whether about Kim Yo Jong or Kim Jong Un himself—could not be more clear: the American president wanted to humiliate the North Korean dictator, remove him from power, and kill his entire family. Trump had hinted at such an outcome before, of course, but what Kim had once been able to dismiss as rhetoric he now viewed as a deeply personal feud.

Kim Jong Un was not irrational. But he was vigilant, to a fault, about threats to his person and to his rule. He had learned that, in the rough-and-tumble politics of North Korea, the survivor was the person who acted decisively, eliminating his adversaries before their plots could take shape. And it is clear from recordings and interviews that, by March 21, 2020, Kim absolutely believed that attempts on his life were real and ongoing—and that his aides were unwilling to question this belief out of fear that Kim would conclude that they too were plotting against him. Now every lesson that Kim Jong Un had learned about how to preserve his grip on North Korea was pushing him inexorably toward the abyss.

THE VIEW FROM THE BASEMENT

Sitting in a cold basement after a missile attack on his family compound, Kim Jong Un quickly concluded that the United States was making good on its threats: the air strikes were an attempt to kill him, the most brazen attempt yet. The evidence before him, at least as he understood it, was quite persuasive on this score.

First, Kim believed that the United States had engineered this crisis, staging the provocation with an American bomber. His aides were adamant that the aircraft had been a military plane, not a civilian airliner. After all, the aircraft had no transponder. What civilian airliner didn't use a transponder? And had it not followed exactly the course of a bomber overflight from only a few weeks before? Moon's speech, whose text Kim's staff in Pyongyang finally managed to relay to him, changed no minds in the basement. Kim saw the speech as more evidence that Moon was no different than any other South Korean leader, that he was simply doing what American leaders told him to do. "Moon's speech, in which he played along with the American ruse, just showed that he could not be trusted," Kim's close aide Jo Yong Won told his interrogators, still insisting that the aircraft had been a military plane. "He was a puppet like the rest."

Second, over the past month the United States had massed a large number of troops, aircraft, and ships on and around the Korean Peninsula as part of the annual FOAL EAGLE/KEY RESOLVE military war game conducted with South Korea. While those troops were present as part of the annual military exercise, North Korean officials had long believed that any war would begin under the cover of this exercise. As a result, Kim's military aides were hypervigilant in looking for any evidence that the war games were no exercise. The fact that the US–South Korean war games in 2020 were bigger than ever loomed large in their estimation.

Third, why was the cell-phone network not working? For many years, the United States and North Korea had engaged in a battle to hack into and disrupt each other's computer networks. In December 2014, North Korea suffered a massive distributed denial-of-service attack that knocked down its internet after President Barack Obama promised a "proportionate response" to allegations that North Korea had hacked the company Sony Entertainment in retaliation for an unflattering portrayal of Kim in the film *The Interview*. And in late 2017, the United States accused North Korea of conducting another large-scale cyber-attack called Wanna Cry. US officials declined to specify what steps the United States took in response. But it is clear that, as a result of the ongoing campaign of hacking and counter-hacking, North Korean military officials had long concluded that any American attack on North Korea was likely to begin with a cyber-attack against North Korea's critical infrastructure, particularly the communications channel used by North Korea's senior leaders.

It is conceivable that aides might have presented Kim with reasons for doubt. Perhaps the aircraft had suffered some kind of electrical problem that disabled the transponder? Maybe the larger war games were nothing more than a reflection of the unusually tense atmosphere? And wouldn't explosions in Pyongyang be expected to result in a huge volume of calls and text messages that might overload the network? But there is no evidence in any of the transcripts that his aides attempted to contradict Kim. This should not be surprising, given that he was already convinced that a plot on his life was afoot. After all, an attempt to deny the existence of a plot would have only led Kim to suspect that the denier was one of the conspirators.

In fact, the small number of Kim's surviving aides remain convinced to this day that the aircraft was in fact a bomber and that the United States staged the provocation as a pretext for an invasion under the cover of the annual FOAL EAGLE/KEY RESOLVE exercise. "History is written by victors," Kim's aide Jo told his interrogators. "And even if this was all a coincidence, how do you explain the missiles?"

Neither Kim nor his aides seriously considered the possibility that the missiles were South Korean or that they had been launched without the approval of the United States. The immediate assumption around Kim was that the missiles were either American or fired on orders from the United States. "We actually did discuss the fact that Moon claimed that he ordered the strike," Jo told his interrogators. "Kim just laughed when Choe said that."

Kim's sister Kim Jo Yong was one of the few North Koreans other than Kim to have spoken with Moon or to have met the South Korean president in person. She played an important role in shaping Kim's thinking at this point. According to Jo, "She smiled and said, very sweetly, 'Don't forget that I too spoke privately with [Moon] Jae-in during the Olympics. He doesn't take a shit without permission from the Americans.' I had never heard her swear before. I was very shocked."

Kim was also receiving inaccurate information from beyond the basement. South Korea had launched only six missiles against two targets, but in the rumors racing through a panicked Pyongyang, the attack had grown to involve dozens of missiles against a much larger number of targets. It is quite common for rumors in a crisis to provide a distorted picture of events, all the more so in a closed society like North Korea, where the most important news usually arrives in the form of a rumor. Even the supreme leader had to pay attention to informal information networks. In the first thirty minutes after the attacks, with sporadic cell-phone service, Kim received conflicting information about the size of the attack and the intended targets, in some cases in reports that were dramatically exaggerated. "I think at one point Choe got a text saying that the zoo had been destroyed and one of the lions had gotten loose," Jo recalled. "We talked for a long time about why the Americans would target a zoo and whether the lion would kill anyone."

Eventually, Choe received a text message informing the party gathered in the basement that the Air Force headquarters had been destroyed. That explained why the Air Force was not in contact with air defense units around the country and was unable to say whether a general attack was under way or not. "The cyber-attack on our communications, the destruction of our air defenses—isn't that how Americans always start wars?" Jo said to his interrogators.

Then, a few minutes later, word reached Kim's sister that the family residence had been hit by another strike. This time Kim's staff in Pyongyang had succeeded in placing a call to Kim Yo Jong in the bunker. She informed her brother that the residence had been targeted and that a small number of staff had been killed or injured. This news marked an important turning point for Kim. "In Kim's mind, there wasn't really any difference between an attack on his house and an attack on him," explained one of Kim's aides in a postwar debriefing. "You have to remember, back then, in North Korea, it was treason to even deface a poster with his picture on it. And you went and blew up his house with a missile!"

South Korea's strike on the Kim residence created one final impression that was a most unfortunate coincidence. North Korean strategists had closely examined Operation Iraqi Freedom, the US military invasion of Iraq in 2003, to understand what a military operation against North Korea might look like. In doing so, they seized on what is generally thought of as a minor footnote in the war. The day before the invasion was set to begin, the United States received intelligence indicating that Saddam Hussein would be at a location known as Dora Farm. The Bush administration raced to design a small strike using cruise missiles in a dawn raid, hoping to kill Saddam as he slept and end the war before it could begin. After reports indicated that Dora Farm had a hardened bunker, two aircraft with four guided bombs were added to the strike package. However, while daring, the strike was a spectacular failure. Like so much of the Iraq War, it was based on flawed intelligence. Saddam had not visited Dora Farm in years. There wasn't even a bunker at the site.

Within the United States, the strike on Dora Farm is largely forgotten—dismissed as a fool's errand, an inconsequential, last-minute improvisation. It received little attention in after-action reports or books about the Iraq War. But in North Korea, military strategists saw something different. They saw a page in the American playbook. They believed that any invasion of North Korea would begin with an effort to isolate Kim Jong Un from his nuclear forces and, in all probability, to kill him. "How did you start your invasion of Iraq? You tried to kill Saddam in his bed and end the war before it started!" Jo reminded his interrogators. "We studied your approach very closely!"

From Kim Jong Un's point of view, the strike on his residence outside Pyongyang was the opening gambit of an invasion. The air defenses that protected him from American bombers were under attack, and he had only intermittent communications by cell phone with what remained of his military. There was every reason to believe that American forces would follow. If Kim Jong Un was going to avoid the grisly end that had met Saddam Hussein, he concluded, he must act decisively to blunt the coming American attack.

"DETER AND REPEL"

North Korea had a single, well-developed war plan. It was based on the realistic understanding that North Korea could not hold out for long against the combined military power of South Korea and the United States.

North Korea's military leaders were rational and competent. They understood that just as the American military had defeated Iraq and just as NATO airpower had toppled Libyan dictator Muammar Gaddafi, the United States could beat North Korea in a conventional war. American military forces were, they knew, far superior to anything that North Korea could field. There was no level of ideological fervor that could blind the North Koreans to this obvious gap between their military and those of their enemies.

The goal of North Korea's nuclear weapons program was to close that gap. Nuclear weapons, the North Koreans believed, would deter any attempt at regime change by the United States. And in the event that deterrence failed, North Korea's military was counting on nuclear weapons to seriously damage the American invasion force and give North Korea the best shot at victory—or at least survival.

Kim Jong Un's grandfather Kim Il Sung had believed that North Korea might be able to use nuclear weapons to destroy American forces in South Korea and Japan, thus preventing an invasion. The United States had, after all, refused to use nuclear weapons against North Korea in the 1950s, in no small part because American military officials believed that the US forces were far more vulnerable to Soviet nuclear weapons if fighting escalated. "Right now we present ideal targets for atomic weapons in Pusan and Inchon," General Joseph "Lightning Joe" Collins had argued in a 1953 meeting. "An atomic weapon in Pusan harbor could do serious damage to our military position in Korea. We would again present an ideal target if we should undertake a major amphibious operation. An amphibious landing fleet would be a perfect target for an atomic weapon at the time when it was putting the troops ashore."

Kim Il Sung and his generals keenly understood that American forces had an Achilles' heel. They would be most vulnerable when they were concentrated, whether in ports or beachheads. As early as the 1960s, Kim Il Sung had told anyone who would listen that North Korea needed atomic weapons to defend itself, for the same reasons that Lightning Joe outlined.

Kim also believed that the horrific casualties arising from the use of nuclear weapons would cause the United States to stop an invasion. "As early as 1965, Kim Il-sung had said that North Korea should develop rockets and missiles to hit US forces inside Japan," according to Ko Young-hwan, a former North Korean diplomat who defected to the United States. Such a strike would produce "casualties of somewhere between 10,000 to 20,000 . . . in order to have anti-war sentiments rise inside the United States and cause the withdrawal of US forces in the time of war." According to Ko, Kim Jong Il believed the same thing: "Kim Jong Il believes that if North Korea creates more than 20,000 American casualties in the region, the US will roll back and North Korea will win the war." Like Saddam, members of the Kim family believed that the United States was casualty-averse and unable to sustain public support for military operations that involved substantial loss of American lives.

Unlike Saddam, however, North Korean military officials would never allow the United States to build up a massive invasion force immediately outside their borders. After carefully analyzing US military operations against Saddam in Iraq and Gaddafi in Libya, North Korean military officials reached the same conclusion as General Norman Schwarzkopf, who commanded US forces during the first Gulf War and who famously admitted that he would have struggled to liberate Kuwait had Saddam continued his offensive into Saudi Arabia. As one commentary that appeared in North Korean state media explained, North Korea was "well aware of [the] foolishness of Saddam Hussein who allowed the deployment of the world's most powerful war forces just at its doorstep." And the commentary made clear that, unlike Saddam, North Korea "would not miss an opportunity but mount an attack by mobilizing all possible forces under its possession in case there is a sign of deployment of armed forces."

Saddam had watched the United States build up a massive invasion force in 1991 and again in 2003. The North Koreans had concluded that was suicide. Saddam's mistake—and Gaddafi's too—was not possessing nuclear weapons that could stop the invasion before it started. "The Saddam Hussein regime in Iraq and the Gaddafi regime in Libya could not escape the fate of destruction after being deprived of their foundations for nuclear development," was how one North Korean statement put it.

This was precisely why North Korea's generals hated the annual American military exercises. Each war game included a large buildup of troops, ships, and aircraft—an agglomeration of military might that could easily be an invasion force hiding in plain sight. North Korea's generals had to watch the exercises extremely carefully for the slightest indication that this was no game. Pyongyang was constantly on guard for the day when the US military exercises turned out to be the real thing. On that day, the North Korean plan was to strike the invaders with nuclear weapons.

All North Korea missile units were trained to execute this plan. They practiced striking US forces with nuclear weapons in port and in their barracks, and they practiced destroying US airbases where airplanes were kept. And to make sure that the United States clearly understood that Kim Jong Un would not sit idly by while the United States assembled his executioners, he posed with maps showing that the DPRK planned to strike

US forces throughout the region. Invariably there would be a map, held down by weights and an ashtray, showing the point where the missile had landed in the ocean. And just as invariably, some North Korean military official had drawn an arc from the splash point down to the intended target—the port in Busan, South Korea, in one case, or the US airbase near Iwakuni in Japan in another. And just to make sure the United States understood all this, North Korea released statement after statement making clear that Kim Jong Un would not hesitate to use nuclear weapons against US forces in South Korea and Japan to stop any invasion by the United States.

Now, trapped in a basement, Kim was certain that an American invasion was gathering steam. And he knew that he must act quickly if North Korean forces were to have any hope of stopping that invasion.

Still, it is one thing to have a plan on paper. It is quite another thing to go through with that plan, particularly when everything hangs in the balance. It would have been understandable if Kim had hesitated. No one, not even Kim Jong Un, would have started a nuclear war with the United States of America unless he was certain that there was no other option, no other way out. Above all, Kim wanted to live—he wanted "regime survival," in the peculiar language of intelligence assessments. But everything he knew about surviving told him that he had to act decisively when the moment came. He could wait—but he could not wait too long. He still had intermittent cell-phone service. How long would that last? Once his cell phone stopped working, it would be too late.

In the end, Kim's cell phone provided the final confirmation he needed. An aide showed him a tweet sent by the American president, time-stamped early in the evening at 7:03 PM Seoul time — nearly an hour before the missiles had been launched. The message was in the president's own distinctive voice. It read:

> **Donald J. Trump** @tehDonaldJTrump
> LITTLE ROCKET MAN WON'T BE BOTHERING US MUCH LONGER!

Kim's English, picked up in boarding school, was passable — certainly passable enough to understand what Trump meant. It was clear evidence, at least to Kim, that Trump knew about the strike in advance. Still, he showed the phone to his sister, who showed it to Choe. Everyone agreed that the tweet's meaning was plain.

It was time to give the order. Waiting would be fatal.

THE ATTACK

At approximately 2:00 AM Pyongyang time, Kim Jong Un gave the order to launch a nuclear strike. The targets: American and South Korean forces on and around the Korean Peninsula.

When Kim Jong Un's order reached North Korea's missile units, commanders roused the troops sleeping in their bunks. Almost immediately, teams of North Korean technicians began driving out to specially prepared launch sites, each carefully selected in advance. Every one of these sites had been cleared of any trees or bushes, then paved with gravel.

The distinctive shapes along the side of the road were unmistakable: each clearing looked exactly like the others. The North Korean troops who had built the sites called them 눈표 —literally, an "eye mark" that a Korean reader might add in the margin of a page, but figuratively an idiom for anyone or anything that stands out.

At each of these sites, a truck pulled up and unloaded its crew of six, who began running hoses out to a decoy. As it inflated, the decoy gradually took the shape of a Scud missile. These decoys had been purchased abroad; sometimes the North Koreans used them as targets in training. With special metallic fabric, they looked almost exactly like the real thing to both human beings and radars.

The decoy crews finished their work quickly—within twenty minutes—and then returned to their bases. By the time they got back, another, more deadly phase of the operation was under way.

At the same time the crews had been inflating the decoys, North Korea began to launch the first wave of its attack—a swarm of drones aimed at missile defenses located throughout South Korea and Japan.

Using drones to attack missile defenses was hardly a novel idea. Iran had, for many years, trained its proxies to attack American-made Patriot defenses by sending cheap drones that used GPS to navigate along waypoints, before diving down on the radar and exploding. Without the radar, the entire battery was useless. And often the missile defense battery would be forced to shoot at the drones, wasting valuable interceptors. After an Israeli battery shot down a $200 quadcopter with a $3 million Patriot missile, there was a lot of talk about defense against drones—but that talk never translated into defenses for the missile defenses sitting in South Korea. At the same time, North Korea released images of drones being used in combat and paraded them through Pyongyang.

Striking American missile defenses was straightforward enough. South Korean and American soldiers routinely took pictures of their bases and uploaded them to Facebook. Soldiers on runs would log their route with a FitBit and upload that to a social media site. The only security measure that South Korea took was placing trees over sensitive military facilities in Naver and Daum—the South Korean equivalent of Google Maps. But since those same facilities were not censored in Google Maps, the ruse merely had the effect of confirming which sites were sensitive.

The single terminal high-altitude area defense (THAAD) system, an antiballistic missile system that US forces had placed in South Korea, was an especially easy target. It had attracted considerable attention in 2017 after being deployed on a golf course in Seongju, South Korea, and the North Koreans knew exactly what it looked like; in fact, a North Korean drone had crashed while taking pictures of the site. The system—and especially its crucial radar—also was visible in satellite images, sitting out in the open. The THAAD system had a radar that could only look forward. It never saw the three North Korean drones that navigated south over the ocean and along the Korean coastline before turning inland and striking it from behind.

Meanwhile, as North Korean units inflated decoys and sent drones to attack missile defenses in South Korea and Japan, Kim Jong Un's missile units had also begun their phase of the operation.

The attack on March 21 largely used North Korea's arsenal of Scud and Nodong ballistic missiles. The Scud was a Soviet missile, although the North Koreans had gotten their first Scuds from Egypt. The Nodong was a larger, even longer-range longer-range version of the Scud developed by the North Koreans, who extended its range to nearly 1,000 miles.

Launching a Scud or Nodong missile requires a period of preparation—soldiers have to use a crane to lift the missile up and place it on the truck that will carry it and then bolt a warhead to it. The most dangerous part of the whole operation is fueling the missile—filling it with toxic propellants that are designed to explode. The safest approach is to erect the missile and then fuel it, but crews can fuel the missile first and then drive to the launch site. Few units will transport a missile filled with explosive fuel and an armed nuclear warhead except in the most urgent circumstances.

These circumstances were certainly urgent. So, with their missiles armed and fueled, the truck drivers and the rest of their crews climbed into the cabins of their vehicles and put on their headsets. The heavy trucks were so loud that the crews inside the cabins could only communicate with one another over radio.

The units themselves had a specific schedule on which they needed to launch their missiles; North Korean military planners knew that in any attack, and especially a preemptive nuclear strike, timing and coordination were crucial. And so the North Korean missile units all went to staging areas where they could hide until it was time to come out.

Like the Iraqis before them, the North Koreans had concluded that digging a tunnel for their missile launchers to hide in might well draw the suspicion of US spy satellites. When possible, therefore, the truck drivers parked underneath highway overpasses or inside road tunnels.

During the Cold War, the Red Army had trained to launch Scud missiles within about ninety minutes of an order. But North Korean crews, like the Iraqis and others, knew that they had no such luxury when fighting the United States. They trained to reduce that launch time to about twenty minutes.

Of course, the North Koreans need not have been so careful. There was no coming air attack. And the launch preparations were being conducted in the dead of night, underneath a thick blanket of clouds, which explains why they were not spotted by US satellites and aerial surveillance.

As the designated launch window approached, the units drove out from their hiding places, parked in pre-surveyed launch spots with their trucks pointing in the direction of their designated targets, and raised their missiles.

North Korean units at nine different locations all over the country fired fifty-four nuclear-armed ballistic missiles against targets in South Korea and Japan, as well as eight more missiles at American forces stationed in Okinawa and Guam. From the first launch to the last, the entire attack occurred in a span of about half an hour.

After each vehicle launched its missile, its location was revealed to American satellites, whose sensors could see the bright burning plumes of the missiles. Kim's military planners knew this would happen, and so North Korean crews had practiced what they called the "double fifteen": within fifteen minutes, the unit needed to move 15 kilometers away—about 9 miles. At the next location, the unit could load another missile, this one armed with a conventional warhead, and fire again. The unit was ordered to repeat this process over and over again until it ran out of missiles or was destroyed.

5

SUNSHINE STATE

AS TRUMP DESCENDED THE stairs leading to the Situation Room beneath Mar-a-Lago shortly after 6:00 AM on the morning of March 21, the crisis had not yet reached the point of no return. Time was slipping away, and quickly, but American officials, even once they became aware of the strike launched by South Korea, simply did not believe that the situation was spiraling out of control.

For the American officials managing the crisis, it was still morning and it was spring. The contrast with Kim's surroundings could not have been greater. In Kusong, it was the middle of the night and there was still snow on the ground. In Palm Beach, on the other hand, March 21 was the kind of bright sunny spring day that illuminates hopes and blots out dark thoughts.

The president and his aides simply did not anticipate that, within less than twelve hours, North Korea would launch a full-scale nuclear attack against US forces throughout South Korea and Japan. In the more than three years that have passed since this historic oversight, many commentators have compared the intelligence failure that struck the United States that day to the US government's failure to anticipate the surprise attack by Japan on Pearl Harbor in 1941, or to take steps to prevent Osama bin Laden from carrying out the terrorist attacks of September 11, 2001. In some quarters, there is even a persistent belief that the senior officials deliberately ignored the warning signs of an impending North Korean attack, or that the attacks were a "false flag" operation designed to justify the postwar impeachment proceedings against President Trump.

We have concluded that there is no evidence of any conspiracy—just a tragic series of mistakes and errors of judgment. The signals of the coming nuclear attack were simply blotted out by the sun that spring day.

MAR-A-LAGO

Jack Francis was in an optimistic mood. All in all, he later explained, the timing of the crisis was fortuitous. So much of his job was keeping bad information, and bad influences, out of the president's ear. If there was to be a serious crisis with North Korea, he recalled thinking at the time, then it was better to have it happen over a weekend in Florida than during the White House workweek.

Francis's reasoning was simple. In Palm Beach, the president was usually isolated. The staff typically remained in Washington. The first lady and their son Barron were in New York. Nor were Trump's other children present. Because it was Saturday morning, his son-in-law and daughter were out of contact while observing Shabbat in Washington, DC, as a family, with their television and smartphones turned off. Of course, exceptions to the electronics ban self-imposed by Jared Kushner and Ivanka Trump could be made in case of emergency, but Francis had arranged to be the person who would decide when to call the White House and ask someone to walk over to the Kushner home. "It was really the best possible situation," said a member of the National Security Council staff who was staying nearby, across the lagoon in West Palm Beach. "There were no obsequious factotums like Stephen Miller and it was up to Francis when and if to awaken the Jarvanka."

Francis wanted the briefing in the Situation Room beneath Mar-a-Lago to be a small affair, one that would settle the president and allow him and the professional staff to manage the crisis playing out between North and South Korea. Francis limited participation in the meeting to just four people: himself, National Security Adviser Keith Kellogg, Secretary of Defense Jim Mattis (who joined by video conference from the Pentagon), and of course the president. Not present was Acting Secretary of State John Sullivan.

The decision to exclude the acting secretary of state from the briefing was not, as press reports initially claimed, the result of technical problems with the video conferencing equipment at Mar-a-Lago. Francis had chosen not to include Sullivan. Trump seemed to dislike Sullivan, possibly because he associated him with Tillerson. The president still resented press reports that Tillerson had called Trump a "fucking moron." More often than not, however, Trump simply pretended not to know who Sullivan was at all.

Francis worried that including Sullivan on the call might provoke Trump to do something unwise, merely out of spite. Francis spoke briefly with Sullivan by phone before the meeting to explain his reasoning. But in the basement beneath Mar-a-Lago, Francis decided to tell the president a different story: he claimed that only Secretary of Defense Mattis would be joining them because the secure video conference software was having some difficulty connecting to the State Department. "They told the president that we were having some trouble connecting to State," according to a Defense Department employee who watched the call with Mattis. "The president made a couple of jokes about Sullivan not being so smart because he couldn't figure out how to work the 'gizmo.' Then the president started ranting about Chuck Robbins." The secure video conference hardware in the Mar-a-Lago Situation Room was made by CISCO, whose CEO, Chuck Robbins, had been critical of a number of Trump initiatives, including the deportation of undocumented immigrants who came to the country as children. The president seemed to hold Robbins personally responsible for what he'd been told were technical problems. "He blew off a lot of steam over John and then Chuck," according to Francis, "but that was okay. Sometimes it helped settle him down."

Francis believed that Mattis was essential to making sure the briefing went smoothly. Although Kellogg and Francis were perpetually rumored to be on thin ice with Trump, Mattis was generally regarded as the most adroit handler of the president's ego. "Mattis somehow managed to moderate Trump's worst impulses," reflected former White House chief strategist Steve Bannon during his appearance before this commission. "I don't know how he pulled it off while getting so much fawning press coverage—the adult babysitting the man-child in the Oval Office and all that." Somehow, as Bannon and other White House insiders had observed, Mattis succeeded in not running afoul of a president who otherwise saw positive coverage of any staff or cabinet member as coming at his expense.

Everyone around President Trump appears to have had a method for managing the chief executive. Many resorted to stalling—agreeing with the president in the moment, but then failing to take any actions to follow up and hoping he would simply forget any action items they had agreed upon. Tillerson had, famously, tried this strategy with the president's proposals to withdraw from the nuclear deal that limited Iran's nuclear energy program. But when the president did not forget, he grew increasingly angry with Tillerson for slow-rolling him and ultimately fired the secretary of state.

Mattis, on the other hand, had survived multiple staff purges with his ability to spin the president around, then gently send him off in the opposite direction. When Trump suggested something crazy, Mattis would compliment the president on his strong instincts. But then, ever so slightly, he would complicate the story, eventually convincing the president that he wanted to do the opposite of what he had just said. Mattis understood that between the president's susceptibility to flattery and disinterest in details, there was ample room to maneuver. Francis was counting on Mattis to use these skills to full effect in case they needed to talk Trump out of doing something crazy, like starting a nuclear war.

Normally, National Security Adviser Keith Kellogg would have been responsible for briefing the president. But Trump disliked long briefings, especially if they began to sound like a lecture. Francis thought that Kellogg's briefings were always too long. So Francis took the lead, succinctly summarizing the situation: The North Koreans had shot down a South Korean jumbo jet, killing everyone aboard. South Korea's president had, to everyone's surprise, announced a limited missile strike on North Korea, which was now under way.

President Trump, Francis explained, needed to put out a statement as soon as possible, condemning the shootdown and urging the parties to stand down. After that, there would be an effort at the United Nations to dramatically increase the pressure on North Korea, with tough new sanctions to punish Kim for what he had done. (Later, Francis admitted to deliberately mentioning the United Nations, knowing that Trump was far more likely to approve of an idea if he thought it came from Nikki Haley instead of Sullivan.)

Francis recalled being surprised that he got as far as he did before Trump started fidgeting and then talking over him. According to Francis, the president was agitated and appeared to still be working through some of the frustration he had expressed during his tirades against Sullivan and Robbins. Trump started by pointing out that he had been right all along: "I told Rex and what's-his-name [Sullivan] that they were wasting their time trying to talk sense into that guy [Kim Jong Un]. He only understands one thing!"

Francis recalled bracing for the request for military options.

"Why don't we hit that little fat kid with everything we have?" the president asked. "What's the point of having all the best nuclear if we don't use it?"

As Francis had hoped, Mattis steered the president back to the proposal for another round of sanctions. "Your instinct, sir, is right on the money," said the secretary of defense, according to a note-taker that Mattis allowed to witness the call from the Pentagon. "Kim Jong Un has to know that if he keeps this up, we will hit him with everything we've got. The South Koreans have just given him a good spanking. We're ready to go too. Now we just need to tell Kim Jong Un that, if he doesn't back down, there is more where that came from."

This seemed to mollify the president, so Francis turned the discussion back to New York. The president's attitude changed when Francis brought up the United Nations for a second time.

"What about Nikki?" Trump asked. "Where is Nikki?" Francis explained to the president that Ambassador Haley was, at that moment, on her way to a meeting with the North Koreans. He did not tell Trump that Sullivan had arranged the meeting, or that Haley had insisted on an invitation only after learning of it from the Chinese ambassador. He certainly did not mention that the Chinese were hosting the meeting. ("Any mention of China," one aide explained, "and BOOM! You were off on a journey to God knows where. Some old Steve Bannon conspiracy theory, usually.") The president indicated that it was good that Ambassador Haley was on the case, then made an off-color remark regarding the ambassador's attributes as an interlocutor.

At that moment, Francis realized that the president was finished with the meeting. "Jack told me that Trump started rehearsing his locker-room talk for later—his golf-game banter," one aide told us later. "That's how he [Francis] knew he had moved on." The president, according to Francis, repeated the remark about Ambassador Haley a second time. "I did wonder how many times his golf buddies would laugh as Trump said it over and over again, as he invariably would."

With the shift in tone, Francis concluded that Trump was now behind his strategy for managing the crisis. The president had agreed, albeit in general terms, to a diplomatic effort. Francis would issue a statement, one that would reframe the president's tweet in a less inflammatory context. The nation's diplomats would go to work in New York. And Trump was off for eighteen holes of golf, followed by a long lunch with his friends.

Typically, with golf and lunch on the agenda, Trump was easy to manage. He might make calls from the golf course, but those calls would be to Francis. As he had the night before, Francis worried that there might be some negative press to the president playing golf amid a crisis. But the White House had dealt with this problem in the past. The White House would often simply refuse to confirm whether the president was playing golf, even if it would later emerge that he had. In one case, a white panel truck just happened to appear parked in a spot that blocked a camera crew from being able to film the president on the green. The truck, it later turned out, was parked in a spot reserved for the Palm Beach County sheriff. Francis declined to discuss these incidents with our investigators, noting that they had occurred before he was chief of staff, but he acknowledged that he had felt confident that he could manage the "optics" of the president's golf outing. And anyway, like most of the president's missteps, it would quickly be buried in the relentless news cycle.

The only other challenge that Francis expected were the mealtimes. Lunch or dinner in an open dining room did raise the possibility of uninvited interactions in which Trump might say something compromising about the situation in Korea. But Francis felt that he could manage those.

There was every chance they might all get through this in one piece, one aide remembered Francis suggesting, and in the long run maybe they would even come out with a big win. "Maybe this is a turning point," the aide recalled Francis saying. "When the Soviet Union shot down a Korean airliner in 1983, what happened?" According to the aide, Francis believed that the international outrage that followed the Soviet Union's 1983 shootdown of a Korean airliner had strengthened the hand of reformers within the Soviet Union, leading to the rise of Mikhail Gorbachev, the fall of the Berlin Wall, and the collapse of the Soviet Union. "Getting rid of North Korea was not quite winning the Cold War," the aide admitted, "but with this president? Jack would take what he could get."

LONG MORNING IN TURTLE BAY

As US envoy Sydney Seiler was pulling into Penn Station shortly after 7 AM, he read about Moon's address—and the South Korean military strike—on his phone. Seiler was a career intelligence analyst who spoke fluent Korean; his background was in translating and analyzing propaganda. He read Moon's remarks in the original Korean and understood immediately that Moon had acted unilaterally. Seiler was pretty sure his meeting was shot. He was not even sure whether the North Koreans would show up to the meeting or not. After all, they would probably want to wait for instructions from Pyongyang, and those orders probably had not yet arrived, given the likely chaos situation on the ground in North Korea.

The North Korean diplomats did in fact attend the meeting, but Seiler was right—it was a total loss. The North Korean ambassador, Ja Song Nam, was unsure what to do. Between the time that Ja had agreed to Sullivan's request for a meeting and the actual meeting, North Korea had come under attack. The North Koreans believed this was an American attack, or at least one carried out with Washington's blessing. Ja, like many North Korean officials at the time, simply could not imagine that South Korea would have taken such an aggressive measure without the backing of its most powerful ally.

Ja, who now lives in California, recalled that his mind was spinning as he entered the Chinese mission. Surely Kim Jong Un would be weighing a retaliation of some sort. But the North Korean Foreign Ministry in Pyongyang was cut off from Kim Jong Un, who at the time was still hiding in the basement at Kusong with limited cell service, and thus Ja's superiors were completely unable to issue instructions to their ambassador in New York. And then there was the matter of the Americans. What diplomatic goals might they have now that they had already used force against North Korea? Ja could only guess. All he knew at the outset of the meeting was that he would have to improvise.

Seiler, for his part, recalled being relieved that the North Koreans had shown up at all—relieved, at least, until the North Korean ambassador opened his mouth. As soon as they sat down in a conference room in the Chinese mission's faux wood-paneled offices decorated with the obligatory traditional landscape painting, Ja launched into a long lecture concerning the various misdeeds of the United States on the Korean Peninsula, starting with the division of the Korean Peninsula in 1945 by Dean Rusk and "that pirate Bonesteel." Seiler smiled. The late Charles Bonesteel III had worn an eye patch later in life that did in fact make him look a little like a pirate, although Seiler understood that Ja was really just using the word as an all-purpose insult, like "brigand."

As Ja's diatribe continued through the Korean War, Seiler calculated how long it was going to last—Ja was progressing at a rate of about two years every three minutes by Seiler's reckoning. At this pace, Ja was likely to go on for more than an hour. Seiler considered his options. He had endured harangues like this before, but he preferred reading them to listening to them. Yet he knew he had no choice but to sit and take it. If he got up and left, it would be the United States that had walked out of the talks—even if there was, at the moment, only one person talking.

Seiler then recalled looking at his Chinese hosts. "They were sitting stone-faced, not moving an inch," he later told investigators. "I admired their discipline." The members of his own delegation appeared to be holding up too. The faces of the foreign service officers who had come with UN ambassador Nikki Haley were impassive; even Haley herself, a politician and not a diplomat, was doing tolerably well, although Seiler could tell she was growing impatient. He found himself looking at the painting. It was a reproduction, but not bad.

Ja later confirmed to investigators that he was stalling in the hope that instructions from Pyongyang might arrive during the meeting. In the meantime, he did not want to give even the slightest impression that he was anything but extremely outraged over the US attack on his country. After all, he recalled, the political officer assigned to his mission would send his every word back home, where it would be scrutinized. "It goes without saying that I had a good relationship with my minder," he later explained, "because no one lasts long if the minder has it out for you. But still, part of getting along is making his job easy. He has to write a report, so you give him something to work with, to prove your loyalty."

After an hour, Ja decided that no instructions would arrive. Having done his duty, he stopped talking. It was now the Americans' turn.

Seiler was brief. Whatever he said, he knew, mattered little. Ja would have to wait for further instructions before offering any real reply. So the US envoy simply expressed outrage over the shootdown of a civilian airliner, demanded that North Korea issue an apology, and explained that the United States had been neither involved in the South Korean launch nor consulted. Seiler glanced at the Chinese ambassador. He noticed an ever so slight note of confusion cross the otherwise steady grimace maintained by the Chinese ambassador when he mentioned this last fact.

Seiler urged Ja to take a message back to his leadership. He very pointedly decided not to issue any threats. The threat of force is often an essential part of a diplomatic process, but as Seiler knew, threats can also backfire, especially if the other side feels that their issuer intends to humiliate the threatened party—or worse. On the train up from DC, Seiler had seen the president's tweet. With South Korea's missiles slamming into North Korea and the president openly taunting the leader of North Korea, Seiler was worried that the United States might be overdoing it already, although at the time he kept those concerns to himself.

As the meeting came to an end, Seiler assured the North Koreans that he would remain in New York and would be willing to meet wherever and whenever the North Korean ambassador suggested. Ja recalled being grateful that Seiler had understood his position, but extremely confused about the American's claim that the US government had had nothing to do with the attacks on his homeland. Yet at the moment, there was little he could do. So the North Korean thanked his Chinese hosts, stood up, and walked out with the rest of the members of the North Korean mission trailing him, returning to his office to wait for further instructions.

The Americans held back, initially just to avoid an awkward elevator ride with the North Koreans, according to one of the US foreign service officers who was present. When the coast was clear, Seiler stepped out of the offices, walked down the hall, and pushed the button for the elevator.

Haley, still furious at having been cut out of the planning for the meeting and resentful of Seiler's role, stopped short of the elevator and took out her phone. She called the Ops Center and asked to speak to the acting secretary of state. According to one witness, as Haley loudly expressed her disappointment to John Sullivan, the Chinese diplomats stepped out of their offices and into the hallway one by one to see what the commotion was about. There they stood, watching the spectacle unfold, as Haley's shouts rang out and echoed down the hallway. Ambassador Haley vehemently denies the story, saying she never lost her temper.

THE NINETEENTH HOLE

In Florida, the spring morning had blossomed into a glorious day. At 10:00 AM local time, Jack Francis and Keith Kellogg were in the Situation Room under Mar-a-Lago, reading a cable from Sydney Seiler recounting the meeting with the North Koreans. The envoy described the meeting as having been inconclusive and unproductive—but he was careful how he framed it. He attributed the inconclusive nature of the meeting to the surprising missile strikes by South Korea, which occurred just before the diplomats convened.

If anything, the cable was boring. A vivid cable, one that tells a good story, can race around an administration as gossip and end up on the front page of the *Washington Post* or the *New York Times*. But Seiler was biding his time, and the last thing he wanted was a headline declaring that the talks were dead. He had delivered his démarche to Ja; now they would wait. The atmospherics were irrelevant.

As Francis and Kellogg reviewed Seiler's readout in the Situation Room at Mar-a-Lago, the president was across the lagoon, at his golf course in West Palm Beach. This disposition —the president in West Palm Beach and his senior staff over the bridge at Mar-a-Lago—held through the morning and into the early afternoon.

Kellogg and Francis spent the day working out of Mar-a-Lago. At 1:16 PM, the National Security Agency (NSA) informed Kellogg that it had detected an unusual pattern of communications in North Korea.

The NSA has a vague, nondescript name because it is charged with one of the most sensitive intelligence-gathering tasks—the collection of "signals" intelligence, or eavesdropping. For many years, even the existence of the NSA was not acknowledged, with employees joking that the acronym stood for No Such Agency. Yet the agency's role in national defense is critical, and there is no clearer testament than its intervention in the unfolding crisis on March 21.

Signals intelligence involves not merely collecting intelligence but also analyzing it. Signals must be separated from noise, and then interpreted. This process may involve breaking codes or recognizing patterns. History now hinged on the latter.

The NSA analysts could not read the North Korean communications because they were encrypted, but the pattern had stood out. These communications looked like nothing that anyone at NSA had ever seen. A report had been made, warning that something unusual was happening. This report had gone up the chain of command and had finally prompted Admiral Michael Rogers, the agency's director, to phone Kellogg.

Kellogg thanked Admiral Rogers for the report, then hung up and discussed the matter with Francis.

The two decided to take no action.

The report was, according to senior officials, "vague and not specific." And the timing was a challenge. After his briefing in the Situation Room, the president had traveled from Palm Beach to the mainland, where he had a 9:30 AM tee time. Typically, Trump's outings on the golf course would last for about four and a half hours, including lunch. At 1:16 PM, when the report arrived, Trump would have been nearly finished with the round of golf, but would not have eaten lunch yet.

Neither Kellogg nor Francis believed that it was wise to interrupt the president, particularly when he was so close to finishing his outing. "We were told [the president] was shooting really well. Sometimes he struggles with his wedge game," explained an NSC staffer. "Our goal was keeping him on an even keel—and no one could see how yanking him off the course would help."

Other White House staffers dismissed the unusual pattern of communications as "chatter," reasoning that it could be anything. It was easy enough for these officials to imagine that the communications warned of some familiar danger when, in fact, it was a warning of an entirely new kind of threat—as we now know.

This is what the historian Roberta Wohlstetter called the "background of expectation"—the assumptions and beliefs that allow us to make sense of confusing and contradictory information. Francis and Kellogg were, at that moment, focused on the possibility that North Korea might respond with another provocation. They were particularly worried about the possibility that North Korea would conduct a nuclear weapons test designed to be shocking—such as placing a live nuclear warhead on a missile and firing it over Japan and out to sea. Testing a live nuclear weapon over the ocean would be very unlikely to cause much long-term harm, but it would demonstrate North Korea's nuclear capabilities in the most vivid way.

Because the background expectation of senior officials was that North Korea was likely to conduct a provocative missile test in response to South Korea's strike, they interpreted the unusual signal pattern as a warning of this expected danger —not as an indication that the crisis had taken a new and dangerous turn. Neither Francis nor Kellogg considered the possibility that the unusual pattern of communications was warning of a large-scale North Korean nuclear attack against US forces throughout South Korea and Japan.

This is not a new or novel problem. Both the Roberts Commission, which was charged with understanding why the United States was unprepared for Japan's attack on Pearl Harbor, and the 9/11 Commission observed that background expectations had helped blind policymakers to these surprise attacks. While there was sufficient evidence to anticipate both attacks, it was only with hindsight that the signals clearly separated themselves from the noise. In 1941, and then again sixty years later in 2001, policymakers were expecting different sorts of attacks in different places—and those expectations blinded them to warnings that seem clear in hindsight.

Something very similar was now happening in 2020. It was inconceivable to American policymakers that North Korea would start a nuclear war with the United States, a war that North Korea was certain to lose. After all, officials knew that Kim Jong Un had no incentive to start a nuclear war unless the United States was about to invade North Korea. And they both knew that no such invasion was planned.

Francis and Kellogg understood that the South Koreans had conducted the missile strike on their own. And they knew that the president's tweet was little more than an offhand comment before a day of golf and banter. It seems not to have occurred to either of them that Kim Jong Un, cowering in a basement and struggling with only intermittent access to communications, might not share their clarity on these points. Nor did it occur to them that his own background expectations might be shaping his decisions in a profoundly different way.

And so the strange pattern of communications was noted by Francis, Kellogg, and a small circle of aides, but nothing was done. The information was too vague. And the president was too close to completing his game. It was better, they all agreed, to let him finish his round of golf, then go to lunch in the clubhouse.

The president shot a 71.*

---

* Former president Trump was emphatic that the commission note his score, which was one stroke under par. While the commission understands that the step of noting the president's golf score may seem out of place in such a document, the former president, after a draft was shared with him for his comment, expressed his concern that "the fact that you didn't publish the number proves that you are just like all the biased reporters who are part of the anti-Trump fake news media that never gives me as much credit as I deserve."

6

A FALSE DAWN BREAKS

FOR MILLIONS OF PEOPLE in South Korea and Japan, dawn broke early on Sunday, March 22. More than thirty-one North Korean nuclear weapons, lifted into space on ballistic missiles, now fell silently back to earth through the night sky before suddenly igniting the day—first with flashes, each brighter than a thousand suns, and then with spontaneous fires that in some cases grew into firestorms. These conflagrations swept through the cities and towns of South Korea and Japan, burning brightly enough to keep the darkness at bay for days.

It is not possible, with mere words, to fully convey the scale or the horror of the suffering to those who did not live through those difficult days. But some accounting of the destruction is necessary in this report. Thus, we have chosen to share the stories of three survivors. It cannot be said that the experiences of these individuals were typical, for there was no typical experience for the millions of survivors, each of whom has endured their own private horror. But perhaps these three stories can begin to explain the struggle for life that followed North Korea's nuclear attack on its neighbors.

Survivors are, by definition, an unusual group. To this day, each wonders why he or she lived when so many others perished. They count and count again the many small items of chance or caprice—a decision to stay at work in one case, a decision to stay home in another—that spared their lives. For observers, however, there is neither rhyme nor reason for who lived and who died. Instead, there is only chance, or perhaps luck—although more than one survivor objected to our investigators' use of that term.

For many of the people who survived, and who saw more death in those two days than they might have expected to see in a dozen lives, the luckiest ones were those for whom morning never came.

SEOUL

After delivering his television address announcing the missile strike against North Korea, President Moon Jae-in and his aides faced a long night. None of them believed that they were on the threshold of a nuclear war, although they did worry—indeed, they were certain—that Kim Jong Un would retaliate in some form. More than anything, they were anxious that the tit-for-tat should remain under control. "We were definitely worried that Kim might punch back," according to Im Jong-seok, Moon's aide, "but our mind-set was all about keeping things from getting too crazy."

At the same time, there was not much for the South Koreans to do. There were no survivors from BX 411, and the missiles had been launched. When Moon and his advisers reconvened in the bunker, they found themselves just sitting there, silently, waiting to learn whether the strike had been a success and checking their phones. Kang Kyung-wha, the foreign minister, noticed Trump's tweet first. She read it aloud, first in English and then translated into Korean.

Kang had studied in the United States, and her English was excellent. But she was never really sure how to translate the taunt implied in "Rocketman"—Mr. Rocket? Rocket Boy? The others around the table quizzed her about the rest of her translation. Did Trump really just suggest that he was about to kill Kim Jong Un? It was ambiguous. "He's really a fool, isn't he?" she said, to no one in particular.

Eventually, a preliminary damage assessment arrived—a few sheets of paper in a folder marked "SECRET," carried by a military aide in a smart uniform. The aide handed the folder to General Jeong, who opened the folder, scanned the contents, then distributed them to the rest of the group in the bunker.

The damage assessment was a single page, but General Jeong nonetheless provided an impromptu briefing. South Korea's intelligence assets were not as extensive as those of the Americans, and they would need to wait for daylight to take clear satellite pictures of the damage. But it seemed that the missiles had reached the targets. There were six large explosions. And based on intercepted cell-phone conversations, it seemed the big building at the Air Force headquarters had fallen down and that there were casualties at the Kim family residence. He also noted that, despite the strike, North Korea's military—already on alert for the duration of the US–South Korean war games—was acting normally, although he cautioned that it was too early to know exactly how the North would respond.

Moon asked a few questions. "General Jeong felt obligated to brief the president, and in turn, Moon felt obligated to ask at least one question to show he was listening," Im recalled. "But there was really no point. We all had copies of the same piece of paper."

They waited in the bunker for at least another hour before General Jeong pointed out that it might be several days before North Korea responded. After all, he said, it would probably take until the morning for the North Koreans to give Kim Jong Un a full and accurate picture of what had happened, and they would likely need a day or so to plan a calibrated response. "I know the president felt some responsibility to see the strike through," Im recalled, "but there really wasn't anything to do in that bunker. General Jeong was doing us a favor, hinting that we could all go home."

Eventually, at 11:24 PM, after sitting in the bunker for nearly three hours, Moon relented and suggested that they all go home and try to get a good night's sleep. He asked his aides to inform him immediately if the military detected any unusual movements in North Korea, such as preparations for a missile test or an artillery barrage. They all agreed that, in that case, they would reconvene immediately. If not, Moon told them, they were to treat the next day like any other Sunday. General Jeong asked for all the copies of the damage assessment, counted them, and slid them back into the folder before locking it in his briefcase.

Moon retired to his residence. Im Jong-seok, the president's aide, telephoned his wife to say that he would stay overnight in a guest room at the Blue House. Im later recalled that he was uneasy, convinced that he was in for a sleepless night. "I decided not to go home," he said later. "I didn't think I was going to sleep much anyway. I don't know why, but I knew the phone would wake me."

The call came at 2:16 AM, when General Jeong woke Im Jong-seok to inform him that the military had intercepted an unusual pattern of communications in North Korea. The communications were mostly encrypted, but the pattern was still unusual enough that General Jeong thought the president should know. South Korean military intelligence had intercepted a great many communications since North Korea's military went on alert at the beginning of the US–South Korean war games a month earlier. But this order looked different. General Jeong said that they had never seen anything like it before. He suggested that some North Korean units, such as the country's missile units, might be moving to a higher state of readiness. Im said that he would wake President Moon.

Moon's residence was only a short walk from the guesthouse where Im was staying. He walked across the courtyard, then asked the household staff to wake the president. Moon emerged from his quarters after a short delay. "I suggested that he call General Jeong," Im recalled later. "Moon said it was enough to reconvene."

Moon and Im briefly discussed where the security council should gather. The Crisis Room was secure, but it was also small and cramped. Moreover, it was cut off from the rest of the government now housed in the Central Government Complex, which was in downtown Seoul and separated from the Blue House by an ancient palace complex. Moon decided that it was better that they meet downtown. They could evacuate back to the bunker if things got out of hand. "Then he said I looked terrible, like I had not slept at all," according to Im. "I told him about my premonition about the phone call. [Moon] Jae-in looked at me a long time, and I got the sense he worried that the stress was starting to get to me. He suggested that I go back to bed for a few more hours."

Im recalled weighing the president's offer before acquiescing, telling himself that it was unlikely that he would have another chance to rest in the next twenty-four hours. "I didn't know that was the last time I would see him," he explained to investigators.

Moon arranged for a motorcade to take him to the Central Government Complex, about a mile away. He was still downtown, with most of his national security team, when, at 5:48 AM, a single nuclear weapon exploded over the city center.

The explosion reduced the Central Government Complex to rubble. President Moon and all of the advisers who had gathered with him apparently were killed in the blast. Like more than one million people in Seoul that day, they simply

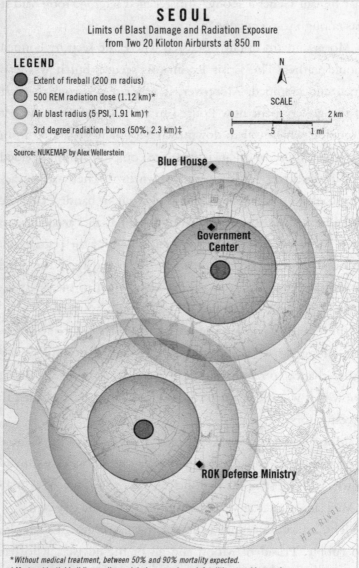

SEOUL

Limits of Blast Damage and Radiation Exposure
from Two 20 Kiloton Airbursts at 850 m

LEGEND

- Extent of fireball (200 m radius)
- 500 REM radiation dose (1.12 km)*
- Air blast radius (5 PSI, 1.91 km)†
- 3rd degree radiation burns (50%, 2.3 km)‡

N

SCALE

0   1   2 km
0   .5   1 mi

Source: NUKEMAP by Alex Wellerstein

Blue House

Government
Center

ROK Defense Ministry

Han River

*Without medical treatment, between 50% and 90% mortality expected.
†Most residential buildings collapse, injuries are universal, fatalities are widespread.
‡Third degree burns extend throughout the layers of skin, and are often painless because they destroy
the pain nerves.

disappeared—incinerated in the fireball or ground into nothing as the massive government building collapsed.

Despite its proximity to the downtown government complex, the Blue House sustained only what is called "light damage." The explosion shattered all the windows, sending shards of flying glass through the buildings. Although Im, lying in his bed, suffered lacerations on the side of his body facing the window, he was not seriously injured. The guesthouse did not collapse on him. A few of the buildings were seriously damaged when the blast wave pushed past them, then reflected off the massive hillside and hit them again from behind. The effect was like a riptide, straining the buildings in one direction, then pulling their foundations out from under them in the other.

Im was able to stumble outside, although he was in a daze. He initially thought it was snowing. "Only after a few moments did I realize that it wasn't snow, but that there were pieces of paper floating everywhere. I picked up one. It was the damage assessment that General Jeong had tucked under his arm."

After the blast knocked down the massive towers in central Seoul and the heavy steel-and-concrete structures fell, millions of sheets of paper from the office buildings now turned to rubble drifted up and wafted through what remained of the shattered city. Many survivors remembered the pieces of paper as a snowfall. Many others found a sort of solace in tracing the pieces of paper that they picked up that day and, for some strange reason they said, could not throw away. Each scrap of paper seemed to help connect many of the survivors to those others with whom they shared that terrible day.

It is not possible, however, that Im picked up a copy of the damage assessment distributed the night before. When the blast hit, General Jeong was in a car driving from the Central Government Complex to South Korea's military headquarters —the blast wave flipped his car, then buried it beneath ten feet of rubble from the buildings it pushed over. When the general's body was recovered, all six copies of the damage assessment were still locked in his briefcase. Im's shock and confusion, it seems, had simply gotten the better of him.

Im then attempted to make his way on foot to the Central Government Complex a mile away, not realizing that it was totally destroyed. There was so much dust and ash in the air that he could barely see or breathe. As he picked his way through the wreckage, his progress slowed to a crawl as his coughing and choking got the better of him. A seemingly endless number of crushed or overturned cars littered the vast, indistinguishable landscape of rubble.

After a nuclear explosion in or near an urban area, collapsed buildings spread a debris field of rubble almost evenly across the blast zone. In Seoul, a modern city with towering skyscrapers, the debris field was more than twenty feet high in some places. Im found that he could not go more than a few hundred yards before he had to turn back.

When Im arrived back at the Blue House, he found it completely deserted. There were no security guards at any of the checkpoints. He was able to walk through the grounds, into the main building, and then down into the bunker without stopping once to show anyone a badge or let them inspect his briefcase. *That's convenient*, he thought: in his haste after the blast, he had neglected to even dress himself, much less pick up his badge and briefcase. He was wearing nothing but the T-shirt and briefs in which he had fallen asleep. Both were soaked with his blood from the wounds he had sustained in the blast.

As Im entered the bunker, he found Admiral Um, sitting alone. Um had also attempted to go downtown after the blast, but he too had found his way blocked. When that failed, he thought perhaps he should make his way to the Crisis Room. The two of them sat there, alone in the bunker, with all the television screens off and the telephones dead.

Im asked if they could go someplace else, but the admiral had already considered that. "No car," he told Im. His driver had fled after dropping him off. The two continued to sit there, with the admiral in his splendid uniform and the civilian in his bloodied underwear. "It was really quiet, and then I heard thunder," Im recalled. "Admiral Um listened for a moment, then shook his head. He just said, 'Artillery.'"

TOKYO

Kenichi Murakami was the chief of the Tokyo Fire Department. He was very proud of that fact. Of course, all around the world, young boys and girls dream of growing up to be firefighters. But in Japanese culture, firefighters are more romantic bandit than simple hero. The traditional ladder-wield-ing fireman depicted in Kabuki theater or in a woodblock print is more likely to be found brawling with sumo wrestlers than putting out fires.

The firemen of Edo—as Tokyo was called during the early nineteenth century—certainly had plenty of fires to fight. Tra-ditional Japanese homes were built of wood and paper, and they were packed close together. Great fires ripped through the city on a regular basis—so often that people began to call the conflagrations *edo no hana* ("the flowers of Edo"). The cultural difference between firefighters in other parts of the world and the *tobi* (firefighters) of Edo can be explained by the simple fact that the latter did not fight fires with water; they had no water trucks or water pumps, just a few buckets and ladders. The primary method of controlling fires at the time was to knock down houses to make a firebreak, which allowed the fire to burn itself out without spreading. Thus, the fire brigades weren't there to fight the fire but to fight any homeowner who might—understandably—resist seeing his home demolished.

A sort of protection racket arose around the firefighters. Af-ter all, it was far better if the *tobi* sacrificed a neighbor's house to the firebreak rather than your own. Naturally, the Edo fire-men became a tough lot—drinking, brawling, and covered in tattoos. Indeed, the distinctive tattoos that mark the *Yakuza*, today's Japanese gangsters, are a relic of the Edo fire brigades.

Modern firefighters in Japan, of course, are a more professional group. The only real links between modern firefighters and the Edo firemen are the acrobatic teams that each department keeps; these are groups of skilled firemen who perform dangerous stunts atop ladders to thrill children. They are well educated and professional, respected for their bravery in the face of great danger. There are a number of women in their ranks. The model for the modern Japanese firefighter is less the Edo fire brigades than the professional firemen who helped battle the firebombing of Tokyo in the final months of World War II. On a single night in 1945, nearly sixteen square miles of the city burned in what was then the largest firestorm in history, and larger than the fire that would engulf Hiroshima a few months later.

Today Japanese people expect a lot from firefighters. And Murakami expected a lot of himself. Ordinarily, he might have been on his way to the office at 6:02 AM, even on a Sunday. After all, he had so many preparations to plan for overseeing the 2020 Summer Olympics, which were set to open in Tokyo in just 124 days. There was much to do. But he was tired. He simply needed a day off, one day when he was not headed into the office while everyone else slept.

Murakami was still in bed, then, when his cell phone buzzed.

⚠

Emergency Alert

Missile Launch

2020/03/22 06:02

A missile was reportedly fired from North Korea. Please

stay inside your building or evacuate to the basement.

(Ministry of Disaster Management)

Five minutes later, at 6:07, a nuclear weapon exploded with the force of 30 kilotons high above Japan's Defense Ministry. This was twice the size of the bomb that leveled Hiroshima. A few minutes later, a second weapon exploded a mile to the north.

Murakami saw both flashes. He called his office, but got no answer.

If Murakami had been on his way to work, he probably would have perished while sitting in his car at an intersection. And had he survived the car journey, he probably would have been killed by the second blast, which severely damaged the Tokyo Fire Department headquarters less than two miles from ground zero. He was very lucky.

He got dressed in a hurry and went outside. As he tried to start his car, he briefly remembered someone telling him that an electromagnetic pulse—one of the side effects of a nuclear explosion—could damage a car's electronics. But the car started. Murakami soon realized that the problem wasn't going to be a dead car; rather, it was going to be the tens of thousands of working ones.

When Murakami got to the highway, he saw a massive traffic jam caused by people trying to flee Tokyo. He got out of his car. His phone was working, but there was still no answer at the Fire Department headquarters. He started to wonder whether there still was an office. He started calling around to other headquarters within the Fire Department. Murakami soon realized that no one in central Tokyo was answering.

He needed to set up a temporary command post. The Olympic Security Command Center (OSCC) was now largely functional and outside of central Tokyo, far from the blast zone. But it was still quite a distance away. Fortunately, the Tokyo Fire Department had a few helicopters to rescue people from burning buildings. The fire chief managed to get in touch with one of his fire stations where a helicopter was based and asked for a ride.

In the helicopter, Murakami had a commanding view of Tokyo. He looked over the endless city and saw that the center of Tokyo around where the Defense Ministry had been was completely leveled. The blasts had knocked down all the buildings for more than a mile, and further out it had stripped others to their bare steel frames. Those bare frames stood like skeletons around the blast zone, keeping watch over the smoldering ruins. And then Murakami noticed what worried him most: fires were breaking out all around the city.

Nuclear explosions release an enormous amount of heat, setting fires that, in many cases, can do far more damage than the blast from the explosion. But fires are hard to predict. Murakami's fire department had trained for all kinds of disasters, including a nuclear explosion. He was prepared for fires to break out in residential areas and at low-rise public buildings constructed of wood. Most of the technical literature works from the assumption that modern cities, built of steel and concrete, are relatively resistant to fire. But the reality can be far more complicated—as Murakami learned when he arrived at the OSCC.

In recent years, Murakami now recalled, there had been a spate of high-rise fires, many of which resulted from the flammable cladding on the outside of the buildings that has become popular because it both improves the appearance of a building and increases its energy efficiency. The Grenfell Tower in London that killed seventy-one people in 2017 was the most famous case, but there had been similar fires in Australia and South Korea. One survey of Melbourne concluded that more than half of the 170 buildings surveyed were a fire risk. In energy-conscious Japan, such cladding was also commonplace.

Now Murakami was witnessing the same effect across his own city: many tall buildings were on fire. These structures might well have been perfectly safe in normal conditions, but the towers were simply not designed to withstand the intense heat of a nuclear explosion. To make matters worse, the widespread loss of power had led to sharply reduced water pressure throughout Tokyo, disabling many sprinkler systems. Fighting fires in high-rise buildings is one of the most demanding tasks any firefighter will ever face. Murakami was facing dozens of fires in tall buildings spread around the disaster area.

Inside the OSCC, Murakami worked hard to coordinate the groups of firefighters throughout the city, but the fires erupted so quickly that he found it impossible to keep up. Told that a building was on fire one moment, he was often informed the next that it was hopeless and out of control—all before he could assign firefighters to deal with the problem.

In the midst of this maelstrom, he received another text:

⚠

Emergency Alert

Missile Launch

2020/03/22 07:23

A missile was reportedly fired from North Korea. Please stay inside your building or evacuate to the basement.

(Ministry of Disaster Management)

Mildly surprised to see that the emergency alert system was still functioning, Murakami felt his spirits lift a bit, before the weight of his situation settled over him once more. He had a responsibility to do his part, even if his efforts seemed to be futile. He decided not to seek shelter, but to keep working. *How can I hide underground when my firefighters are out there?* he later recalled thinking.

The next missile fired was not a nuclear one. North Korea had a small stockpile of nuclear weapons, most of which had been fired in the opening attack. Over the next twenty-four hours, Murakami's phone would continue to receive missile alerts. Eventually, he remembered something he had read about World War II. During the war, after Allied bombers dropped incendiaries to set fire to German and Japanese cities, the Allies would launch a second wave of bombers with explosives — to kill the firefighters attempting to put out the fires. In Syria, the same kind of strikes were called "double taps" — one strike against a target, then a second strike to kill the first responders. As his firefighters were trying desperately to extinguish the blazes breaking out all over Tokyo, Murakami realized that the North Koreans were trying to stop them. They were trying to kill his firefighters so that Tokyo would burn.

These follow-on missiles, armed with conventional explosives, were frightening, but far too inaccurate to really hamper the firefighters. Soon enough, the strikes dwindled. Over the course of the first day, the firefighters responded to warnings of incoming missiles by calling the warheads *sumo-tori* — a sly reference to the sumo wrestlers who had brawled with their predecessors of yesteryear.

As the day dragged on, the fires burning throughout Tokyo began to draw air in toward the city center. March is the windiest month in Tokyo, and so, at first, Murakami merely worried that the stiff breeze might fan the flames at the individual fire sites, making the job tougher and more dangerous. But as the force of the winds continued to climb, his heart sank. It wasn't a March wind at all. In fact, the morning had been perfectly calm.

The fires were growing in strength and starting to make their own weather. This was the beginning of a firestorm.

Not every nuclear explosion unleashes a firestorm. In August 1945, Hiroshima burned in one, but Nagasaki, nestled among the mountains, did not. Predicting whether a firestorm will or will not develop is nearly impossible—it's so difficult, in fact, that the US military has never even attempted to calculate deaths or damage from fire in its models of nuclear war. Fire is simply too unpredictable, too wild, for neat and tidy calculations.

As the wind speed topped 70 miles per hour—the same as a typhoon—Murakami realized that the unthinkable was happening. Tokyo was now a city of metal and glass, not wood and paper. But it would burn just as it did during the Second World War when the Allies dropped incendiary bombs on it.

Modern firefighters, even with all their equipment and technology, are as helpless in the face of a firestorm as an Edo fireman with his buckets and ladders. Murakami understood that he could not put out a fire of this size and scale. He would have to treat it like a wildfire, containing it until it burned itself out.

What he needed to make this tactic work were firebreaks. But how to make firebreaks in a city? The firemen of Edo might knock down a house made of wood and paper with their hands, but modern steel-and-concrete structures? Murakami took out a map and began to locate the natural firebreaks—rivers, open spaces, hillsides—throughout Tokyo. He began to order the crews to retreat to these points, leaving much of central Tokyo to burn. "I thought about those old guys, the ones who fought fires with not much more than their ladders," he said later. "I felt totally helpless. Maybe firefighting today isn't so different after all."

BUSAN

Oh Soo-hyun shared a name with a doctor in a Korean soap opera. She was a doctor too, though beyond that single point of comparison, she was completely different from her fictional counterpart. The television Oh was rich and sheltered. The emergency room doctor in Busan, South Korea, was competent and thoroughly middle-class. The television Oh had a father who ran the hospital. The doctor in Busan had only her mother, who lived in a small hamlet two hours outside the city.

Korean dramas about doctors typically feature the archetype of the "genius" doctor—a person with something resembling the magical power that most cultures attribute to healers. Oh knew that the only genius when it came to practicing medicine was working hard and paying attention. Still, she cherished little moments of, if not genius, then ingenuity—fitting an extra patient into her schedule, for instance, or bending a rule to help someone. This was especially true for patients from her hometown, who came to the city only when they had a serious problem. If she thought a patient didn't have a lot of money, she might do a test herself rather than make a referral to one of her specialist colleagues. If it proved unnecessary, she wouldn't charge the patient for the test.

Lately, her supervisor had cautioned her about bending such rules. The warning was a mild one, but Oh took things seriously. She'd started to have a recurring nightmare in which her bosses discovered every single bent rule or infraction and then insisted that she pay them back for all the hospital resources she'd wasted. On the morning of March 22, she was tired, having spent another night wrestling with that unwelcome dream.

Still, Oh didn't exactly stop bending rules. At 6:02 that morning, she was doing it again—walking down a hallway and carrying a blood sample she'd drawn herself, quite against the regulations, from a patient who was now seated in one of the examining rooms at the end of the hall. She was just one step from the giant window that looked out over the courtyard when there was a giant flash—"like someone taking a picture in an old-time movie," she remembered later.

She dropped to her knees just as the blast ripped through the hospital, slapping the glasses off her face and smashing the blood sample against the wall. She shouted for the chief resident. He was in his office, badly cut by debris. The entire hospital was in chaos. The windows were blown out, beds were overturned, and parts of the ceiling had collapsed. There was blood and glass all over. Patients were screaming. Others were lying motionless. At the end of the hallway, Oh's patient was dead. So too were the technicians in the laboratory she'd been heading to with the blood sample. In fact, Dr. Oh was the only doctor on staff who was not seriously injured—but without her glasses.

She quickly grabbed as many bandages as she could and began treating the injured, cleaning their wounds and dressing them one after another. Working steadily on the wounded patients and doctors inside the hospital, she was so focused on her work that she did not realize that thousands of maimed and dying residents of Busan were gathering outside.

Busan had billed itself as the "medical hub" of Asia. In the developing world, there are usually about six hospital beds for every 1,000 people. In South Korea, that number was nine beds for every 1,000 people, and in Busan it was nearly twenty-one. With more than 72,000 hospital beds, Busan was as well equipped to handle a massive humanitarian crisis as any city in the world.

But the scope of the humanitarian crisis now facing Busan was extraordinary. Two 20-kiloton nuclear weapons had detonated over the docks in the city's harbor. The explosions killed almost 100,000 people and seriously injured more than 400,000, many of whom were too injured to move. Those who could move—or those whose friends or family members were able to carry them—were now descending on the city's hospitals by the tens of thousands.

The nuclear weapons that had killed and injured so many did not discriminate among their victims. The bomb does not spare doctors or nurses. Many hospitals in Busan were ravaged by the explosions and their aftereffects. St. Mary's, less than a mile from one of the detonation points, was totally destroyed. And Pusan National University, where Dr. Oh was working, had a direct line of sight to the other explosion. With nothing to shield it from the blast, it had suffered terrible damage, although so far it had not collapsed. Thankfully, Busan is nestled in the mountains. So although the port district and its medical facilities had been partially leveled, the surrounding areas were somewhat shielded. Other hospitals, nestled in Busan's mountains, had been largely spared—but now they, not to mention the surviving doctors, nurses, and orderlies at the stricken hospitals, were overwhelmed.

As Dr. Oh began to treat the wounded, she noticed that, in addition to abrasions and lacerations, patients began appearing with terrible burns. Quickly she realized that she was running out of supplies, from medications to treat the burns to simple bandages. She kept treating one person after another. By this time, she recalled, that spark in her personality that had led her to try to see each patient as a person who deserved a bit of special treatment had disappeared entirely. She moved mechanically from one patient to the next, treating the same problems over and over again. She worked for seventeen hours straight, desperately trying to care for the wounded. When she attempted to sneak off to sleep, just for a few minutes, a group of wounded people found her and excoriated her for sleeping while they suffered, left untreated.

As March 22 stretched on, Dr. Oh began to realize that there were simply too many patients to treat. She needed to make decisions. Which injuries were too light to bother with? Which were too severe to bother with? It was no use treating someone who was just going to die. And where were the other doctors and nurses? She remembered reading a study that said, after the Fukushima accident in Japan, many doctors, nurses, and clerical staff simply did not show up for work. Absentee rates were especially high among clerical staff. Where were they now that she needed help? She was angry—and then she felt a pang of guilt, as she wondered whether the absent colleagues she was cursing were among the dead or dying.

There were so many patients dying now. They were dying inside the hospital, and they were dying outside, in the parking structures and in the street. The worst part was that there was no one to take the bodies away, and no place to take them. The smell inside the hospital was unbearable. A colleague told her that she should eat, but the thought of food sickened her.

It was only at the end of the first day that she noticed new doctors and nurses had begun appearing.

Local authorities had been able to organize a relief effort: the surviving hospitals in the port district were being staffed up with doctors from the countryside, and the wounded were being evacuated to hospitals throughout the region. One of the first decisions made by the authorities was to shut down the operations at Pusan National. Severe damage had made it structurally unsound, and most of the staff were casualties themselves. As the new doctors arrived to organize the evacuation of the patients, they reassigned the doctors on the scene, mostly either sending them to another hospital to get care for wounds that had been neglected or just sending them home for some sleep.

Soon, one of the new doctors noticed Dr. Oh. She was past the point of exhaustion, having worked nonstop for more than twenty-four hours with neither food nor sleep. She was bandaging a patient who was long dead. The doctor stopped her, sat her down on a chair, and asked where she lived. Dr.

Oh mentioned her mother's address in the countryside. He walked her over to an evacuation point and sent her home.

NORTH KOREA'S STRIKE IN CONTEXT

In the early-morning darkness of March 22, North Korea had conducted a limited nuclear strike against US forces throughout South Korea and Japan. Kim had targeted US bases throughout the region as far as Okinawa and Guam. His forces fired nuclear-armed ballistic missiles at a total of twenty-one military targets, most of which were US bases. Overall, in the course of forty minutes, North Korean units at nine different locations all over the country fired fifty-four nuclear-armed ballistic missiles against targets in South Korea and Japan as well as eight more missiles at American forces stationed in Okinawa and Guam.

Fewer than half of North Korea's missiles successfully delivered their nuclear payloads to their targets. Both the US military and the South Korean military claim that the missiles that did not arrive were probably stopped by their defenses. Other experts believe that the missiles simply broke up during flight, as some North Korean missiles have been known to do.

Of the nuclear warheads that struck South Korea, Japan, and Guam, most missed their intended target by a significant distance—up to a kilometer and sometimes more. In some cases, this resulted in significant casualties in neighboring communities. In other cases, the warheads detonated harmlessly at sea. Not one of the eight missiles fired at US bases in Okinawa

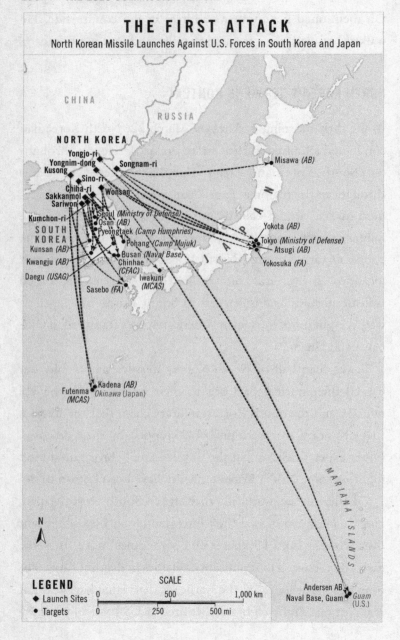

THE FIRST ATTACK
North Korean Missile Launches Against U.S. Forces in South Korea and Japan

CHINA

RUSSIA

NORTH KOREA

Yongjo-ri
Yongnim-dong   Songnam-ri   Misawa (AB)
Kusong
       Sino-ri
Chiha-ri   Wonsan
Sakkanmol
Sariwon
                                                                  Yokota (AB)
Kumchon-ri   Seoul (Ministry of Defense)
              Osan (AB)   Tokyo (Ministry of Defense)
SOUTH   Pyeongtaek (Camp Humphries)   Atsugi (AB)
KOREA
Kunsan (AB)   Pohang (Camp Mujuk)   Yokosuka (FA)
Kwangju (AB)   Busan (Naval Base)
                 Chinhae
                 (CFAC)
Daegu (USAG)   Iwakuni
                         (MCAS)
        Sasebo (FA)

JAPAN

                      Kadena (AB)
Futenma   Okinawa (Japan)
(MCAS)

N

MARIANA ISLANDS

LEGEND   SCALE
◆ Launch Sites   0   500   1,000 km   Andersen AB
                                                  Naval Base, Guam   Guam
● Targets   0   250   500 mi   (U.S.)

and Guam struck its target. Some failed to arrive, while the remainder landed in the water off the coast. The only fatalities reported in Okinawa and Guam arose from traffic accidents when the bombs went off.

The metropolitan areas of Seoul, Pyongtaek, Daegu, and Busan in South Korea and Tokyo and Yokohama in Japan were the hardest hit. All told, about 1.4 million people died as a result of the attacks on March 22, 2020, while more than five million were severely wounded. Most of the casualties were in these urban centers.

Among the six million people killed or wounded in North Korea's nuclear strikes that day were about half of the ninety thousand American troops stationed in the two countries, as well as nearly thirty thousand of their dependents. The American service men and women deployed in Korea and Japan, along with their families, paid a steep cost—often the ultimate cost—to fill that role. Their sacrifices and examples will not soon be forgotten.

And yet this was not to be the final sacrifice of March 2020. Although North Korea had expended a significant fraction of its nuclear arsenal in the March 22 strike, Kim Jong Un retained about a dozen high-yield thermonuclear weapons and intercontinental ballistic missiles (ICBMs) that could reach the United States.

Kim Jong Un hoped that the loss of US forces in the region and the horror of the casualties that day would cause the United States to halt what he believed was a coming invasion of North Korea. And if the bloodshed in Asia did not do the trick, Kim Jong Un hoped that the big missiles he was holding back, the ones that could strike the United States, would force Donald Trump to see sense. Tokyo was lost. Was Trump so eager for revenge that he was willing to risk Trump Tower as well?

Kim was now betting his life that, having suffered through the terrible day of March 22, the United States had had enough.

7

FUMBLE

IN THE HOURS BEFORE North Korea launched its nuclear strikes on South Korea and Japan, senior White House officials had become convinced that Kim and his generals were planning something significant.

The warning that reached Keith Kellogg and Jack Francis at 1:16 PM on March 21 had been followed by additional warnings, all based on communications intercepts that documented encrypted communications flowing from North Korea's military command out to missile units throughout the country. And yet, even as the evidence that North Korea was preparing a large-scale missile attack accumulated, White House officials were working on the assumption that North Korea would conduct a series of missile tests in response to the South Korean missile strikes on Pyongyang and Chunghwa —nothing more.

At most, a few officials expressed concern that North Korea might arm one missile with a nuclear weapon and fire it over Japan and out in the ocean as a demonstration. This would be a momentous and extremely dangerous development, to be sure. And the possibility of a North Korean retaliation up to and including such a test caused great consternation in the Trump administration as the hours passed on March 21.

No one in Washington, DC, or at Mar-a-Lago seems to have realized what was in store. The political crisis now bearing down upon them was not another North Korean missile test. It was a second war on the Korean Peninsula.

WARNING

As the warnings accumulated on the afternoon of March 21, Francis and Kellogg had made the decision to leave Mar-a-Lago and travel over the bridge to the mainland. Trump was lingering over lunch, and while no one on his staff wanted to disturb him, Francis now felt that it was important that the chief of staff be physically near the president. Other former members of the Trump administration suggested later that Francis was still worried about the appearance of the president being at a golf club, and that the decision to move was intended solely to give the impression that the president was taking meetings and calls while at the club. In his interviews with members of this commission, Francis strenuously denied those allegations.

Francis was expecting that North Korea would launch a number of missiles, but he was expecting a launch like those in 2006, when North Korea fired seven unarmed missiles into the sea. If there was to be a repeat of a missile launch such as that one, he knew, a statement would need to be made and the president would need to be the one to make it. "At this point," one staffer recalled, "[Francis] mostly wanted to be near the president to make sure that, after the test, he could get the president back to Mar-a-Lago so any statement came from there, not the golf course." Francis said that this is a mischaracterization of his motives. His only concern, he told the commission, was moving the president as soon as possible back to the secure facility at Mar-a-Lago, where he would be able to more effectively coordinate and manage the government response to any provocation or attack.

About ten minutes after four o'clock, Francis was in the car traveling from Mar-a-Lago toward the Trump International Golf Club. At that moment, the first North Korean missiles, just launched from sites throughout the country, were breaking through the clouds over South Korea, Japan, and Guam and coming into full view of US early warning satellites, which detected their brightly burning exhaust.

The satellites relayed the missile detections to a ground station in Germany, which passed the data back to North American Aerospace Defense Command (NORAD) in Colorado Springs, which determined that the bright flashes really were missiles.

Once confirmed, a "missile event" shot up the chain of command.

At 4:14 PM, while Francis was still in the car en route to the golf club, his military assistant called him to explain that there were "several launches" from North Korea. At 4:17, the assistant called him back to say that the number was now about two dozen, and that the missiles were headed toward targets in Japan and South Korea. Francis understood immediately that this was an attack, not a missile test.

Later he recalled being surprised by the number of missiles. Francis was not alone in this reaction. A recurring theme in the recollections of various officials is surprise at the number of nuclear-armed missiles fired by North Korea, in spite of the fact that the total number of missiles fired in the first phase of the Second Korean War—sixty-two projectiles—was well within the range of the classified estimates on which policymakers had been briefed several times throughout 2019. Those estimates —including one from September 2019 entitled "North Korean Stockpile Continuing to Expand"—seem to have had little effect on shaping the expectations of senior White House officials. "There are so many briefings about this stuff," one NSC staffer explained. "The briefers used to joke by saying, 'Don't worry, there won't be a quiz.' But there was."

Francis and other White House officials, according to a number of people involved in the deliberations, simply did not process how rapidly the ground was shifting under them. The North Koreans were advancing their nuclear arsenal at a breathtaking pace. The expansion was carefully tracked by the US intelligence community and dutifully relayed to policymakers. But the reality of what was happening did not seem to sink in with US political leaders. Perhaps it was all just happening too quickly, or perhaps they could not reconcile their notions of North Korea as a backward "hermit kingdom" with reports of the aggressive and technologically sophisticated research-and-development campaign taking place inside the country. One way or another, top officials within the Trump administration appear to have missed the signals.

The year 2017 had been a particular turning point. The previous year, Kim Jong Un had posed in a photograph with a mock-up of a North Korean nuclear weapon. That image contained small details that, to experts, hinted at highly classified knowledge about far more advanced nuclear weapons designs. The mock-up was a ball made of pentagons and hexagons, like a soccer ball but far more complex. The actual geometric shape is called a "chamfered truncated icosahedron." The analysts just called it the "disco ball."

The disco ball had one curious feature: an enigmatic metal object sticking out of the top, clearly designed to hold something. But that something was missing. US nuclear weapons designers speculated that the holder was designed for a component called a "pulse-neutron tube." This is the same technology used to treat patients with tumors. A nanoscale pulse-neutron source—a tiny device that fires neutrons through a relatively simple fusion process—can be surgically implanted next to a tumor, where it can bombard the growth with neutron radiation. Put a larger version of the same device in a nuclear weapon and it can fire those same neutrons into the center of the weapon just before it explodes, making the bomb vastly more efficient and opening up new design possibilities.

In September 2016, North Korea tested the weapon whose mock-up had appeared in the photo. The explosion shook the ground with the force of about 20,000 tons of TNT—more powerful than either of the nuclear weapons the United States had dropped on Hiroshima and Nagasaki. The test prompted a frantic review inside the CIA and other parts of the intelligence community.

American analysts quickly concluded that North Korea's nuclear weapons might be far more efficient than they had thought previously. In practical terms, "more efficient" meant that North Korea could make more bombs from the same amount of nuclear material. While the advances surprised some CIA analysts, others pointed out that the United States had demonstrated these technologies in the 1950s and 1960s and that other nuclear powers, including the Soviet Union and China, had followed suit by the 1970s.

After reassessing the status of North Korea's nuclear development, the highest estimate of how many nuclear weapons Kim Jong Un could have jumped from forty to sixty. (The low end remained at thirty.) The same intelligence report also concluded that North Korea could be adding as many as twelve nuclear weapons a year to its arsenal—each using a composite of plutonium and highly enriched uranium and each small enough to fit on a missile.

One month after this report was completed, North Korea

released a second series of pictures of Kim Jong Un, this time standing next to a different model of a nuclear bomb. This weapon—which analysts nicknamed the "peanut" after its shape—was a thermonuclear weapon. And sitting in its metal holder was a black pulse-neutron tube.

Hours after releasing the picture, North Korea detonated a massive nuclear explosion, demonstrating that the bomb modeled in the photo was already part of its nuclear arsenal. That explosion was ten times bigger than the explosions that leveled Hiroshima and Nagasaki.

Policymakers were routinely briefed on the revised assessment that the US intelligence community produced after this weapons test. The new report indicated that North Korea's nuclear stockpile was even larger and more sophisticated than had been previously thought. This information was widely available to the president, his staff, and members of Congress. The estimate that increased the number of North Korean nuclear weapons from forty to sixty had even been leaked to the *Washington Post* in the summer of 2017.

Yet neither the classified briefings nor the leaks seem to have changed how senior officials saw the threat from North Korea. According to aides, it was only after the first reports of a nuclear explosion in Seoul that Francis realized that the vast majority of the missiles in flight were armed with nuclear weapons. "I don't know why it didn't really click until then," said one former White House staffer, "but it didn't. These briefing papers talk about deuterium and tritium and plutonium—it's like reading a periodic table in chemistry class. It's different when someone tells you that the missiles are in the air. Then it's for real."

THE SECOND HOLE

Francis realized that North Korea was conducting a nuclear attack, but he was not at all certain of its scope. American analysts had been able to determine some of the targets of North Korea's attack by calculating the trajectories of a number of the missiles that were already airborne, but not all of them—and the launches seemed to be continuing. With so many missiles being launched, there was also a chance that the radar had missed some.

Francis made a snap decision that at least a few of the missiles might be headed for the United States. Whatever his original motivations for seeking out President Trump at the golf club, at this point his focus shifted to a single, new objective: getting Trump to safety as quickly as possible.

When his car arrived at the Trump International Golf Club, Francis walked into the dining room, where the president was still sitting, talking to guests, lingering over a leisurely lunch. The president, Francis later recalled, seemed upset at the intrusion; he did not rise to greet his aide. And so Francis knelt down next to the president and whispered in his ear: "North Korea is launching a major attack. We must seek shelter immediately."

There was, Francis knew, an old bomb shelter beneath the

tee on the second hole. Trump in fact had bragged about it often. "It was built of four and a half feet of steel and concrete," he told one reporter. "I got bids from demolition companies. It would have cost me three and a half million to rip it out. So instead of ripping it out, I fixed it up for $100,000. We used it for elevation . . . and now, when members tee off on the second hole, they're teeing off from the top of a bomb shelter."

Francis quickly commandeered a golf cart and asked the president to get in. The president told Francis to get out and to sit in the passenger seat. As the president drove Francis toward the bomb shelter, golfers on the course—who were unaware of the impending attack—waved at the president. He waved back. One golfer posted a picture of the two driving to the shelter on his Instagram account with the caption: "Why does Jack Francis always look so sad? Smile like President Trump! He is MAKING AMERICA GREAT AGAIN. #MAGA."

As the president and the rest of his staff gathered in the shelter, which was now used for storage, Francis thought through what to do next. They were safe from all but a direct hit with a very large nuclear weapon, but there were no secure conference lines, and his cell phone didn't work inside. This was just a makeshift solution, one that Francis realized would quickly need to give way to something better. They would need to return to Mar-a-Lago once it was clear that none of the more than thirty missiles that had been launched—the latest estimate from his military assistant—were headed toward Florida. Until then, he was stuck.

Francis recalled that his first thought was to wonder how he could contact Mattis. He could turn, of course, to the military aide carrying the president's Emergency Satchel. The "nuclear football" could communicate directly and securely with the National Military Command Center in the basement of the Pentagon.

But Francis did not want to open the satchel. In fact, he did not even want to draw Trump's attention to it. He resorted to walking out of the bunker to get reception on his cell phone, making a few short calls, then coming back in to manage the president's growing discomfort. Someone asked Francis if he had taken up smoking, which he recalled finding amusing under the circumstances.

The president, aides recalled, was becoming confused and disoriented. He wanted to know what was happening. Eventually, Francis realized that it would be better if Kellogg stood outside the shelter door, maintaining contact with the command center in Colorado Springs and with the Pentagon, while Francis focused on managing the president's growing anger.

Especially disquieting to Francis was one particular line of Trump's questioning: he wanted to know why Mattis wasn't retaliating immediately—and with nuclear weapons. After all, hadn't Mattis promised in that morning's briefing that, if Kim kept up his aggression, the United States would hit North Korea with "everything we've got"?

Francis tried to explain to the president that as far as they could tell, North Korea's attack was being conducted against South Korea, not the United States. That meant that North

Korea had not yet used its nuclear-armed ICBMs, the big missiles that could reach the United States. American intelligence estimates suggested that North Korea possessed around a dozen of these missiles. Any nuclear strike against North Korea—any strike against North Korea at all—would have to be integrated into a full air campaign to find and destroy those missiles before they could be launched, Francis explained. That would require hundreds of aircraft and could not simply be ordered up on a moment's notice.

The president grew increasingly aggrieved, constantly returning to the meeting that morning, constantly invoking what he called "my general's promise" that the United States was ready to "hit [Kim] with everything we've got." At this point, Francis asked Kellogg to step back into the bunker to see if he could make headway with the president. Kellogg explained that mounting a major air campaign against North Korea, even with so many US aircraft already on the Korean Peninsula to participate in the war games, was not something they could order up in just a day or so. Kellogg's explanation quickly appeared to turn into an argument with the president, who even on a normal day had little patience for his national security adviser. And this day was not normal.

As the tension in the room grew, Francis realized that they had a major problem: the president simply did not believe that North Korea's long-range missiles worked. Indeed, prior to this moment, aides had noticed that, from time to time, the president would make comments indicating that he was skeptical that North Korea could strike the United States. In a phone call with the president of the Philippines, Trump had said that "Kim's missiles keep crashing." And in tweets, he referred to the fact that Kim's "button" might not work.

Aides had generally chosen not to confront the president on this issue. One reason for their reticence was that it was rarely a good idea to correct the president. But aides also felt that it was better to err on the side of letting the president underestimate North Korea. He had, after all, said quite publicly—in a tweet—that he would never allow North Korea to develop the ability to strike the United States. And so, after North Korea tested a series of missiles that could do just that—testing one missile in July 2017 that could strike most of the United States and then, in November 2017, testing an even larger missile that could reach them here at Mar-a-Lago—aides appear to have developed a tacit strategy of not contradicting the president when he said the missiles did not work. After all, no one knew what he might do when confronted by the fact that North Korea had done the one thing he had said would never happen while he was president—test a missile that could strike the United States.

Instead, aides subtly redefined what it meant for missiles to "work." Mike Pompeo, who had lasted in the president's inner circle as long as anyone, had figured out, when he was the director of the CIA, how to carefully move the goalposts by referring to North Korea's ability to build a *reliable* ICBM. What was a reliable ICBM? Using this vague and malleable term allowed aides to keep putting off the day of reckoning. They could constantly refer to North Korea's growing stockpile of nuclear-armed ICBMs as a future threat rather than force the showdown that each of them dreaded. But it left the president continuing to think that North Korea's missiles did not work.

Now this strategy was backfiring. Aides were frantically trying to explain to Trump that while, yes, they had said the missiles were not reliable, neither were they completely unreliable. Some would surely reach the United States, Kellogg explained, with terrible consequences.

The president was undeterred. He insisted that the missile defense systems deployed in Alaska would simply shoot down any missiles that North Korea managed to launch at the United States. "We have missiles that can knock out a missile in the air 97 percent of the time," he insisted, "and if you send two of them, it's going to get knocked down."

"It was weird," one aide explained. "Normally we just didn't correct him, especially not when it was an excuse not to do something crazy. But now, all of a sudden, all this stuff was working against us. And we didn't know how to push back. Every time Francis or Kellogg corrected the president, he grew more stubborn."

"Out of the blue," the aide continued, "he said, 'I want to hit them both right now.' And Francis just asked, 'Both?'"

Trump, according to multiple people we interviewed from the bunker, was adamant that China was behind the attack. Wasn't China giving the North Koreans their missiles? Wasn't China not enforcing sanctions? Wasn't China really responsible for what was happening? "Isn't that what Steve told us was happening all along?" the president asked, referring to a frequent theme of his former chief strategist, Steve Bannon, who famously believed that China, not North Korea, was the main threat to the United States.

Over the past few years, aides had seen Trump claim that North Korea was a Chinese puppet or that Kim Jong Un never acted without the approval of China's leader, Xi Jinping. Those who briefed the president had long stopped pushing back on these theories. Crazy or not, there was no talking Trump out of them. But now the president's theorizing had taken a dangerous turn. Trump was now proposing to fight two nuclear-armed adversaries.

Not only was the president now suggesting that the United States retaliate with nuclear weapons against both China and North Korea, but he was also standing less than twenty feet from a military aide who was holding the communications device designed specifically to allow him to give such an order.

Using the "football," the president could, on his own authority and with no second vote, bypass the secretary of defense and directly instruct the National Military Command Center to order a nuclear launch. The NMCC would transmit his orders directly to launch units. The entire system was designed to allow the president to fire all of the land-based nuclear-armed missiles sitting in silos throughout the Great Plains in the tiny window of time between the moments when satellites detected the launch of enemy missiles and when those missiles arrived. There was no requirement to notify the secretary of defense or the chairman of the Joint Chiefs of

Staff, let alone to seek their authorization. The entire system was designed around the possibility that there might not be any time for such actions.

The only check on the president's authority was the requirement that he authenticate his voice by reading an alphanumeric code printed on the "biscuit"—a card sealed in a foil wrapper. Some presidents had asked an aide to carry the biscuit. Other presidents kept it themselves. Jimmy Carter famously sent a suit coat to the cleaner with his biscuit in a pocket. Trump had marveled at the little card and the power it represented. It was in his pocket. All he needed to do was call the NMCC using the football, which he was legally entitled to do.

The president now seemed to recall the briefing he had received about these procedures—or perhaps to become aware of the military aide standing in the bunker with him. Because he suddenly turned his full attention to the soldier. "I just remember the president said, 'Come over here!' to the major with the football, gesturing with his hands," one aide recalled.

What happened next is a matter of some dispute. The president, Francis, and others have asserted that the president was simply asking for the football so that he could review the briefing book located inside it, the book that contained the different options for a nuclear attack.

The military aide, however, in the Article 92 hearing for his court-martial, explained that he was uncomfortable with the president's tone and demeanor. He said that he was concerned that he was about to be given an order that he believed was unlawful. He understood the president's gesture to be a request for the football to order a launch, not merely to review the options.

Everyone present agreed that the major took a few steps toward President Trump, but then paused and looked at General Francis. "What are you looking at him for? I am the president," Trump said, according to another aide who was in the bunker. "And then," this aide added, "he kind of lunged for the briefcase."

The major jumped back, but the president had his hand on the handle. "They pulled back and forth," the other aide recalled, "with the president screaming, 'You're fired! You're fired!' at the poor guy." From prison, the major confirmed that there was a brief struggle. "His grip was really strong for a seventy-year old man. He was very angry. I just kind of jerked the satchel out of his hands, really hard, maybe too hard, then he fell over." During the scuffle, President Trump sustained minor injuries.

After the major recovered possession of the satchel, he quickly left the bunker, in violation of normal procedures for the handling of the device. The president's Emergency Satchel would remain outside the normal requirements for custody for the next few hours, until Francis sent one of the other military aides to retrieve it.

Following the major's flight from the bunker, an awkward hush fell over the group. President Trump remained on the floor, seated, with one hand on his head. Francis recalled that the normally combative president appeared to be avoiding eye contact with his aides. The chief of staff felt relieved when, after several long minutes, the stillness was interrupted by a message from the Pentagon: no missiles were believed to be headed toward the United States, and a helicopter was en route to the fairway outside the bunker entrance to retrieve the president and his closest aides.

Francis helped the president to his feet, and then a small number of them exited the bunker. At 6:02 PM, a US Marine Corps helicopter landed near the second hole. They climbed in and flew the few minutes back to Mar-a-Lago in silence.

THE TANK

The Joint Chiefs of Staff conference room is located deep inside the Pentagon. Occasionally a news story refers to it as the "Gold Room," but almost no one calls it anything other than "the tank."

The room was small, dominated by a large conference table. Throughout the morning of March 21, Secretary of Defense James Mattis had sat at the head of this table. The retired Marine general was surrounded by senior military officials and civilian staffers. On the table in front of them were stacks of briefing books that detailed the operations plan for defending South Korea, a plan that called for US forces to drive deep into North Korea to remove Kim Jong Un from power.

Mattis had spent the morning looking over the plans, "just in case this Korea thing got out of control," he later told investigators. An aide in the room joked that the scene was a kind of tableaux, like Leonardo's *The Last Supper*. "Except that we're the ones planning the crucifixion," he recalled Mattis noting dryly.

The operations plan for defending South Korea had evolved over the years. The current plan, OPLAN 5015, was a pre-emptive attack—it called for a surprise attack with airpower and special forces to remove Kim Jong Un and pave the way for a rapid ground invasion of North Korea to nip any threat in the bud. As North Korea's nuclear and missile capabilities had grown, planners in the United States had increasingly come to think that the best defense of South Korea was a good offense. The entire operations plan was premised on the United States acting decisively to kill Kim Jong Un before he could order his rocket forces to use their nuclear-armed missiles.

The plan described a conventional invasion; it did not re-quire the use of nuclear weapons any more than had the inva-sion of Iraq. There was, of course, an annex to the plan that provided for the limited use of nuclear weapons, but Mattis had quickly rejected that on the morning of March 21, for the same reasons that his predecessors did in Iraq in 1991 and again in 2003. After the First Gulf War, Air Force offi-cials made clear that the possibility of using nuclear weapons in the conflict had never been seriously considered. "The nuclear weapon's only good against cities," observed retired general Chuck Horner shortly after the end of that war. "It's not any good against troops in the desert, I mean it takes too many of 'em, so the problem you have is, you have a war where if you kill a lot of people, particularly women and children, you lose the war no matter what happens on the battlefield." In fact, although it was not widely known at the time, President George H. W. Bush had ruled out the use of nuclear weapons in 1991. "No one advanced the notion of using nuclear weapons," wrote Brent Scowcroft, who had served as Bush's national security adviser, "and the President rejected it even in retaliation for chemical or biological attacks." The Bush administration's public statements, however, had been ambiguous. Why clear things up for Saddam?

Mattis had much the same outlook as Horner, Bush, and Scowcroft. During the counterinsurgency in Iraq, he famously told his Marines to "take off your sunglasses and let them get to know you. Play soccer with the kids, and don't worry if you lose. Shake a lot of hands and chat them up." Mattis, like Horner in 1991, could see no upside in killing large numbers of civilians indiscriminately. He had seen up close, and painfully, the brutal insurgency that gripped Iraq once the local population started to turn against their liberators.

But like Bush and Scowcroft, Mattis was reluctant to be completely clear about this outlook, for fear of encouraging Kim Jong Un. To be sure, he had dropped hints about his attitude toward nuclear weapons. When Mattis was out of government, he worked closely at Stanford with George Shultz, Ronald Reagan's former secretary of state. Shultz believed in the elimination of nuclear weapons. Later, as secretary of defense, Mattis was careful to talk about the importance of nuclear deterrence, but he also voiced a Marine's skepticism that a bomb could do what muddy boots could not. Asked about a proposal for a new tactical nuclear weapon, he responded, "I don't think there's any such thing as a tactical nuclear weapon. Any nuclear weapon used any time is a strategic game changer." Mattis had also deflected questions about whether the United States might place nuclear weapons in South Korea.

So it was in keeping with his prior statements that, practically as soon as he began reviewing OPLAN 5015 on March 21, Mattis decided that nuclear weapons were largely off the table. If the United States had a shot at Kim in some remote mountain bunker, Mattis told his commanders, and if there was no reasonable conventional alternative for getting at him, then he was willing to recommend using one or two nuclear weapons to kill the North Korean leader. Otherwise, Mattis said, the most important targets in North Korea were mixed in with cities and towns, and it was out of the question to use nuclear weapons against them—there were just too many innocent people around and the conventional invasion force would do the job soon enough.

Over the course of the morning, Mattis had carefully reviewed and approved the primary details of OPLAN 5015 and ordered a series of steps to increase the military's readiness to execute it. The United States really was about to hit North Korea with "everything we've got"—or something close to it.

There was only one catch. OPLAN 5015 had been conceived of entirely as a preemptive strike—a massive effort by air, sea, and ground forces to invade North Korea and kill Kim Jong Un before he had a chance to order North Korea's nuclear-armed missile units to fire. OPLAN 5015 was premised entirely—indeed, depended—on the United States going first.

At 4:16 PM, around the time Francis received the call en route to the golf club, the same warning reached Mattis at the Pentagon: North Korea was conducting a massive surprise attack on US forces throughout South Korea and Japan. One thing, Mattis recalled, went through his mind: *Fuck*.

MAR-A-LAGO

After the helicopter returned President Trump to Mar-a-Lago, Francis attempted to restore some semblance of normalcy around the president. But it was tough going. Francis noticed that the president was bleeding from a slight cut over his eye, a result of his fall in the bunker. Normally the president was loud and pushy. At his best, he was a big, fun blowhard. At his worst, he was a bully. But this, Francis observed, this was something different. Trump was sullen and withdrawn.

Once Mattis appeared on the screen in the Situation Room, the president focused entirely on the military options that the secretary of defense explained to him. Francis was struck by how long the president was able to focus on what Mattis was saying. "Normally, after a minute or two, the president would look bored and start tugging at his ear," an aide recalled. Not now. Trump seemed engaged and respectful, and he was asking questions—good questions. Francis would later recall, with all sincerity, that it was the most presidential he had ever seen Trump behave.

It occurred to Francis that the president was fixating on the secretary of defense and his briefing because Mattis had not been in the shelter during the struggle with the military aide. "Mattis wasn't there for the altercation," another aide recalled. "He was the one person who hadn't seen the president humiliated."

Mattis was not only unaware of what had transpired in the bunker but also distracted by the war he was having to improvise. Almost immediately, US and South Korean forces near the DMZ had returned the artillery fire that had rained down on Seoul, suppressing it. It was not clear whether the North Korean artillery pieces were destroyed or had simply been pulled back into caves, but one way or another the shelling had stopped.

Mattis was now telling the president that the main goal was to shift from defense to offense. The war plan they had been considering was designed as a preemptive action, but North Korea had beaten them to the punch and now the United States had to catch up.

Luckily, Mattis explained, while North Korea's nuclear weapons had done enormous damage throughout South Korea and Japan, a number of important US airbases in the region had survived. These included—crucially—the airfields on Okinawa and Guam, whose bombers were intact and within striking distance of North Korea.

The Air Force even now was targeting Kim Jong Un's network of surface-to-air missiles, Mattis said. The goal was not to avenge BX 411, but to establish complete air superiority over North Korea. This mission was going to take twenty-four hours, Mattis explained, but they had no choice but to wait it out: the United States could not safely send pilots to find North Korean missiles as long as the air defenses remained in place. Once the air defenses were down, the really heavy air strikes would begin. As for the prospect of further North Korean nuclear attacks, Mattis was convinced that the worst was over. North Korea had already expended much of its small stockpile of nuclear weapons, he said, and he was confident that American airpower could find the rest of them, along with the leader who had ordered the holocaust. They would find and destroy North Korea's remaining missiles and kill Kim Jong Un.

The longer Mattis talked, the more the White House aides began to notice what he was *not* saying: his remarks contained no mention of nuclear weapons. North Korea had just launched a massive and surprise nuclear attack on US troops and US allies. The loss of life had been catastrophic. Kim Jong Un had precipitated the bloodiest day in human history. And yet, as Mattis laid out for the president a massive air campaign against North Korea that would be followed in short order by ground troops flowing into the region and then into the hermit kingdom, he did not mention nuclear weapons. Only at the end, with the question lingering unasked, did Mattis mention in the most offhand way that this would all be done with conventional forces.

"We're going to win either way, with or without nukes," Mattis explained. "Kim [Jong Un] is the guy wearing the black hat. We're wearing the white hat. We're there to liberate the North Koreans, not murder them." Mattis said that the United States did not need nuclear weapons to knock down North Korea's air defenses, destroy any remaining ballistic missiles that threatened the United States, and ultimately remove Kim Jong Un. In fact, he said, nuclear weapons might get in the way.

Mattis had anticipated more argument, or at least debate, about the plan he was proposing. But he was unaware of the events that had transpired at the golf course—although he would recall sensing that there was something strange about the mood in Mar-a-Lago. Then again, he explained later, he always found video conferences off-putting.

The aides in the Situation Room at Mar-a-Lago, meanwhile, waited to see how President Trump would respond. "The president had talked about ordering a nuclear strike on China," an aide explained, "so yes, we were worried about his reaction. Everybody just wanted to leave it to Jim [Mattis]." Every aide who was in the room told this commission that they believed the altercation in the golf course bunker had colored the deliberations. But in the moment, they could not be sure how.

Finally, Mattis finished. Trump thanked him. "Okay, general," the president said. Then Trump stood up and walked out of the Situation Room.

An aide asked Francis whether someone should accompany the president. Francis said no. He instructed the kitchen staff to send the president dinner, whether he asked for it or not.

The President later ordered dinner himself. The staff, largely immigrants, later explained that no one knew who Francis was or precisely what his relationship to Mr. Trump was.

Only then did Francis ask another military aide to find the president's Emergency Satchel and the missing major. The aide to whom he gave this order seemed confused about why the satchel wasn't with the president, but Francis didn't explain. According to Francis, he simply repeated what he had said already: "The satchel was separated from the president at the golf course. You need to drive over and get it, and sit with it in the Situation Room." The aide recalled that Francis was more succinct the second time: "He just said, 'Football, golf course, sit in room. Understand?' I understood well enough to stop asking stupid questions."

After the aide left to retrieve the satchel, Kellogg asked Francis if, given the events of the past few hours, it was really a good idea to bring the football back into play. "Where else can we put it?" Francis said, not really asking.

Francis later explained that he was no longer worried about the president giving any unexpected orders. The United States was at war, but that war was being run out of the Pentagon. "We were just snowbirds," Francis explained, "wintering over in Florida."

There was a second reason why Mattis did not propose using nuclear weapons—a reason that he withheld from the president. The North Korean strike had been a massive attack against US forces throughout South Korea and Japan. It had killed hundreds of thousands of civilians. But Kim had held back those of his nuclear missiles that could strike the United States.

These missiles were a real danger, and Mattis knew it would be next to impossible to find them all. Nor did he have much confidence in the missile defense system in Alaska. The odds were far better that one of the big missiles would deliver its powerful thermonuclear weapon all the way to New York or Los Angeles or Palm Beach than the odds that they could shoot it down. Kim knew that as well as he did. Yet Kim had been reluctant to use them. Why?

Mattis reasoned that Kim still thought he might wriggle out of this. Perhaps, thought the secretary of defense, Kim was hoping the Chinese or the Russians would negotiate a way out for him. Mattis had no intention of letting that happen. He was pissed.

The strikes on South Korea and Japan were not simply among the worst atrocities in human history. They were also a cowardly attack on America and those who served it. Kim had killed tens of thousands of US service personnel and their family members. Whatever happened, Mattis later recalled, he was going to make sure that Kim Jong Un died in North Korea. There would be no comfortable exile and no negotiated settlement. This was to the death.

Still, if Kim wanted to delude himself, Mattis was happy to let him. The ex-Marine thought he might be able to string along the young dictator, buying valuable time for the Air Force to find those missiles. If Kim waited too long in hopes of saving his own skin, it might be too late for him to order a follow-on strike against the United States. By the time he realized that the United States would never accept a diplomatic solution, Mattis hoped, Kim's missiles would be gone, lost to air strikes or cut off from communications networks. "If we hit North Korea with nukes that day," Mattis recalled, "then Kim would have used his [nuclear weapons] for sure. I needed to give the Air Force time to find them. I knew it was a long shot, but we had to try."

8

A WORLD WITHOUT NORTH KOREA

KIM JONG UN WASN'T going to just sit in a basement, waiting to die. As he saw it, he had the upper hand. His missile units had delivered a terrible blow against US forces throughout South Korea and Japan, leaving Seoul, Tokyo, and Busan in flames. The launch units had almost immediately relocated, reloaded, then begun launching missiles armed with high-explosive warheads into the areas they had just struck with nuclear weapons. North Korea's artillery force had also opened up on Seoul. South Korean forces returned fire to suppress the artillery strikes, but for most of the day it was North Korea that was on the offense, delivering one punishing blow after another.

Now Kim intended to press his advantage. Immediately after giving the order to launch the attacks on South Korea and Japan, he changed locations and then spent the day waiting for the United States, reeling from the shock of the attack, to seek some sort of settlement. He believed that as soon as the American public saw the horror unfolding in South Korea and

Japan, they would collectively demand a cease-fire to save their own cities from the same fates.

Kim was hardly the first world leader to misjudge an opponent. While he waited throughout the day for word that his diplomats in New York had reached a cease-fire, an American military commander was putting in place the pieces of the campaign to topple Kim.

The supreme leader was expecting a response. It would come when night fell.

KIM GOES TO MYOHYANG

As soon as Kim had ordered his missile units to repel the invaders massing in South Korea and Japan, he had decided to move to safety. He was in the middle of the country, but his wife and children were in Wonsan, a port city on the coast. As they sat in the basement in Kusong, Kim's aide Choe Ryong Hae had suggested that the family compound in Wonsan would surely be a target. They should all move to safety. But where?

Kim had choices. There was no shortage of palaces throughout North Korea, almost all of which were equipped to allow him to wait out a conflict in relative comfort. There was a large palace complex along the border with China, with tunnels leading into the mountains around Mount Baekdu. Kim's father, Kim Jong Il, had overseen the construction of a massive underground complex there over the course of many years.

This was where the elder Kim had always planned to evacuate in case of an emergency.

To Kim Jong Il, the residence near Mount Baekdu had represented North Korea's strategic depth. Even in 1950, during the Korean War, when United Nations forces drove northward and were on the verge of capturing the entire peninsula, they were still nearly forty miles from this strategic spot when Chinese troops poured across the border and saved Kim Jong Il's father, Kim Il Sung, and with him the Kim family dynasty. For Kim Jong Il, then, the residence near Mount Baekdu was as far as possible from the threat posed by South Koreans and their American masters. He was certain that if American forces approached this location, China would intervene again. And in the worst case, he could simply slip across the border and into a comfortable exile. After all, Kim Jong Il had been born in the Soviet Union, at a Soviet military camp where his father was training as a guerrilla. Kim Jong Il knew that his life might end as it had begun—outside Korea. He had prepared carefully for this eventuality, hiding assets abroad to ensure that any exile was far more comfortable than his childhood in that Soviet military camp.

Kim Jong Un was a different man from his father and grandfather. He had been raised amid incredible wealth and privilege. He could not have imagined life as a normal person if he tried—and there is no evidence that he ever did. There was not going to be any comfortable exile for Kim Jong Un. China, looming just over the border, looked nearly as threatening as South Korea. Kim had ordered the execution of his uncle and the assassination of his half-brother because he believed both were conspiring with Beijing to overthrow him. He was careful to manage the relationship with China, but he wasn't going to just show up on China's doorstep and plead for mercy.

Instead, Kim Jong Un decided that he would head to the interior of the country, to the Myohyang Mountains. Kim's grandfather had kept a large lakeside palace there, surrounded by steep and fog-shrouded mountains. It was a beautiful and historic location, but it had other advantages as well.

Kim Il Sung had died in a residence near the lake—suddenly, of a heart attack—in 1994. Kim Jong Il, disliking any place associated with death, had avoided it in the following years. Kim Jong Un, the grandson, knocked it down. He then ordered the construction of a new airstrip nearby. The airstrip was placed right next to the train station built by his father, who was afraid to fly. The runway was at the mouth of a valley dotted by large and luxurious hotels meant to lure foreign visitors. The lakeside villa was all the way up the valley, and over the hill. In 2019, Kim ordered the construction of a magnificent new palace at the site. The high peaks were beautiful to look at, but they also provided protection. North Korean workers had dug tunnels deep into the shelter of the soaring mountains.

This new palace complex at Myohyang would be Kim Jong Un's final redoubt: in the middle of the country, surrounded by more than a million North Korean soldiers under arms, and shielded beneath a thousand feet of granite. Invaders from the south, or the north, would have to fight their way through hundreds of kilometers to reach him. In the meantime, Kim would be safe from air strikes and even the largest American nuclear weapons—if it came to that. Kim's calculation was simple: He would hold out as long as possible. Once Trump realized that there was no easy victory, no quick decapitation, the American president would have to face an ugly reality. If the Americans did not cease their provocations, the horror Kim Jong Un had inflicted on South Korea and Japan would arrive on Trump's doorstep.

And so Kim Jong Un flew fifty miles toward the interior of the country, to the site of his grandfather's death, with the confidence of a man who had been born to rule. When his plane touched down, he climbed into a car that followed a winding road up to the magnificent palace. The car parked in front of what looked like the mouth of a cave, but with a pair of heavy steel doors just ever so slightly ajar. Kim slipped between the massive steel doors and disappeared beneath the mountain.

THE AIR CAMPAIGN TAKES SHAPE

While Kim hid beneath a mountain, the man responsible for finding and killing him sat in a large, comfortable office with a commanding view of Pearl Harbor. Admiral Philip Davidson was the commander of US Pacific Command. It would be his responsibility more than anyone else's to rid the earth of North Korea and Kim Jong Un. He had about twelve hours to figure out how to do it.

Davidson had found himself commanding US forces throughout the Pacific with almost no background in Asia. In his previous job, Davidson had the unenviable task of sifting through hundreds of disciplinary cases arising from a bribery scandal. He had to dole out punishments to officers who were implicated in the scandal but had escaped federal prosecution. This wasn't the sort of job that makes a man many friends. But it did require making unpopular decisions and seeing them through to the end.

By contrast, Davidson's predecessor, Harry Harris, was a celebrity—popular with the press and fawning politicians for his blunt remarks, which made perfect headlines. At times, Harris had ruffled feathers. The Chinese government in particular reportedly had sought Harris's removal after a number of remarks that Beijing viewed as inflammatory. (Both the Chinese embassy and the Trump administration officials deny that any specific request had been made for Harris's removal.) Although some found Harris undiplomatic, Trump did not: he eventually nominated Harris as the US ambassador to Australia, before changing his mind and sending him to South Korea.

One of Harris's favorite chestnuts had been that Pacific Command was ready to "fight tonight." Harris had repeated the mantra often in speeches; it appeared in press releases and was popular on social media. In one case, the phrase caused a minor panic when, after a North Korean missile test, Trump retweeted a tweet from Pacific Command with #FightTonight and briefly caused reporters to think the United States might be about to strike North Korea. Davidson wasn't flashy like that. He lacked Harris's showmanship. But now Davidson was tasked with making "fight tonight" more than a hashtag.

Davidson understood that it was not possible to plan an air campaign from scratch in so little time. He would have to work from existing plans for contingencies on the Korean Peninsula. If the Pentagon does one thing, it develops and continuously updates plans, including rapid reaction plans in the event of a surprise attack. Still, every plan rests on certain assumptions, and North Korea's nuclear strike was invalidating many of those assumptions. As Davidson recalled to the members of the commission, "There is an old adage: no plan survives first contact with the enemy." Davidson was now leading an effort to review these plans, decide what was still possible and what was not, and figure out how it might all fit together.

Davidson counted himself lucky on two counts. First, the United States had an unusual number of aircraft and naval assets in the region already, thanks to the ongoing war game. These assets included three aircraft carrier groups that contained all the forces called for in the various war plans he was weighing against each other.

Second, neither Okinawa nor Guam had been seriously damaged in the North Korean attack, despite the fact that Kim had fired two nuclear-armed missiles at each base. The major hubs for American military effort were still in action.

Even with these advantages, however, it didn't seem like enough—but then again, no commander, Davidson explained to us, ever thinks he has enough. And while he wished that his force was bigger, it was nevertheless a formidable assemblage that could and would bring the fight to Kim Jong Un. "Fight tonight" was for real.

Davidson's first task would be to use his aircraft to destroy North Korea's surface-to-air missiles. Without these missiles, Kim Jong Un would be naked, with no way to defend himself against air attacks. North Korea's fighter aircraft would be easy enough to shoot down; the country's Air Force, American pilots used to joke, was one of the finest aviation museums in the world.

Kim Jong Un might have a million soldiers, but once his air defenses were down, those units would be pinned down by heavy bombardment that would destroy their morale. Davidson expected American soldiers to march across the border with almost no resistance, encountering only North Korean troops exhausted from heavy bombing. After all, that was what happened in 1991 when the United States entered southern Iraq. After the First Gulf War, military analysts were confused by a strange inconsistency. Although bombardment had destroyed enormous amounts of equipment, like tanks, the number of people killed was surprisingly low. It turned out that Iraqi units, facing heavy bombardment, had simply deserted their equipment, leaving it to be destroyed. Davidson was hoping that when South Korean and eventually American ground troops moved into North Korea, they would find burning tanks and surrendering crews.

Davidson designed a second set of strikes, using smart bombs, to destroy so-called high-value targets in North Korea. These would include communications, infrastructure to produce nuclear weapons and ballistic missiles, and—if the Americans were lucky—the highest-value target of them all: Kim Jong Un himself. But Davidson knew that killing Kim or catching some of the ballistic missiles would be like winning the lottery. A man or a missile can move around and hide. What airpower was really good at was pinning these targets down and cutting them off from communications. Then ground forces could sweep in and finish the job.

The Americans would need to move fast. The longer the war dragged on, the greater the chance that Kim Jong Un would use his nuclear-armed missiles against the United States. Everything depended on speed.

THE TWIN LAKES INCIDENT

Just before the first missiles struck Seoul, the North Korean Foreign Ministry finally had sent instructions to their chief diplomat in New York, Ambassador Ja Song Nam. The supreme leader demanded an immediate cessation of hostilities from the United States. Moreover, the instructions contained a clear threat that Ja was to deliver: if the United States did not cease its attacks on the DPRK, the supreme leader would "reduce the US mainland into ashes and darkness."

Ja had read the instructions with some discomfort. They implied that Pyongyang believed that South Korea's missile strikes on Pyongyang and Chunghwa were the beginning of a larger American military operation. He had dutifully cabled back home reports covering both President Moon's speech, which clearly described the strikes as limited, and US envoy Sydney Seiler's assurance that Seoul had not informed Washington before launching the attack.

The North Korean ambassador received no immediate reply. He remembered wondering if he should send the cables again when he saw the first reports of massive explosions in Seoul and Tokyo on television. "My heart sank when I saw what happened," Ja recalled. "I wondered how anyone could make such a mistake."

Ja had his instructions, and he intended to fulfill his responsibilities. But first, he decided, he needed to leave New York City immediately. He was worried for his own safety, and that of his staff. The North Korean mission was a small, nondescript office in a drab building on the East Side of Manhattan with a greeting card shop on the first floor. It was hardly a well-defended embassy compound in the event that outraged local citizens decided to avenge Seoul or Tokyo. And of course, New York City was certainly one of the places Kim Jong Un would target for "ashes and darkness" if things continued to get out of hand.

Ja announced to his staff that they needed to leave immediately. He told them to quickly "secure" the office, and they obliged — shredding the most sensitive documents, destroying computers, and smashing their phones. He then brought the entire delegation downstairs and crowded them into a few embassy cars. He told his driver to wait a moment, then stepped into the card shop.

Back inside the car, he gave the driver an address and then he called Sydney Seiler. "I was worried," Ja later recalled, "but as a diplomat I knew how to play a role. I told him that since the supreme leader would soon totally destroy New York City and the other imperialist outposts throughout the country, he would need to drive to Haskell if he wanted to meet with us." Ja gave Seiler the address of a Holiday Inn Express in Haskell, New Jersey.

Seiler was caught off guard. He recalled confirming that Ja was on his way to Haskell by asking, "Like Eddie?"

Ambassador Ja had picked the site because it was as far from New York City as North Korean diplomats were legally allowed to travel—almost exactly twenty-five miles from the center of Columbus Circle. He also liked the fact that the hotel was sandwiched between two large hills. Even if a North Korean nuclear-armed ICBM missed New York City by many, many miles, the hotel would be safe.

Seiler and Ambassador Haley argued about whether they should take the meeting. Seiler felt that it was his obligation to hear the North Koreans out. The situation, he said, was spiraling out of control. Haley, on the other hand, thought there was nothing further to discuss. She was needed in New York, moreover, to channel the international outrage over the nuclear strikes into a concrete plan to remove Kim Jong Un from power.

They agreed that Seiler would be the one to drive to meet Ja. Haley declined to allow him to take any of her staffers to serve as a note-taker. "She said that she wasn't going to send anyone on a fool's errand," Seiler recalled, "and that everyone wanted to stay in New York—where the action was."

As Seiler crossed the George Washington Bridge on the way to New Jersey, he noted that traffic was extremely heavy for a Saturday evening. The news of nuclear explosions in South Korea and Japan had not produced a full-blown panic in American cities, but clearly plenty of people were beginning to leave New York all the same. On a normal day, the drive to Haskell might take forty-five minutes, but it took Seiler that long just to get across the river and into the Garden State.

As Seiler sat in traffic, he recalled, he felt a growing sense of anger about the North Korea attack. It would be hard, he worried, not to hold the ambassador personally responsible. "As a diplomat, you have to sort of learn to mentally separate the person from the policy," Seiler said. "But this was really hard. I had lived in Seoul and was so sick and angry about what had happened. I was trying to keep my composure. I am not at all a violent person, but I worried I might punch him."

When Seiler finally arrived at the Holiday Inn Express in Haskell, a clerk at the front desk smiled at him and asked if he was looking for "Mr. Eddie." Ja had been confused by Seiler's question. When Seiler said yes, the clerk directed him to the hotel's meeting room. Seiler wandered around a bit before he found the "Twin Lakes Meeting Room." There was a small sign on the door, left over from a law enforcement seminar.

"I just thought having the meeting in the 'Twin Lakes Room' was going to sound a heck of a lot better in the inevitable State Department history than the 'Holiday Inn Express Summit,'" Seiler remembered. "And then I laughed out loud. I mean, what were the chances that we'd even live to write a history? Why was I worrying about that? I guess everyone reacts to stress differently."

Seiler recalled that he knocked once, just as a courtesy, then opened the door. The entire North Korean mission to the United Nations was in the room, milling around. Ambassador Ja stepped up to him and, without a word, handed him a card. It said, "HAPPY BIRTHDAY, MOM."

Seiler was very confused. "I was experiencing a lot of emotions: anger, sadness, black humor," Seiler recalled. "And then that card. What could I do? I opened it."

The ambassador's handwriting was messy, and the message had been scribbled in haste. It read:

"I would like to seek asylum for myself and my staff. This is my decision alone. No one else knows this yet."

Seiler was stunned. In retrospect, he later admitted, the ambassador's decision was an obvious possibility, but one that he had neglected to consider in the rush of emotions. Defection simply had not occurred to him. "Initially, I had no idea how to react. I just thanked him for the card and asked where the restroom was," Seiler explained. "Then I stepped outside and called the State Department Ops Center."

The mass defection of the Korean mission surprised not only Seiler but also the State Department and the US intelligence community. From time to time, of course, North Korean diplomats had defected. But never in a large group. In fact, there had been only a single mass defection of North Koreans—a group of thirteen restaurant workers in Ningbo, China, who fled to South Korea in 2016.

Ja had read about this defection, and its details had informed his planning. In organizing the defection, the restaurant manager had not told the twelve young women working as waitresses the purpose of their exciting trip abroad until the very last moment. Some probably guessed what was happening, but his ruse was designed to protect them as well as their families back in North Korea, who could plausibly claim that their sisters and daughters had been tricked into following him. "I probably didn't need to be so cautious in this circumstance," Ja told interrogators, "but I had carefully planned how I might leave for a long time. In fact, the only detail I didn't plan was which card to buy. With so much stress, I couldn't choose! I said to myself, 'Ja, don't be stupid, it doesn't matter, just pick any one.'"

North Korea had traditionally combated defections with the carrot-and-stick approach of choosing loyal people with strong ties to the regime, while threatening retribution against family members as a deterrent. Ja and his family had done very well for themselves under Kim Jong Un, far better than the vast majority of North Korean citizens. But all that was over now, Ja reasoned. To Ja, Kim was finished. Dead men offer no inducements and threaten no punishment. Defunct countries don't need ambassadors, and they can't kill defectors. His main concern was whether his family would survive the coming war. Ja was certain that the United States would prevail, but he wasn't so sure about what would come next. In particular, he was concerned that his surviving family members might be targeted by their neighbors.

More than anything else, Ja was motivated by a strong desire to resettle his family abroad, ideally in the United States. "I was a big shot in Pyongyang," Ja explained. "Not everybody likes a big shot, especially one from the big city."

Some critics have charged that the loss of the DPRK mission eliminated an important channel for diplomacy. Some press reports even speculated that the Central Intelligence Agency continued to run the mission in the hours that followed, in an effort to deceive North Korea. There is no evidence to support these notions. By the time Seiler reported the defection, the president and his advisers had already settled on an air campaign to remove Kim Jong Un from power. Moreover, the North Korean diplomats had already destroyed the communications equipment in their Manhattan office, so there was no way for US intelligence to pretend that the mission was still operational. The Federal Bureau of Investigation (FBI) did not plan to secure the North Korean office space until early the next morning. They never got the chance.

MYOHYANG HDBT

When night fell on North Korea, the United States began striking targets throughout the country. High on the list were the palaces where Kim Jong Un might be hiding.

Throughout the course of the war, the United States never had an accurate fix on Kim Jong Un's location. The Myohyang complex was deemed a secondary target; US planners had assumed that Kim Jong Un would most likely do what his father would have done: flee to the complex near Mount Baekdu.

Still, US military planners covered their bases, drawing up plans to heavily strike multiple palace complexes, including Myohyang. In doing so, they were guided by a single analytic insight. Kim Jong Il had been deathly afraid of flying and took trains everywhere, but Kim Jong Un was an avid fan of aviation, having even learned to fly his own plane. Kim had ordered the construction of runways at his most important palaces—in Pyongyang, Wonsan, and, of course, Myohyang. The North Koreans had laughed at how careless the South Korean military officers had been when they revealed the location of so many missile bases on social media. No one told Kim that his runways, often set next to the train stations built for his father, would be used to guide American missiles and bombs to him and his family.

At 6:48 PM Pyongyang time, only a few minutes after sunset, explosions began to rip through the newly constructed palace complex at Myohyang. The site was struck with no less than a dozen cruise missiles. They targeted not only the palace's buildings but also the systems that provided electricity and ventilation to Kim's bunker beneath the mountain. Although he was far too deep for American missiles or bombs to reach directly, there was another possibility—what the military calls "functional defeat," or effectively turning the bunker into a tomb. At the very least, the bombs would make life very unpleasant for those inside by striking the entrances and the life support systems. With no electricity, it would be dark in the bunker. The increasingly foul air would be hard to breathe. Food would spoil, and toilets would not flush. Kim would be cut off from communications. The explosions might also trigger avalanches that would send rocks cascading over the entrance of the bunker, blocking the door.

The strike on the Myohyang HDBT ("hard and deeply buried target") was only partially successful. The explosions did not bury Kim in his bunker. They did, however, knock out the bunker's electrical systems. Without power, there was no heat and the air filtration system stopped working. Personnel on-site opened up doors and vents to let in fresh air. Kim could breathe and was still in contact with his forces, but over the course of the night the temperature in the bunker dropped. His children in particular found the extreme cold of the March night difficult to endure.

The strikes, according to transcripts of the meeting recovered from the Myohyang bunker after the war, caught Kim and his family off guard. They had believed that a diplomatic effort was under way in New York. They expected the Americans to try to reason with the supreme leader, not kill him —not when he still had so many ICBMs up his sleeve.

KIM JO YONG [KIM JONG UN'S SISTER]: Do we have an answer from New York?

CHOE RYONG HAE [KIM'S AIDE]: I think this is the answer. It is fairly clear to me.

KIM JO YONG: [inaudible]

KIM JONG UN: They were just stalling. Trump doesn't care about South Korea or Japan. He said so himself.*

KIM JO YONG: [inaudible]

KIM JONG UN: He needs to know Americans will die too. We have to show him we have the will to see this through.

CHOE RYONG HAE: What good is a world without [North] Korea!

The last statement is one that we find elsewhere in the historical record as well. Several North Korean prisoners of war made it when asked why Kim Jong Un had been willing to use nuclear weapons or to escalate the conflict at crucial moments. The phrase came up again and again in interrogations, much to the confusion of the interrogators. "What good is a world without North Korea?" Former regime officials would

---

* Kim Jong Un appears to have been referring to a comment attributed to Trump: "If there's going to be a war to stop Kim Jong Un, it will be over there. If thousands die, they're going to die over there. They're not going to die here." Trump denies ever saying this.

simply repeat this rhetorical question, as though its meaning was obvious. "You think it sounds crazy, but you are totally wrong," Choe Ryong Hae later explained to this commission's investigators from his holding cell at [REDACTED]. "You don't understand anything about war. How many people did you kill just because you don't want to understand?"

Choe's comment, he explained, was a reference to something Kim Jong Il had said—a reference that Kim Jong Un would have understood all too well. Choe pointed out that the statement was little more than a repackaging of a quotation by China's Mao Zedong, who had dismissed the threat of nuclear attacks on China with a similar statement. It was nothing more than a Leninist idea that war is decided not by weapons but by the will of the soldiers and their leaders. "If war is a test of weapons, then you Americans would always win," Choe explained. "But you lost in Vietnam and Afghanistan and Iraq. That's because war is a test of will. Capitalists aren't willing to blow up the earth, because you care only about money. The supreme leader understood what I meant: with his strength of will, surely we would prevail."

According to Choe, Kim continued to see the conflict as a personal struggle with Donald Trump. One of them would have to back down and accept defeat. For Kim, it was clear that Trump the "property developer" would back down. After all, for Kim Jong Un defeat would mean the loss of everything— his rule, his family, his life. Donald Trump, on the other hand, could simply stop and walk away, suffering nothing more than the same short-lived sting of embarrassment that had befallen many other defeated imperial powers.

Kim's plan was to respond to every American escalation with an escalation of his own, until the price was simply too high for Trump. The news that the first attack had not produced the expected public pressure on Trump to stop the attacks was disappointing, but not unexpected. This was a struggle to death, and Kim believed that the winner would be the one who had the will to carry on to the bitter end.

The transcripts give no record of Kim giving an order to use long-range nuclear weapons against the United States. Choe said simply that, after the conversation, he understood what Kim wanted. When Kim had ordered the strikes against South Korea and Japan, he had also ordered that the long-range missile forces be dispersed. Their orders were clear: if North Korea came under attack, they could retaliate against their targets in the United States. Still, Choe said, he managed to contact the Strategic Rocket Force Command on his cell phone to convey the order.

He recalled being somewhat evasive, unsure whether his calls were being intercepted.

"The medicine doesn't seem to have cured the patient of his madness," Choe recalled telling the Strategic Rocket Force commander. "Trump is a big man. The supreme leader wants to give him a stronger dose."

Then Choe accompanied Kim's children as they made their way back over the hill to a hotel at the mouth of the valley.

THE GREAT MISSILE CHASE

Davidson had tasked the Air Force with hunting down North Korea's long-range missiles. The priority during the first day of the air war was to find and somehow disable the small number of big missiles that could reach the United States with their massive thermonuclear weapons—and to do so before Kim had a chance to launch them. Davidson knew he had a narrow window of time, but he hoped that Kim would hesitate—and that his hesitation would be fatal.

The analysts working at the CIA and in other corners of the intelligence community had a good idea where North Korea stored most of the missiles that threatened the United States. On March 21, 2020, the US Air Force struck these sites heavily, with cruise missiles launched from ships and aircraft. But North Korea had stored many of these missiles in tunnels, which made them difficult to reach with a single air strike. Destroying a deeply buried target often required striking it over and over, in the same spot, with each successive explosion digging a bit deeper. What's more, the intelligence provided to the US aircrews participating in these missions, while impressive, was far from perfect. It was impossible to know where every last missile had been stored or even how many there were. As one senior Defense Intelligence Agency official admitted, "There was no accurate accounting of mobile launchers or where they were based or hiding." US intelligence analysts are supremely talented, but they are not omniscient—and no one should have expected them to be.

North Korea's long-range ballistic missiles, including the massive Hwasong-15, were mobile — that is to say, they could be transported by massive trucks. These vehicles were slow and cumbersome, but the North Koreans had been able to disperse them at the same time Kim gave the order for its short- and medium-range missiles to attack targets in South Korea and Japan. Some of these missiles were moved to secondary tunnels a safe distance away from the primary tunnels where they were regularly stored. Others were hidden under highway overpasses, in road tunnels, or in caves.

As a result, the massive series of air strikes that targeted North Korea's known missile bases destroyed few, if any, of Kim's intercontinental ballistic missiles. This illuminates one of the reasons that OPLAN 5015 was premised as a preemptive strike: Air Force officials believed that it was essential to destroy these ICBMs before North Korea could disperse them. Their concern was sometimes shrouded in euphemisms like "left of launch" and "pre-boost phase intercept," but the jargon all meant the same thing: destroy the missiles before they could be launched. And the best time to do that was when the missiles were still sitting on the trucks in garages at known locations.

But with North Korea's preemptive nuclear strike against US forces in South Korea, Japan, and Guam, the United States had lost the element of surprise. North Korea's remaining missiles were already on the move, the truck drivers heading for secure places to hide from the retaliatory strikes that might be coming. Thus, the Air Force was forced to play catch-up and chase after Kim Jong Un's missiles just as it had scrambled to find Saddam's Scuds in the 1991 Gulf War. In that war, allied war planners had neglected to target Saddam's small force of Scud missiles, judging it to be militarily insignificant. But what they did not anticipate was that Saddam would lob missiles at Israel, creating a political crisis. Allied commanders threw large numbers of aircraft and special forces at the mission of "Scud hunting," only to fail miserably.

Although the conflicts were separated by nearly thirty years, technology had not changed quite as dramatically as might be imagined. Some of the F-15E Strike Eagle fighter jets used in the air strikes on North Korea were the same aircraft that had hunted the Scuds in 1991 in Iraq, although these aircraft were now joined by the F-35, a stealth fighter with far greater capabilities. Crucially for this nighttime raid, both aircraft had much improved targeting pods that allowed the pilots to see better in the dark.

While the planes' better new sensors allowed the pilots —and the controllers communicating with them—to see far more than ever before, they did not tell the pilots and controllers where to look. The Air Force was quickly forced to develop a strategy similar to how it handled Scuds during the 1991 Gulf War: identifying "launch baskets" from which North Korean missiles might be expected to be fired, and then sending aircraft to patrol in figure-eight patterns over these areas, dropping bombs at preset intervals on possible launch sites. The idea was to harass the launch units, using the aircraft like artillery to force the missile crews to stay hidden and to keep them from launching. Of course, if a pilot saw a vehicle moving into the launch basket or preparing for a launch, then her priority immediately changed to destroying it.

This approach had worked poorly during the 1991 Gulf War. Afterward, the United States could not confirm that even a single one of Saddam's Scuds had been destroyed prior to its launch. Pentagon officials had hoped that improvements in technology might see them through during another such conflict—that the next time would be different. But North Korea was different in other ways that complicated the missile chase.

North Korea was a more challenging environment than Iraq, particularly since many of its launch sites were located in remote and mountainous regions. In Iraq, the launch baskets were easy to identify because Iraq's missiles were short-range: if the Iraqis wanted to launch a missile at Israel, there was only a small area of the Iraqi desert close enough to Israel for the missile to reach its target. But against North Korea, the Air Force was looking for missiles that could fly all the way to the United States. All of North Korea essentially was a launch basket.

This made the criteria for where the Air Force should send its fighters to patrol more nebulous. In telling the pilots where to look, military intelligence analysts were often forced simply to guess. These guesses were educated, of course; the analysts had some idea of where the missiles were stored, approximately when they were told to disperse, and how fast the launcher trucks could drive. North Korea's poor road network helped narrow down the trucks' possible locations: for instance, the big trucks were far too heavy to travel off-road.

US analysts were largely correct in drawing their launch baskets, although a few missiles were launched from outside these areas. But the analysts had created these accurate launch baskets by making them very, very large, and thus a large number of aircraft were required to patrol them.

The approach, whatever sense it made on paper, was simply not effective enough to protect the United States. About a dozen Hwasong-14 and Hwasong-15 missiles were successfully launched against the nation during the early-morning hours of Sunday, March 22.

Air Force officials have argued that their efforts did, in fact, suppress the number of launches. "From the perspective of limiting damage to the United States," an Air Force history argues, "it is important to remember how many missiles were not launched because missile crews were evading detection by the air campaign." Still, there is no evidence that the air campaign was effective in destroying any mobile missiles, of any range. "In the end," the history concludes, "the best one can say is that some mobile launchers may have been destroyed [prior to firing their missiles]."

The pilots simply could not find the missiles prior to launch. Instead, once a launch was detected, controllers ordered aircraft to fly to the launch location to destroy the launcher before it could escape to reload and fire again. North Korean missile units, like the Iraqis in 1991, practiced a tactic that America military officials called "shoot-and-scoot": firing their missile and then moving the large vehicle to safety. "Those guys were like cockroaches who disappear when the kitchen light goes on," observed Captain Tom McIntyre, an American pilot.

The North Koreans adopted a slightly different shoot-and-scoot strategy. They built huge trucks that could erect the missile on a massive metal firing table and then "scoot" before the projectile was even fired. The truck simply brought the missile to the site and erected it. By the time the crew fired the missile, the precious launcher was long gone to pick up another payload. American pilots reported their frustration in arriving on the scene, only to see little more than a hunk of metal and a burn mark on the ground. "We started calling the trucks 'deadbeat dads,'" another US pilot recalled, "because there was an erection, but they would split town before we could make 'em pay up."

In many cases, the first that pilots saw of the ICBMs were the massive flashes of the huge missiles as the crews launched them toward the United States. "It's a huge flame and your first reaction is that it's a SAM and you want to make a defensive reaction," recalled McIntyre. "Then you see that it is going straight up. So AWACS [the Airborne Warning and Control System, an aircraft that functions as an air-based traffic control system] is yelling and hollering for us to get on it and we're heading for the coordinates as fast as we could go. It was about twenty-five miles away from us, but when we got there, we went up and down the road and all I could find in the targeting pod was a hotspot on the ground."

Even when the pilots saw a launch, it was usually from a great distance, and there was nothing they could do to stop it. It simply isn't possible for aircraft to engage enemy missiles as they lift off.

Many pilots recalled the helpless feeling of watching the huge missiles powering up into space, carrying huge nuclear weapons that the pilots knew were headed toward the United States. "You just think, *I hope those guys in Alaska have a shot*," one pilot recalled. "Then you go try to find the son of a bitch that did it."

9

WHEELS UP

NORTH KOREA FIRED THIRTEEN nuclear-armed long-range missiles against the United States of America. The first missile was fired at 1:02 AM Pyongyang time on March 22 — midday on March 21 on the East Coast of the United States. It would take approximately forty-five minutes to reach its target in the United States.

A number of questions have been raised about why the United States was not able to defend against these missiles, and about the conduct of the president in the forty-five minutes between the launch of the first missile and its impact in the United States. In particular, many citizens have wondered whether the government might have done more to protect its citizens or, at the very least, to warn them of the coming danger.

MAINLAND FIREPOWER STRIKE PLAN

The American targets that Kim Jong Un ordered North Korea's Strategic Rocket Force to destroy with nuclear weapons did not come as a surprise. The targets had been chosen far in advance and clearly identified in North Korean propaganda.

In 2013, Kim Jong Un had even gone so far as to pose for a picture as he sat at his desk, approving the list of targets in the United States. Behind him, his aides had erected a world map labeled "Mainland Firepower Strike Plan." They carefully drew lines from North Korea toward four different locations in the United States.

Let us reiterate: Kim Jong Un's nuclear war plan was not a suicide note. It was a strategy to win the war, although it was a desperate gambit taken as a last resort. Still, there was a grim logic to the four places shown on the map. Two of the targets were military in nature—the naval bases in Pearl Harbor and San Diego that housed the American fleet. These strikes were intended to interdict the supply lines that would stretch from the United States to sustain military operations on the Korean Peninsula.

Modern warfare requires immense support. For the invasion of Iraq, the Navy moved more than 56 million square feet of cargo and 4.8 billion gallons of fuel. To visualize these amounts, imagine you are standing in Washington, DC. The cargo that you need to ship to the Middle East to supply the attack looks like a line of cars stretching past Denver and into the Rocky Mountains. And the fuel is enough to fill a train stretching all the way to Santa Fe, New Mexico.

The invasion of North Korea would require a similarly massive naval operation, but North Korea would not let that happen without a fight. Kim Jong Un had ordered the Strategic

Rocket Force to use its nuclear weapons to break these supply lines, leaving US troops in Asia hungry and out of ammunition, tanks sitting idle, and planes grounded from lack of gas.

The other two targets on Kim's map were chosen to make clear that the United States could not prosecute a war against Kim with impunity. If the president of the United States was going to try to kill Kim Jong Un and his family, Kim wanted to make sure the president knew that he and his family were at risk too.

Washington, DC, was Kim's third target, and an obvious one. But the fourth place on the map had been a bit of a mystery, partly because the precise location was obscured in the picture that North Korea released in 2013. One of the generals was wearing a hat, and his head was in the way. Where was the fourth location? A few people estimated that the target was someplace in Texas, perhaps Austin. At the time the governor of Texas had claimed that North Korea was targeting Texas because of its excellent business climate. Others joked that Kim's real grievance involved Texas barbecue, or maybe not being invited to South-by-Southwest.

But Kim wasn't joking. Intelligence analysts realized the target was something altogether different—and it wasn't in Texas at all.

The fourth place on the map was Barksdale Air Force Base, near Shreveport, Louisiana. The choice of Barksdale puzzled American analysts for some time, until the reason dawned on them. On September 11, 2001, President George W. Bush had been evacuated on Air Force One from an appearance in

Florida. With Washington under attack, the crew decided that they could not return to the Capitol, so Air Force One had landed at Barksdale Air Force Base instead.

The message from Kim Jong Un to the US president was: you can run, but you can't hide.

ALERT

American satellites detected each of the thirteen nuclear-armed intercontinental-range ballistic missiles that North Korea fired toward the United States, just as those same satellites had detected all of the other, shorter-range missiles that North Korea had launched over the previous days.

The missiles that Kim fired on March 22, however, were different. Short-range missiles popped up and fell back down, captured by the satellites for only a few moments. But these missiles—the big ones—kept climbing as their engines pushed them higher into space before burning out and lofting their heavy nuclear warheads toward their targets.

The list of locations that Kim now targeted was importantly different too from the list that he had released in 2013. As threatened, North Korea fired missiles at the fleet in Pearl Harbor and San Diego, as well as at the White House in Washington, DC. But it also launched ICBMs at New York City, which, owing to its landmark Trump Tower, had edged Barksdale off the targeting list. Each of these four cities was targeted with three thermonuclear weapons. North Korea also fired a single nuclear-armed missile at Mar-a-Lago.

The first missile launch at 1:02 AM in Korea set off a grim race between the missile and the satellite warning system. Each missile, once launched, would take between thirty-eight and forty-one minutes to reach its target in the United States. The lone exception was the very first missile fired, which was targeted at Mar-a-Lago. Since its destination was much farther away from North Korea than the others (more than 7,500 kilometers), the missile would take nearly forty-five minutes to arrive. This meant that before it struck Mar-a-Lago at 12:47 PM, there would be forty-five minutes to detect the launch, warn the president, and move him to safety — ideally the safety of Air Force One, which, once in the air, would be virtually invulnerable to attack.

Warning the president consisted of a series of steps, each of which consumed precious minutes. It took one or two minutes for the missile to break through the clouds and be seen by the satellite. It took another minute for the satellite to identify it and alert a ground station in Karlsruhe, Germany. It took another two minutes for the crew in Karlsruhe to confirm the alert and send it to the North American Aerospace Defense Command in Colorado Springs. NORAD then took another two minutes to confirm the attack and call the president's crisis coordinator — his chief of staff.

Francis's military assistant was informed of the launch at 12:09. He called Francis at 12:10. The chief of staff now had three minutes to decide whether to tell the president. At 12:13, feeling sure there was an attack under way, he told the president.

Everything had gone perfectly, but eleven minutes had slipped away, leaving slightly more than half an hour to move the president to safety.

Francis knew that much of the remaining half-hour was already spoken for. It was one thing to tell the president that a missile was on its way, but it was quite another thing to do something about it. In this case, the president would need enough time to get from Mar-a-Lago to the airport, board Air Force One, and get airborne. The trip from Mar-a-Lago to the Palm Beach International Airport was a ten-minute drive in a motorcade in the best of times with a police escort and no traffic. But the Southern Avenue Bridge was now clogged with people trying to get as far away from Mar-a-Lago as they possibly could. The president could use the helicopter again, Francis thought, but it would still take a few minutes to walk to the helicopter, several more minutes to get to the airport, and then several minutes more to board Air Force One and take off. Assuming the helicopter was a viable option, Francis concluded, they needed to be in it within the next ten minutes —by 12:20 PM. "I thought we had enough time," Francis recalled later, "but we couldn't dilly-dally."

President Trump was having lunch on the terrace at Mar-a-Lago and refused to move. The Secret Service was adamant that Mar-a-Lago was no longer a safe location for him. "We need to get you to Air Force One and get you airborne," a Secret Service officer remembered telling Trump. But the president was reluctant to leave. No one could tell him where they were going—clearly Washington was not safe—and his staff found that it was difficult, if not impossible, to persuade the president that North Korea's missiles could reach Mar-a-Lago. According to one participant, Trump kept repeating a line they had all heard before: "all his *rockets* are *crashing*." Kellogg struggled to explain that not every rocket had crashed and that, regardless, they would be far safer from all kinds of threats, rockets or not, once they were in the air. But Trump remained adamant that the Situation Room beneath Mar-a-Lago was the safest place for them to be. "We did tests, and the foundation is anchored into the coral reef with *steel and concrete*," a staff member recalled Trump boasting. "That sucker's going nowhere!"

At 12:18, after the discussion drew the interest of other diners, Trump agreed to go down to the Situation Room, but he was still adamant about remaining at Mar-a-Lago. Another argument ensued. Keith Kellogg, who, according to participants, was shouting by now, said that if the secretary of defense had been present, he too would insist that Trump leave for the airport immediately: "Jim would say the same thing," Kellogg pleaded. "He would say get on the goddamned plane."

The remark about Mattis seemed to upset the president. "That's enough," he said curtly and stood up. "I have an idea. A really brilliant idea. You just keep having your meeting by yourself. I'm done." With that, he walked out of the room, accompanied only by his Secret Service detail.

Francis recalled being as confused as anyone else in the

room. The president's staff had seen him get angry and walk out of interviews before, but never meetings. Francis looked at his watch: 12:23. They could leave as late as 12:25 and still make it to the airport, although it would be close. He decided to give Trump two minutes to come back—but no more. He was prepared to ask the Secret Service to carry the president to the helicopter if necessary.

When Trump had not returned one minute later, Francis stepped out of the Situation Room and walked down the corridor to find him.

In the corridor outside the SCIF, Francis ran into a Mar-a-Lago employee. "One of the kitchen staff looked at me and just said, 'Mr. Trump said you can find your own way home,'" Francis recalled. "I ran back up the stairs and saw his helicopter taking off."

The president departed Mar-a-Lago at 12:25 PM, on schedule, although not quite as Francis had planned.

WEEKEND WARRIORS

As the North Korean missiles climbed into space, they came into full view of the radars linked to the only US line of defense: the missile defense system sitting in Alaska. Consisting of forty-four ground-based interceptors (GBIs), mostly located in Alaska, the system was crewed by members of the Alaska Army National Guard. It would be the responsibility of these Guardsmen to shoot down the missiles. "There's no big red button to put that [interceptor] in play," Colonel Kevin Kick, the unit's commander, explained. "It all happens with a click of a mouse."

The Alaska National Guard had a narrow window for those mouse clicks. A long-range missile is nearly impossible to hit during the period when its engines are firing; the limitations of time and space are simply too great. And once the warhead begins to fall back to earth, it reaches twenty times the speed of sound, making it virtually impossible to intercept.

But between those two moments is a window in which the hot nuclear warhead is coasting silently through the freezing cold of outer space. It is in these few moments, during the middle part of its journey—called "midcourse"—that the warhead is theoretically vulnerable. But to stop it the nation's defenders must act quickly. Within minutes of detecting an enemy missile launch, American missile defenses must fire their interceptors to catch the warhead in this critical stage of its flight. Each interceptor releases a small "kill vehicle" whose only purpose is to slam into the nuclear warhead and destroy it, by impact alone, in what is called a "hit to kill." Of the forty-four interceptors the United States maintained, forty had been placed in Alaska to ensure the best possible shot at any missiles fired from North Korea.

The Alaskan missile defense system—which has been temporarily mothballed pending an independent review of its technical performance—was called Ground-based Midcourse Defense (GMD) to distinguish it from other missile defenses, such as those based on ships or those designed to intercept missiles in other phases of their trajectory. But the most distinguishing feature of GMD was that, in 2020, it was the only missile defense system that could defend the United States against missiles from North Korea.

Even among missile defense advocates, however, there was little love for the system as it was deployed in Alaska. Like so many other defense decisions, the GMD system was a product of compromises and technical limitations. A panel of eminent scientists and engineers had been asked by the Defense Department to review the state of American missile defenses. The panel proposed replacing the system in Alaska entirely, calling the defense it offered "fragile" and mocking the "hobby shop" approach of the people who built it. They proposed designing all-new interceptor missiles and all-new radars and implementing an entirely new concept for how the system would operate. And these were the system's friends.

It should not be surprising, given these reviews, that GMD had a terrible test record. In actual flight tests, its success rate was right at 50 percent—a coin flip. In nearly twenty years of testing, the system had worked only nine out of eighteen times. Only one of those eighteen tests involved shooting at an ICBM like the ones North Korea was firing that day. Even worse, these estimates had been padded by excluding tests that had to be scrubbed for bad weather or technical malfunctions. The system's defenders—that is, those who wanted to fix it

—knew that it needed many, many more tests. "There's no way to prove out the design—let alone its reliability—without more flight tests," one of the panel members complained. "It's stupid."

But tests were expensive, costing nearly $300 million each. And there was another, bigger problem: failed tests sent the wrong message. They showed that the system was not working. Defense officials were worried that Kim Jong Un would be emboldened as he realized how ineffective the system was. Administration after administration had scaled back testing, resorting to classifying ever more information about failures. One document plainly admitted that the "deterrence value" of the system was "decreased by unsuccessful flights."

In short, the only missile defense system charged with protecting the United States against Kim Jong Un's ICBMs simply did not work—but the Defense Department refused to fix it, worrying that the tests required to do so would simply show the North Koreans that the system was a failure. This explains why the Obama and Trump administrations both spent billions of dollars to increase the number of GMD interceptors, but far less to actually improve them.

Instead, the Department of Defense came up with another plan: to fire a lot of interceptors at every missile and hope one of them got lucky. In March 2020, this concept of operations meant that each mouse click sent four interceptors flying into space for every North Korean missile coming at the United States. The reasoning was simple math: If each interceptor had a fifty-fifty chance of stopping an ICBM, four tries should be enough. What are the odds of flipping a coin and getting heads four times in a row?

Critics noted that this approach was based on an impoverished understanding of statistics. "I think this reasoning is flawed," explained one scholar who would later be interviewed by the commission. "It assumes that the *failure* modes of the interceptors are *independent* of one another. But, in practice, if one interceptor *fails* because of a design flaw, say, it's much more likely that others will do so too for the same reason."

And indeed, GMD had plenty of design flaws, many of which were well known prior to March 2020. One test failed because of a manufacturing defect—a faulty circuit board that short-circuited when bits of solder or wire shook loose during the violent process of launching the interceptors into space. More than thirty of the forty-four interceptors had these defective circuit boards, but although this defect was publicly reported years earlier by the *Los Angeles Times*, the Missile Defense Agency decided that "no corrective actions" were needed for the old circuit boards, while deciding to change the manufacturing process for the new ones. That left more than thirty interceptors with the old boards. "If there's a foreign object in one unit, it's sort of whistling past the graveyard to assume that that's a once-in-a-lifetime event," one of the panelists who had reviewed the system told the *Times* reporter.

Another problem that confronted the nation's missile defenders on the morning of March 22 was also an issue of simple math. A total of forty-four interceptors was enough to defend against eleven North Korean missiles. But North Korea had fired thirteen missiles at the United States. And to make matters worse, each missile released a pair of decoys to fool the "kill vehicles" trying to find the warheads in space. A system designed to deal with only eleven North Korean nuclear warheads now faced the task of finding thirteen real ones hidden among more than two dozen fakes.

There is no agreement, even among experts, as to whether the GMD system successfully intercepted any North Korean missiles on March 21. This is a problem that has plagued previous assessments of missile defense effectiveness. The real world is not a video game, even if the computer screen in the fire control unit displays gamelike messages like "probable kill" if it believes the intercept worked. At best, analysts can sift through reams of data from sensors and reach a probabilistic judgment as to whether a missile was intercepted or simply broke up on its own. There is always the danger, of course, of seeing what one wants to see in a pile of confusing and sometimes contradictory data.

We do know that, of the thirteen missiles North Korea fired at the United States, six failed to deliver nuclear weapons against our homeland. These missiles either broke up in flight or had warheads that disintegrated as they reentered the earth's atmosphere. Some experts claim that these six missiles may not have been armed at all.

According to the Department of Defense, the fact that six

of the thirteen nuclear warheads failed to reach the United States was powerful evidence that the nation's missile defense system functioned well under demanding conditions. Indeed, they claimed that the system worked better than could reasonably have been expected, managing to pick out and destroy six of the eleven nuclear warheads it had the capacity to intercept, for a success rate of more than 50 percent. What the system did, explained one official, was "give us a limited capability to deal with a relatively small number of incoming ballistic missiles, which is better than nothing."

Critics disputed, however, that any North Korean missiles were intercepted at all. It is far more likely, they argued, that the missiles broke up in flight or that the warheads disintegrated upon reentry. They noted that some North Korean missile tests had failed, including those whose mocked-up warheads burned up as they reentered the atmosphere.

Our investigators commissioned an independent review of the data provided by the Pentagon, but this review was not able to confirm any intercepts. The author of the review noted that "the data used by the Army raise many questions that create uncertainty over how much confidence can be placed in what the Army used to assess warhead kills.

"The method used by the Army to assess warhead kills appears reasonable on first inspection but on closer scrutiny serious questions can be raised," the report continued. It concluded that "the Army does not appear to have sufficient data to assign high confidence to its claims."

"A PROTOCOL NO-NO"

President Trump's helicopter landed on the tarmac at Palm Beach International Airport at 12:28 PM, three minutes after departing Mar-a-Lago and nineteen minutes before the anticipated impact of the North Korean ICBM. The engines of Air Force One were already running—a sign of urgency that one official traveling with the president characterized as "normally a protocol no-no."

Air Force One would wait for the president, but no one else. "My boss," the pilot explained to us later, "called and told me to depart as soon as the president got on board." A small number of presidential staffers who had been staying nearby at the Hilton Palm Beach Airport Hotel had managed to board the plane before Trump arrived; Francis had arranged for his military assistant, who had been staying at the hotel, to get as many people on board as possible. One of the staff members remembered the unusually tight security protocol, with the Secret Service checking identification in addition to badges and bomb-sniffing dogs. "They were drooling all [over] the luggage," she recalled. "I had dog spittle all over my bags."

After the president's helicopter landed, he walked across the tarmac and then carefully ascended the ramp stairs leading up to the airplane. Before he settled into his seat, he told the pilot, "Let's get the hell out of here."

Air Force One was wheels up at 12:37 PM. The pilot and crew recalled the particular violence of the takeoff. "It was a full-thrust departure," one recounted, "up like a rocket." The passengers were shaken by the sudden ascent. "We were climbing so high and so fast," said another, "I started to wonder if we'd need oxygen masks."

The pilot was racing to get the plane up high enough, and out far enough over the ocean, to ensure a safe distance from any nuclear explosion. He also directed everyone on board to close the aircraft's window shades so as not to be blinded by the flash.

The president's blind was still up when, at 12:48 PM, a 200-kiloton thermonuclear weapon detonated over Jupiter, Florida. By chance, he escaped being blinded, but it was due to more than luck that Air Force One itself survived. The plane was designed to be far more survivable in a nuclear environment than any commercial airliner, and the pilot had, in any event, gotten the aircraft far enough away from the epicenter of the blast.

After the flash caught his eye, President Trump looked out the window, watching the fireball form slowly and rise up into the atmosphere. He observed the scene for a few seconds before the pilot banked the plane hard and headed farther out to sea.

"The president just said, 'Absolutely beautiful,'" recalled a staffer. "I started to cry."

10

BLACK RAIN

SATURDAY, MARCH 21, 2020, marked the worst catastrophe in American history.

North Korea's nuclear strikes were carried out over the course of six hours. Of the thirteen nuclear weapons fired against the United States, seven delivered their powerful thermonuclear weapons onto the country and its citizens.

One nuclear weapon, aimed at Mar-a-Lago, struck Jupiter, Florida. Another nuclear weapon destroyed Pearl Harbor. A third struck Manhattan. Two nuclear weapons, probably aimed at the White House, missed wildly but fell on northern Virginia, their explosions separated by about an hour. Two more exploded off the California coast near San Diego, missing the port by enough that no one was killed.

In attempting to create a definitive and official account of this unparalleled national tragedy, we discovered that written accounts failed to convey accurately for millions of Americans what that day was like. The same event can mean many different things to many people. The commission found as many perspectives on the horror as there were survivors for us to interview.

Perhaps all that unites these individuals is the powerful sense that the portrayal of the events of March 21 by the media and political figures has been misleading, inaccurate, and heavily sanitized. We on the commission have come to have enormous sympathy for those who suffered through those terrible days.

Thus, rather than attempting to offer a definitive account of the events of March 21, 2020, the commission has opted to collect the stories of more than a dozen survivors. Their voices can convey what our words cannot.

EMERGENCY ALERT

Following the first reports on social media that North Korea had used nuclear weapons against South Korea and Japan, there were isolated reports of panic across the continental United States, Alaska, and Hawaii. The traffic leaving major US cities picked up as some people sought to evacuate. Social media posts showed empty store shelves as Americans tried to prepare for the same kind of cataclysm that had befallen their Asian allies.

On the whole, however, most Americans did nothing. For as long as anyone could remember, war was something that happened to other people, in other places. They were not warned that this was different, nor were they told to prepare.

Few Americans, even those in positions of power, expected that North Korea would strike the United States. Many doubted that North Korea even had such weapons, while others were confident that the Pentagon had a plan to protect Americans. And above all, perhaps, the dull pressure of everyday life held many Americans to their routines.

North Korea's first missile was fired at Mar-a-Lago in the middle of the night in Korea, at 1:02 AM Pyongyang time. A second missile followed fourteen minutes later, headed for Pearl Harbor.

Florida has no system for alerting citizens to a ballistic missile attack. In fact, Hawaii is the only state that does. As a result, it was the Hawaii Emergency Management Agency that provided the first warning to the public that North Korea was attacking the United States. At 6:24 AM local time—just before dawn—a text message appeared on phones throughout the state of Hawaii.

⚠

Emergency Alert

BALLISTIC MISSILE THREAT INBOUND TO HAWAII.

SEEK IMMEDIATE SHELTER THIS IS NOT A DRILL.

Josh Goshorn, an electrical engineer from Carmel, California, was on vacation on Oahu with his family. He was getting ready to go surfing as soon as the sun broke over the horizon —what is called "dawn patrol"—when his phone lit up. "It was scary for sure," he later explained, "but there had been a false alarm before. I was still planning on going out, but my wife Molly called me and said, 'Joshua, come home now, the kids are really freaking out.'"

Despite the obvious escalation over the past twenty-four hours, very few people took shelter. Hawaii had been testing warning sirens consistently since 2018, and many people simply assumed that this warning was either yet another exercise or a false alarm. After all, a false alarm with identical wording had been mistakenly sent in 2018. Most people believed that March 21 would be a day like any other.

"I wondered who was going to get fired this time," Goshorn recalled thinking.

ASTRONAUTS

After that lone warning, the nuclear warheads began landing throughout the United States. The first hit Florida, where the nuclear weapon aimed at Mar-a-Lago fell up the coast in Jupiter. Then a nuclear weapon hit Pearl Harbor. New York was next, suffering a direct hit from a nuclear weapon that exploded over Trump Tower in midtown Manhattan. A nuclear weapon, presumably aimed at the White House, missed and exploded in Arlington, Virginia, followed by another an hour later and a few miles away. Finally, another nuclear weapon that had been aimed at Pearl Harbor fell in Honolulu.

All told, seven nuclear weapons, each exploding with a force twenty times greater than the bomb that destroyed Hiroshima,

THE SECOND ATTACK
North Korea Missile Launches Against
the United States Homeland

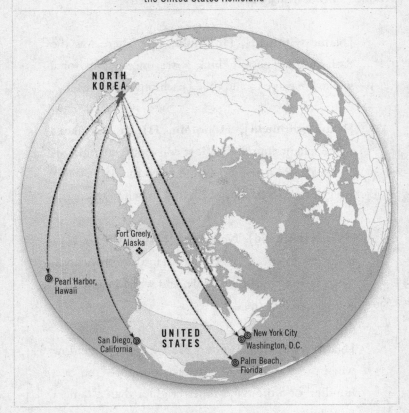

brought death and destruction to the United States over a six-hour span.

For most Americans affected by the attack, memories begin with the flash. Survivors almost uniformly remark on the intense white light followed by pitch blackness—a darkness both literal and figurative. The blast wave that arrived shortly after the explosion's flash engulfed survivors in a black cloud of ash, broken glass, and other debris—cutting them, breaking bones, and blotting out the sun.

[Name withheld], Honolulu, HI: There was the flash and darkness. I think I was unconscious for a while. We came to and called each other's names.

[Name withheld], Honolulu, HI: It was like a white magnesium flash. I lost consciousness right after or almost at the same time I saw the flash. When I regained consciousness, I found myself in the dark.

[Name withheld], New York, NY: When the blast came, my friend and I were blown into another room. I was unconscious for a while, and when I came to, I found myself in the dark.

[Name withheld], Jupiter, FL: I was at the window when the flash went off. It was so bright—ten or a hundred or a thousand times brighter than a camera flash bulb. The flash was piercing my eyes and my mind went blank. The glass from the windows was shattered all over the floor. I was lying on the floor too.

[Name withheld], Arlington, VA: I cried out, and as soon as I did I felt weightless, as if I were an astronaut. I was unconscious for twenty or thirty seconds. When I came to, I realized that everybody, including myself, was lying at one side of the room. Nobody was standing. The desks and chairs had also blown off to one side. At the windows, there was no glass in the panes, and the window frames had been blown out as well.

As the survivors regained consciousness, they found themselves surrounded by dead and injured people. Many survivors were seriously injured themselves but in the shock did not realize it. Only slowly did they begin to reckon with the death and destruction that they now saw all around them.

HAIR LOSS

With the United States under nuclear attack, Colonel Tom Miller, the pilot of Air Force One, had to decide where to take the president, who at the moment was accompanied only by Secret Service agents and relatively junior staff. None of them were in a position to make a strong recommendation about a destination. "I'd never heard the word 'decapitation attack' before," one aide recalled. "There are still missiles out there and the Secret Service says to the president, 'We don't think it's safe for you to return to Washington.'"

Given that Barksdale Air Force Base had been literally targeted on a map released by the North Koreans, Colonel Miller decided that the best thing to do would be to cruise off the coast until the situation became less chaotic. "The pilot says at that point, 'Let's just go cruise around . . . for a little bit,'" said the communications systems operator aboard Air Force One. "That was our Pearl Harbor. You train for nuclear war, then you get into something like that. All the money they pumped into us for training, that worked. We could read each other's minds."

Aides recalled the surreal feeling of knowing that the country was coming under attack, but being unable to do anything about it. They had no cell-phone reception and nothing to do. They simply waited, watching cable television as the first scenes of horror unfolded in Florida and Hawaii. "We were able to get some TV reception," one aide recalled. "They broke for commercial. I couldn't believe it. A hair-loss commercial comes on. I remember thinking, in the middle of all this, *I'm watching this commercial for hair loss.*

"SHE WAS ALIVE AND WE WERE SO GLAD"

Over the next few hours, the horror of the day repeated itself again and again, immeasurably. The nuclear weapon that fell directly on Manhattan exploded with the force of 200 kilotons —about ten times the power of the bomb that leveled Hiroshima. The two bombs that hit the Washington metropolitan area leveled much of the northern Virginia suburban area —home to more than three million people—but missed the White House, which was largely empty. And another nuclear weapon fell on Pearl Harbor.

On the ground, survivors were beginning to collect themselves. In New York City, Nikki Haley's apartment building at UN Plaza had been heavily damaged in the explosion, but it was still standing. She recalled that the windows had been blown out and the building had bent over so far under the pressure that she felt it might snap, before it rocked back violently, swaying like a ship on rough seas. "When I came to, I was anxious to know what happened to my son," she recalled. "I thought, *I have to go, I have to go and find him.*"

There was no electricity or water, and the building's windows had been blown out. Haley lived in the penthouse, fifty stories above the city, and the wind was fierce. Although injured, she walked down the interior stairwell all the way to the ground level and then began to make her way down FDR Drive toward the school where her son had spent the morning in a spring tennis program.

"I saw a young boy coming my way," she told the commission later. "His skin was dangling all over and he was naked. He was muttering, 'Mother, water, mother, water.'" she recalled. "I thought he might be my son, but he wasn't. I didn't give him any water. I am sorry that I didn't."

In the confusion and horror that followed each nuclear strike, the main impulse of many survivors was to move to safety—either to find help or offer help to others. Many survivors also tried to find friends and family members. This was difficult in the darkness, with collapsed buildings and mangled cars blocking roadways.

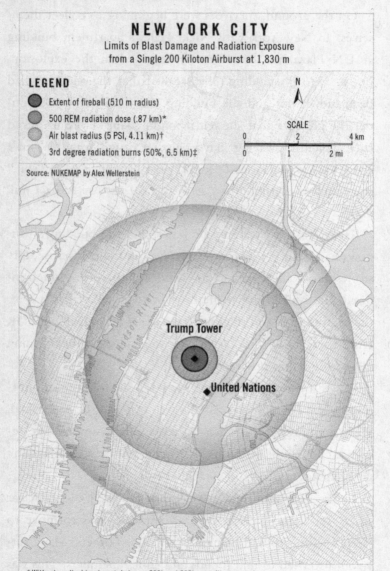

NEW YORK CITY

Limits of Blast Damage and Radiation Exposure
from a Single 200 Kiloton Airburst at 1,830 m

LEGEND

● Extent of fireball (510 m radius)
● 500 REM radiation dose (.87 km)*
● Air blast radius (5 PSI, 4.11 km)†
● 3rd degree radiation burns (50%, 6.5 km)‡

N

SCALE

0   2   4 km

0   1   2 mi

Source: NUKEMAP by Alex Wellerstein

Hudson River

Trump Tower

◆**United Nations**

*Without medical treatment, between 50% and 90% mortality expected.
†Most residential buildings collapse, injuries are universal, fatalities are widespread.
‡Third degree burns extend throughout the layers of skin, and are often painless because they destroy the pain nerves.

[Name withheld], Arlington, VA: I looked next door and I saw the father of a neighboring family standing almost naked. His skin was peeling off all over his body and was hanging from his fingertips. I talked to him, but he was too exhausted to give me a reply. He was looking for his family desperately.

[Name withheld], Jupiter, FL: I really thought I was dying because I drank so much water. I don't know how many minutes passed, but anyway I found something like a piece of wood, but it was very soft and sticky. I touched it. It was actually my friend's leg. She was alive, and we were so glad to see each other.

For many survivors in urban areas, the most intense memories in the immediate aftermath of the strike were the enormous amounts of rubble and ash left by the tall buildings that collapsed—and the cries in the darkness coming from underneath the debris. Many people were buried completely, while others were simply trapped by debris or so seriously injured that they could not move.

[Name withheld], New York, NY: I couldn't see anyone around me, but I heard somebody shouting "Help! Help!" from somewhere. Then I realized that the cries were actually coming from beneath the rubble I was walking on.

> **[Name withheld], New York, NY:** I found one of
> the other kids in the school alive. I held him in my
> arms. It is hard to say this: his skull was cracked open,
> his flesh was dangling out from his head. He had only
> one eye left, and it was looking right at me. First, he
> was mumbling something, but I couldn't understand
> him. I held his hand, and he started to reach for some-
> thing in his pocket, so I asked him, I said, "You want
> me to take this along to hand it over to your mother?"
> He nodded. I thought I could take him along. I guess
> that his body below the waist was crushed. The lower
> part of his body was trapped, buried inside of the de-
> bris. He just [refused] to go, he told me to go away.

With the widespread destruction and collapse of infrastructure, millions of people began to simply walk out of the destruction zone. Over the course of the afternoon and well into
the night, millions of people walked along expressways and
over bridges to escape the misery and suffering within the cities. While many eventually made it home after walking ten
or even twenty miles, many tens of thousands did not, falling
along the way; the escape routes were littered with the bodies
of men, women, and children.

RAVEN ROCK

The president, over the course of the first few hours of the
North Korean attack, grew increasingly agitated in his isola-

tion. He insisted that aides put him in contact with Secretary of Defense Mattis. Communicating with anyone, however, was nearly impossible. As reports of nuclear explosions in the United States appeared on television, the volume of text messages, social media postings, and telephone calls quickly overwhelmed the communications infrastructure. Moreover, government officials were beginning to follow procedures to evacuate to safety.

"Communications systems were overwhelmed with traffic," one aide recalled. "Key officials were being evacuated in Washington, DC, and cell calls that got through were breaking up. Information was mixed with rumor. We had to switch to the military radio network. The president couldn't reach key people on regular phones because people like the secretary of defense had abandoned buildings in DC. Cell phones were useless because the networks were saturated."

During this early period, Mattis was engaged in the important process of shifting Department of Defense operations out of the Pentagon and into Site R, the massive underground complex in rural Pennsylvania. Mattis had given orders to transfer operations to the Pentagon's deep underground, alternative command center as soon as the first missile launch had been detected. Although the complex was kept on a sort of warm standby, it would still take time—more than an hour—to get the staff into the facility and activate all of its communications systems. Mattis himself was in the air, en route to the site. During this period, he was simply not available to the president.

Unable to reach his secretary of defense, the president implored his remaining aides to find a way to contact his wife and children. He was particularly concerned about his wife Melania and their son Barron, who had been staying at Trump Tower. He was also demanding to talk to his daughter Ivanka and her husband Jared. They lived in Washington. Both cities were now under attack, and the president was desperate to know that his family members were safe.

"WHEREVER THE FIRE TOUCHED, IT BURNED"

If New Yorkers remember the rubble, people in Honolulu and northern Virginia—both largely suburban areas with wood frame houses—remember the fire. The intense heat of the explosions lit fires that grew steadily into firestorms, swallowing everything and everyone in their paths.

> [Name withheld], Honolulu, HI: We felt terribly hot and could not breathe well at all. After a while, a whirlpool of fire approached us from the south. It was like a big tornado of fire spreading over the full width of the street. Whenever the fire touched, wherever the fire touched, it burned. It burned my ear and leg. I didn't realize that I had burned myself at that moment, but I noticed it later.

> [Name withheld], Arlington, VA: I still felt very thirsty, and there was nothing I could do about it.

What I felt at that moment was that Virginia was entirely covered with only three colors. I remember red, black, and brown, but, but, nothing else. Many people on the street were killed almost instantly. The fingertips of those dead bodies caught fire, and the fire gradually spread over their entire bodies from their fingers. A light gray liquid dripped down their hands, scorching their fingers. I, I was so shocked to know that fingers and bodies could be burned and deformed like that. I just couldn't believe it. It was horrible.

[Name withheld], Arlington, VA: The houses on both sides of the railroad were burning, and the railway was the hollow in the fire. I thought I was going to die there. It was such an awful experience.

[Name withheld], Honolulu, HI: I could see people running in the dark. Some of them were on fire, and some of them were just rolling around on the ground. Gradually it became lighter. And just then, the sun broke through the clouds. The light appeared in many different colors, red and yellow, purple and white.

In Honolulu, it began to rain—giant drops of rain, blackened with the soot and ash from the fires. With so many people suffering from burns and especially thirst—a primary symptom of radiation poisoning—the rain initially seemed welcome. But it did not extinguish the growing fires.

> **[Name withheld], Honolulu, HI:** The fire and the smoke made us so thirsty, and there was nothing to drink, no water, and the smoke even disturbed our eyes. As it began to rain, people opened their mouths and turned their faces toward the sky and tried to drink the rain, but it wasn't easy to catch the raindrops in our mouths. It was a black rain with big drops.

In northern Virginia, the massive fire isolated the city of Alexandria. The two nuclear weapons had devastated much of the area to the north and west of the city, trapping its surviving residents between the growing fires and the Potomac River. As the fire swept into the city, survivors attempted to flee, but were chased by the flames into the water.

> **[Name withheld], Alexandria, VA:** It was all quiet and the city was wrapped, enveloped in red flames. Mr. W—— came to help me. He asked me if I wanted to swim across the river. The bridge was burning, and the river was very high. I had no choice. I could barely see by then, though. And Mr. W—— took my arms and told me to swim across the river together with him, so together we went into the river and began to swim. When we reached the middle of the river,

WASHINGTON, DC /NORTHERN VIRGINIA

Limits of Blast Damage and Radiation Exposure from
Two 200 Kiloton Airbursts at 1,830 m

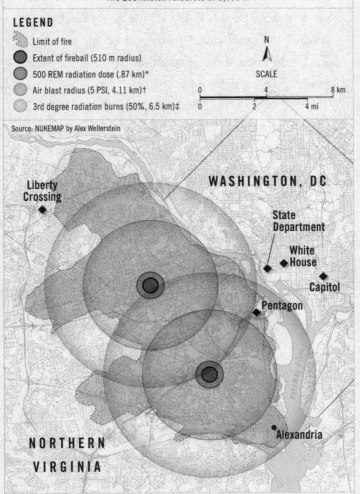

LEGEND

- Limit of fire
- Extent of fireball (510 m radius)
- 500 REM radiation dose (.87 km)*
- Air blast radius (5 PSI, 4.11 km)†
- 3rd degree radiation burns (50%, 6.5 km)‡

N

SCALE

SCALE: 0 — 4 — 8 km
0 — 2 — 4 mi

Source: NUKEMAP by Alex Wellerstein

WASHINGTON, DC

Liberty Crossing

State Department

White House

Capitol

Pentagon

Alexandria

NORTHERN

VIRGINIA

*Without medical treatment, between 50% and 90% mortality expected.
†Most residential buildings collapse, injuries are universal, fatalities are widespread.
‡Third degree burns extend throughout the layers of skin, and are often painless because they destroy the pain nerves.

I could no longer see anything, and I was starting to feel faint. And as I began to feel faint, I also began to lose control. Mr. W—— encouraged me and helped me to reach the other side of the river. Finally, we reached the other side. What surprised me so much was all the cries of the children for help and for their mothers. It just didn't stop.

[Name withheld], Alexandria, VA: I was pushed into the river with many other people. And since I thought it would be dangerous to stay on this side, I swam over to the other side. It was so frightening.

[Name withheld], Alexandria, VA: An awful thing happened when I reached the other side, and was relieved. I was suddenly spun around by the current. And then large pieces of hail begin to fall, and my face started hurting. So I plunged my face back into the water over and over again. I was spun around again and again. It just didn't stop.

[Name withheld], Alexandria, VA: The water was swirling around me, and later I learned that was a tornado. And my friends somehow managed to survive it. [*Interviewer: Did you think you were going to die?*] Yes. The faces of my family came to my mind one after another. And I really thought I was dying because I swallowed a lot of water too.

[Name withheld], Alexandria, VA: Later on in the evening, when we were sitting around without having much to do, most of the people had already fled and the city was still burning. We could hear voices calling "Help!" or "It's burning. Help us!" The voices, they weren't from nearby but from far away. We didn't know just where those voices came from, but it became quiet by midnight.

EVASIVE ACTION

While Air Force One was loitering out over the Atlantic Ocean, air traffic controllers in Jacksonville, Florida, detected an unidentified aircraft heading toward the president's plane. The controllers radioed the pilot. "When controllers asked if we were aware of an unidentified plane bearing down on us, we didn't have a clue," he recalled. "I kept thinking that the sky is huge and the chances of one aircraft finding another are just infinitesimal. But I worried that maybe we were followed as we took off."

The pilot had few options. "Air Force One has defenses to protect against attack," he explained, "but no offensive capability. So I changed course. As we veered west, the other plane did not follow: it was simply an airliner with a malfunctioning transponder."

The passengers aboard the aircraft recall that the report from Jacksonville, although it turned out to be a non-issue, changed the mood aboard Air Force One. The president had

grown increasingly agitated that he was unable to reach Melania or Ivanka. He had been in the air for two hours, and there
were now television reports of nuclear explosions in New York
City and Washington, DC. He did not know if his wife and
daughter were dead or alive. Staff members could see quite
clearly that Trump Tower had been near the epicenter of the
blast. Some thought the president could see that too. Still, no
one said anything.

Trump now insisted that they were no safer in the air than
on the ground. The president began to demand that the pilot land the plane. But where? Florida, Washington, and New
York were clearly not safe. And Barksdale Air Force Base,
George Bush's first stop after leaving Florida on 9/11, had
been clearly marked on Kim's map of nuclear targets — it could
be attacked at any time.

There was brief discussion about attempting to get the
president to Camp David, largely because it was close to both
Washington and Site R. But in the end, the pilot proposed
flying to the US Strategic Command Underground Command
Center — the underground bunker in Omaha designed to allow the United States to fight and win a nuclear war.

No one objected.

RADIATION SICKNESS

Those who survived the blast — the intense heat of the fireball and the hailstorm of broken glass and debris — now faced
dealing with severe radiation burns and the onset of radiation

sickness. The scale of the casualties completely overwhelmed local medical services, many of which had seen their facilities destroyed in the explosions and their doctors and nurses killed. The suffering was especially difficult in suburban areas that were densely populated but relied heavily on road networks to move people around. The accounts of burns and radiation sickness made for some of the most difficult testimony that this commission heard, and are equally challenging to read.

[Name withheld], Honolulu, HI: It was very, very hot. I touched my skin and it just peeled right off.

[Name withheld], Arlington, VA: There was a sticky yellowish pus, a white watery liquid coming out of my daughter's wounds. Her skin was just peeling right off. And nine hours later, she died. [*Interviewer: You were holding her in your arms all that time?*] Yes, on my lap. I held her in my arms. When I held her on my lap, she said, "I don't want to die." I told her, "Hang on, hang on." She said, "I won't die before my brother comes home." But she was in pain and she kept crying.

The surviving doctors, nurses, and volunteers were quickly overwhelmed. There was often no power or water, and medical supplies were soon exhausted. Of the tens of thousands of individuals who attempted to walk out of the affected areas, many were attempting to head home, although many others were descending on hospitals or even doctor's offices, seeking help. Over the course of the day, many people suffering symptoms of fatal radiation sickness attempted to walk to safety but fell and died along the way.

Most of the survivors who managed to reach hospitals or other places where they hoped to find medical assistance were disappointed to encounter tens of thousands of other sick and dying people and only a handful of doctors and nurses, many of them seriously wounded themselves.

[Name withheld], Arlington, VA: There were too many people. We took care of the people around us by using the clothes of dead people as bandages, especially for those who were terribly wounded. By that time, we somehow became insensible [to] all those awful things.

[Name withheld], Honolulu, HI: I felt someone touch my leg. It was a pregnant woman. She said that she was about to die. She said, "I know that I am going to die. But I can feel that my baby is moving inside. I don't mind if I die. But if the baby is delivered now, it does not have to die with me. Please help my baby live." There were no obstetricians. There was no delivery room. There was no time to take care of her baby. All I could do was to tell her that I would come back later when everything was ready for her and her baby. This cheered her up. She looked so happy. So I went back to work taking care of the injured, one by one. There were so many patients. But the image of that pregnant woman never left my mind. Later, I went to the place where I had found her before. She was still there, lying in the same place. I patted her on the shoulder, but she said nothing. The person lying next to her said that a short while ago, she had fallen silent.

Despite being overwhelmed, many doctors and nurses worked tirelessly to aid people, even as their own condition deteriorated from fatigue or radiation poisoning. For many survivors, the heroism of ordinary people like these is a recurring memory of those horrible days.

Moreover, despite claims to the contrary by some people —including former president Trump—we have found no evidence of widespread looting or violence. Specifically, a systematic investigation into the activities of the National Guard and Army units deployed to maintain order reveals no evidence at all that there was organized criminal activity, much less widespread executions to combat it. Despite this, Trump has repeatedly referred to such events, saying, "It was on television. I saw it. It was well covered at the time. Now, I know they don't like to talk about it, but it was well covered at the time."

The commission believes that these rumors stemmed from conspiracies spread on the internet claiming to show military vehicles transporting the bodies of executed looters. These images, many of which are hosted on sites maintained by the Russian Federation, in fact show the vehicles that were required to recover and bury the more than one million people killed in the attack whose bodies were not pulverized or vaporized. Hundreds of thousands of people died in the initial explosions, and tens of thousands more died by the hour. The Army and the National Guard had to organize the enormous logistical effort associated with removing these bodies as quickly as possible. For many, the presence of large numbers of such vehicles, filled with bodies — the "death cabs" — is a stark memory of the days following the attack.

[Name withheld], Honolulu, HI: As military trucks came into the city, they started loading bodies into truck beds. I saw three soldiers try to lift a burned body, but they dropped it to the ground, losing their grip when the skin sloughed off.

[Name withheld], Arlington, VA: When I came to, it was about seven in the evening. . . . I found myself lying on the floor. A soldier was looking in my face. He gave me a light slap on the cheek, and he said, "You are a lucky boy." He told me that he had gone with one of the few trucks left to collect the dead bodies. . . . They were loading bodies, treating them like sacks. They picked me up from the riverbank and then threw me on top of the pile. My body slid off, and when they grabbed me by the arm to put me back onto the truck, they felt that my pulse was still beating, so they reloaded me onto the truck, carrying the survivors. I was really lucky.

It was this heroic effort to retrieve and bury the dead, we believe, that gave rise to the rumors and internet conspiracies.

For many survivors, the overwhelming horror of that day, and the days that followed, is not a story of looting and violence, but a tragic tale of complete strangers desperately trying to help one another in hopeless circumstances. Gillian Mackenzie, a book editor in Manhattan, was close enough to the blast that she was buried in ash and debris. Workers at a McDonald's in Lower Manhattan pulled her out of the ash and gave her water, saving her life. Far from former president Trump's claims of mass looting and violence, she said, it was a day when "ordinary people saved each other."

THE MOLE HOLE

Air Force One landed at Offut Air Force Base in Omaha, Nebraska. As soon as the president stepped off the plane, he was taken to the gleaming headquarters of Strategic Command — the military entity responsible for waging and winning nuclear wars. But instead of entering through the front door, Trump was taken beneath the concrete plaza near the building's entrance to the Operations Center. Officially called US Strategic Command Underground Command Center, it was better known as the "Mole Hole."

Down inside the Mole Hole, President Trump was escorted to an empty office. Despite the spartan accommodations, STRATCOM was in perfect communication with the other underground facilities maintained by the Department of Defense, as well as with the bunkers beneath the White House and Mar-a-Lago.

For many Americans, even in the months leading up to March 2020, the prospect of nuclear war had seemed remote. For the Pentagon, however, nuclear war was an ever-present possibility, and it had drawn up "continuity of government" plans that would ensure the survival of the government even in the event that American society itself completely collapsed. Over the past decade, Congress had authorized billions of dollars in funding to build secure underground facilities where US leaders could be safe from a nuclear attack. The construction of a new command center at Offut alone had cost $1.2 billion, and it was only one of six underground complexes that were now involved in coordinating the response.

These complexes included Site R, the alternate Pentagon where the secretary of defense was now organizing the attack on North Korea; Mount Weather in the Blue Ridge Mountains, where most government functions had relocated once the first nuclear weapon struck northern Virginia; NORAD's alternate communications site at Cheyenne Mountain in Colorado; and the underground bunkers beneath the White House and Mar-a-Lago. In addition to these sites, which were now central to the federal government's disaster management effort, members of Congress were huddled in yet another bunker underneath Fort Leslie McNair in Washington, DC. The Trump administration did not, however, attempt to establish contact with members of Congress in their bunker. "One of the awkward questions we faced [in planning for this sort of scenario] was whether to reconstitute Congress after a nuclear attack," recalled one official present with the president in Omaha. "It was decided that no, it would be easier to operate without them." Congress would remain in session, but the Trump administration did not make contact with them for six days.

The "continuity of government" efforts on March 21 went largely according to plan. Once he was in Omaha, the president was in regular communication with the secretary of defense at Site R and Jack Francis at Mar-a-Lago. (Aides recalled that Francis told everyone that he had volunteered to remain behind at Mar-a-Lago to assist those suffering in Jupiter.) Thanks to these communication links, the president was now receiving a steady stream of reports on both the attacks under way against the United States and the progress of the air war against North Korea.

With the reestablishment of communications, however, the scope of North Korea's nuclear attack was now clear and President Trump's anxiety about his family was growing. He was increasingly insistent that staff put him in contact with members of his family, particularly his wife Melania and his daughter Ivanka. Ivanka and her husband Jared Kushner had been in

Washington. The Secret Service had whisked them to safety at the White House and escorted them down into the Presidential Emergency Operations Center beneath the White House. They were soon put in contact with the president.

There was, however, a delicate task remaining. After the president spoke with Ivanka, he continued to ask why he had not been able to speak with Melania. For the staff around the president, the grim reality was plain enough: Manhattan had been hit directly with a 200-kiloton nuclear weapon, and Trump Tower was almost directly beneath the centerpoint of the massive explosion. The president's son Barron had spent the day outside the city, visiting a friend in Connecticut. He was unharmed. Melania Trump, however, had been home in their penthouse atop Trump Tower at the time of the attack. News helicopters were now showing the enormous devastation throughout the country. In the images from Manhattan, block after city block had been leveled. Trump Tower had simply vanished.

None of the staff pointed out this obvious reason for their inability to make contact with Melania. After all, President Trump was known as a person who did not take bad news well. Moreover, the staff around the president were relatively junior people who had been able to get aboard Air Force One because they were staying at the Hilton next to the airport; the more senior staff who had been at Mar-a-Lago or the Colony Hotel were still in Palm Beach. They simply did not have the kind of personal relationship with the president that was now needed.

Who would tell the president? After a teleconference between Francis and Ivanka, the two decided that they needed to find Hope Hicks.

Hope Hicks was, in many ways, a surrogate daughter for Trump. Staff had sometimes joked that Hicks was the "real daughter," making Ivanka the "real wife." She was also well known as someone who could deliver bad news to Trump. "When a bad story would come up, she would volunteer," explained a former Trump aide, "saying, 'I'll just go and tell him; I got it.' We all had to do it, she was just better at it." "She's like a security blanket for the boss," said another.

Hicks had left the White House in 2018 and was now living in Los Angeles, having started a boutique public relations firm specializing in crisis management. Summoned by telephone, she was entrusted with delivering the worst possible news to the president, who was surrounded by virtual strangers in Omaha, and she had to do it from her office in Los Angeles, using an unsecured line.

When Hicks was connected by phone with Trump, she gave it to him gentle but direct. Trump Tower, she explained, had been completely destroyed. Melania had been there. No, she told him, there was no chance that Melania had survived. No, she admitted, no one had seen her body. But, she felt compelled to add, it was not likely that her body would ever be recovered. She cried a bit. The president thanked her for calling and hung up.

"He was silent for a long time," said one of the staff members present, "and then he said something to the effect that losing Melania was such a waste of a talented life." Another staffer recalled the president's comment differently, but declined to repeat his precise language, citing the need for decorum. Yet another staff member recalled the president's comment verbatim: "What he mumbled was, 'There was nothing in the world like her.'"

CONCLUSION

THE LEGACY OF THE North Korean nuclear attacks is complex and challenging even now, over three years later, as the United States attempts to recover from the devastation of March 2020.

The number of people killed was enormous. In South Korea and Japan, the first wave of strikes killed more than 1.4 million people, while seriously wounding over five million others. The second wave, which struck the United States, killed another 1.4 million people and seriously wounded 2.8 million more. All told, nearly three million people died in the span of about forty-eight hours, and almost eight million people were left in desperate need of medical assistance.

For our country, Saturday, March 21, was only the beginning of what has been an unparalleled period of challenge and recovery. In particular, government authorities were slow to understand the scale of the unprecedented public health emergency that unfolded in the wake of the attacks. There were suddenly millions of people with serious injuries requiring immediate medical care. These demands overwhelmed a public health infrastructure that was itself severely damaged in the nuclear attacks. Nearly half of the nine million people who were seriously injured on March 21 slowly succumbed in the days and weeks after the attack. For many survivors, the grief that accumulated as friends and relatives died day after day was a much greater emotional burden than the sheer terror of the first day.

Within the United States, we continue to struggle with this challenging public health legacy. Even now, three years later, our public health situation has yet to fully stabilize, as evidenced by the frequent outbreaks of deadly diseases such as cholera and typhoid since the attacks. These outbreaks have had complex causes, but nearly all the factors that have contributed to them trace back, in one form or another, to the events of March 2020.

The radiation released by a nuclear explosion has many long-term health effects on a person, including suppression of the immune system. The public health implications of entire populations with compromised immunity are wide-ranging and severe. Public health officials are preparing for dramatic increases in cancers such as leukemia in the coming years. The immediate crisis, however, is that millions of the tens of millions of people with severely compromised immune systems remain vulnerable because they have been displaced and still lack reliable access to clean water and sanitation.

The epidemics that have swept the United States over the

past three years also appear to be attributable to the exploding populations of pests in affected areas, which are almost certainly another consequence of the nuclear attacks. In particular, the slow pace of recovering and disposing of millions of bodies allowed the population of rats and other scavenging animals to skyrocket. These large animal populations are important vectors for the transmission of disease; epidemiologists interviewed by the commission believe that they are probably responsible for the first-ever recorded outbreak of plague in the New York City area.

The heavy burden of caring for the displaced population, punctuated by frantic efforts to combat the epidemics that have periodically broken out, is a major reason for the slow progress of reconstruction in affected areas, which understandably frustrates the hundreds of millions of people who are anxious for the government to restore the normalcy of prewar life and rebuild the country. The commission notes that it is extremely important that this reconstruction work continue apace, particularly because the window of time to complete it is shrinking. The many long-term health consequences of radiation exposure are already beginning to manifest in rising numbers of cancers and other health problems. The challenge associated with providing for the long-term care of many millions of citizens will be an increasing burden in the decades to come. Unless the nation rebuilds vital infrastructure in a timely fashion, it may find itself starved for resources as other long-term effects arise and demand our collective attention.

The displacement of such a large group of people has had important long-term impacts. The most visible impacts are the total destruction of Manhattan and the relocation of federal government operations to the Mount Weather facility in Berryville, Virginia. The reconstruction of Manhattan, which is overseen by a public-benefit corporation, represents an enormous investment by the federal government, as well as New York State and New Jersey. Although the reconstruction has proceeded relatively smoothly, there are considerable doubts about when or whether financial and other industries will return to the city as reconstruction advances. It is more clear that federal government functions will eventually return to Washington, although when remains uncertain. Although the city of Washington itself was largely spared destruction, more than 80,000 federal jobs were located in northern Virginia and the area was home to more than 100,000 federal workers. It was simply not possible to sustain normal government operations in this environment, although reconstruction activities continue to be directed from offices in suburban Maryland. In Hawaii and Florida, too, the task of reconstruction has been daunting and, for many, the pace far too slow.

The tragedy of March 2020 is not, it should be noted, merely a Korean, Japanese, or American tragedy. Extraordinary amounts of black smoke from burning cities has led to a period of global cooling, which is almost certainly responsible for the recent rise in food prices around the world—which in turn is believed to be responsible for the famines that have struck Africa, South Asia, and China over the past few years. Global temperatures have fallen by an average 1.25 degrees Celsius in each of the past three years, resulting in shorter growing seasons. In the United States, corn and soybean production has fallen by an average of 10 percent from prewar levels, and continues to drop. There has also been a significant fall (20 percent) in Chinese middle-season rice production. The best estimates made available to the commission suggest that there are now around one billion people experiencing extreme food insecurity as a result of the cooling temperatures. The outbreaks of famine and disease throughout the developing world pose an important challenge for the reconstruction of Korea, Japan, and the United States.

There were successes during this period. The air and ground campaign executed by US Pacific Command in particular was effective and inspired. Although many Americans are understandably outraged by the failure to prevent the launch of thirteen nuclear-armed missiles against the US homeland, the air operation and subsequent ground invasion resulted in the near-total destruction of the North Korean army within less than forty-eight hours, with fewer than one hundred combat deaths for US forces. The campaign was largely a brilliantly executed improvisation. If the surprise nuclear attack by Kim Jong Un was a tactical victory, it was also a colossal strategic blunder that led to his downfall. This was, presumably, obvious to Kim as he sat beneath the mountains. According to a surviving aide, Kim could hear the sound of gun-fire from US and South Korean special forces as they entered the underground complex in the moments before he took his own life.

There was also the incredible heroism of the many millions of Americans who ignored their own injuries that day to help others who were suffering. Strangers cared for one another. They rescued people from rubble, they bandaged wounds, they shared food and shelter. Sometimes there was nothing at all they could do except simply sit with a stranger so that person did not die alone. Their courage and sacrifice that day is an inspiration to us all and a reminder that we can, if we choose, act in the face of seemingly hopeless circumstances.

It is this spirit that the commissioners believe we must now bring to our most urgent task — reconstruction. In Korea, the success of the military operation to remove Kim Jong Un from power has opened the door to reunification of the Korean Peninsula. But both Korea and Japan — the world's eleventh- and third-largest economies and major American trading partners — are in ruins. The cost of rebuilding our economies is immense. In the United States, these efforts are expected to cost $30 trillion to $40 trillion over the next decade — with the costs associated with rebuilding Manhattan alone estimated at between $15 trillion and $20 trillion. This is a formidable challenge that, above all, requires that our country come together and act with a unity of purpose.

Although the commissioners are mindful that many Americans believe that some officials should be held responsible for the course of events that led to the nuclear attacks against the United States, this would be a mistake. It would only serve to inflame partisan passions again, without bringing back the millions of dead. Although it is possible to disagree with specific decisions taken by senior officials, the commission found that they made the best decisions they could with the information that was available to them at the time. They acted in the same way that any senior official of any political party would, given the circumstances. It would be a mistake to politicize the tragic events of March 2020.

With President Trump's decision not to seek reelection in November 2020, it is important to look forward, not backward. The president set an example for the nation when he announced that he would not run for reelection, sparing the country what would likely have been an extraordinarily divisive election following his impeachment and subsequent acquittal in the Senate on a party-line vote.

With President Pence's election, the commission believes we now have an opportunity to turn the page on this terrible moment in our nation's history. During the public hearings that this commission held throughout the country as part of our inquiry, all of us were astonished by the partisan animosity and recrimination on display. We were struck in particular by the lack of civility characterizing many of these discussions, and we found reprehensible the continuing assertions by many media figures and political partisans that the attacks were, in fact, conducted by federal government officials, such as the intelligence community, to discredit President Trump and his presidency. Though it should be plain enough, we feel compelled to say directly that there was no "deep state" conspiracy to explode nuclear weapons throughout the United States. There were no mass executions by Army and Army National Guard troops keeping order. There is no evidence that large numbers of Jews evacuated New York before the attacks. Kim Jong Un is not alive, nor is he living in Russia. And as their wounds and burns attest, the millions of survivors are not "crisis actors." It is shocking to us to see that these opinions appear widespread and persistent online, as well as in many parts of the United States not directly affected by the attacks. They are false.

As noted at the beginning of this report, the members of this commission have been surprised by how many times they were asked one question in particular at these public hearings. While the answer to this question has been elusive, they feel it is important enough to mention it again in closing.

Should the United States seek the elimination of nuclear weapons? Some people believe that the large-scale destruction experienced by the United States is a powerful demonstration of the danger of nuclear weapons and that, as a society, we should commit ourselves to their elimination. These people believe that the United States should abandon its nuclear arms and join international legal agreements prohibiting the development, possession, and use of such weapons.

Others, however, disagree. They believe that North Korea's large-scale use of nuclear weapons demonstrates that warfare, including nuclear warfare, remains a significant threat to the United States of America. Far from prohibiting nuclear weapons, these people believe that the United States must maintain a robust nuclear force to deter the sort of attacks launched by Kim Jong Un on the nation and its allies. The task of deterring another nuclear war, these skeptics argue, should take precedence over unrealistic efforts to prohibit these weapons.

This is an important and challenging policy question. There are many strong and differing opinions, even among the commissioners. Ultimately, however, they agreed that it lay beyond the scope of their mandate. The commission's task was to understand how the nuclear war came about and to provide the American public with the facts of the situation in the most objective way possible. They have done this. To go further and ask what implications those facts might have for issues such as nuclear strategy or foreign policy would be to engage in speculation. Such speculation, in the current partisan environment, they felt, would only serve to further inflame passions and undermine the fragile national unity upon which our recovery depends. This commission of politicians and other distinguished public servants was asked to answer the simple question of what happened. Now that they have completed their task, they return to their lives as private citizens who each possess one vote in our great Republic — one vote that counts exactly the same as every other American citizen's.

Jeffrey Lewis, PhD
On behalf of the 2020 Commission
Mount Weather Emergency Operations Center
Berryville, VA
May 1, 2023

STATEMENT BY FORMER PRESIDENT OF THE UNITED STATES DONALD J. TRUMP

APRIL 2, 2023

The so-called 2020 Commission is a total Witch Hunt and just more Deep State FAKE NEWS.

The Democrats will NEVER accept that I defeated Crooked Hilary even though 3 million illegals voted for her.

They can't stand that I won the Republican nomination by defeating seventeen candidates, often described as the most talented field ever assembled in the Republican party, and then beat their candidate.

Now the Democrats want to blame me for the Nuclear War (which was very terrible) and that they caused. The SAME nuclear war that killed Melania who was so beautiful.

The Democrats like Lyin' Chuck Schumer will never admit that I almost made a deal with Rocketman. It would have been a very good deal for the world. And the Phony media says negotiations "collapsed" but never admit that it was the Democrats that didn't want a deal and said that it was terrible (although they did and very often). Crooked Hilary, Lyin' Chuck and the Democrats did every thing to kill the deal because they can't stand me winning. VERY DISHONEST.

Fortunately, we have many great Americans who remain

very supportive of our Great President Mike Pence and the Make America Great Again agenda. Like me, they love the United States of America and are helping to take our Country back and build it up much better than it was before, rather than trying to burn it all down.

ACKNOWLEDGMENTS

I am deeply indebted to Hidehiko Yuzaki, the governor of Hiroshima prefecture, for inviting me to be a member of his roundtable on disarmament. Visiting Hiroshima each August is a profoundly moving experience. Every time I visit Hiroshima, I find myself wondering how to persuade more people to listen to the stories of the Hibakusha — the Japanese people who survived the bombings of Hiroshima and Nagasaki in 1945. I made the decision to use their real testimonies to describe the horror of the fictional nuclear war in these pages. I did this because it is easy, as Americans, to let the slightly stilted grammar of a translation create a false sense of distance between ourselves and the very real people who suffered and died. But they were and are people, just like we are, and our fate might well turn out to be the same. The testimonies presented in Chapter 10 are largely drawn from interviews presented in the television program *Hiroshima Witness*, produced by the Hiroshima Peace Cultural Center and NHK, Japan's national public broadcaster. These interviews were translated into English by the college students Yumi Kodama, Junko Kato, Junko Kawamoto, Masako Kubota, Chiharu Kimura, and Kumi Komatsu, who were advised by Laurence Wiig, and they are now posted at the Atomic Archive. I want people to read the stories of the survivors. I hope that I did right by them.

Along the same lines, John Hersey's 1946 book *Hiroshima* is probably more responsible than anything else for my interest in nuclear weapons. While there really is a South Korean television drama with a doctor named Oh Soo-hyun, the Dr. Oh depicted in Chapter 6 is a fictional homage to the very real Dr. Terafumi Sasaki, who was profiled in Hersey's *Hiroshima*. Everyone who cares about the fate of this world and the danger posed by nuclear weapons should read Hersey's book and the stories of the Hibakusha, and then visit the city of Hiroshima. Do it and you will understand.

Similarly, I used many stories from 9/11—particularly those relating to events on Air Force One. If you are interested in that day, I found Garrett Graff's oral history "'We're the Only Plane in the Sky,'" published in *Politico*, to be completely spellbinding.

All of the casualty estimates were created using Alex Wellerstein's incomparable Nukemap website.

I am also thankful to a slew of local friends, including Josh and Molly Goshorn, who let me use their real-life experience with the false alarm in Hawaii, and Jay and Chloe Dolata, who let me sit for hours at Carmel Belle writing.

I am grateful to the suggestions of those who read drafts of chapters, including Joe Cirincione, Ian Martin, Adam Rawnsley, Peter Scoblic, and Erin Simpson. I am shamelessly stealing your suggestions and taking credit for them.

Bill Potter, the director of the James Martin Center for Nonproliferation Studies, and my colleagues at the center were tremendously supportive. Melissa Hanham, Josh Pollack, and Dave Schmerler helped me think through so many scenarios and picked up the slack when I was overextended. Grace Liu provided translations and notes on Korean culture.

I am grateful to Mike Madden at the *Washington Post* for commissioning the op-ed that was the germ of the idea that grew into this book.

My literary agent, Gillian MacKenzie at MacKenzie Wolf, was a tireless advocate for this book project, reading chapters as soon as they were finished.

My editor, Alex Littlefield, and the entire team at Houghton Mifflin Harcourt have been a joy to work with, even on some of the more emotionally difficult chapters. Cynthia Buck did an incredible job copyediting the manuscript.

Finally, and most important, I am grateful to my wife, Jill, and our three children—Sebastien, Julian, and Alma. They bore the brunt of the many weekends I spent writing instead of parenting.

NOTES

1. THE SHOOTDOWN OF BX 411

page

3   *on October 22, 2005, a British Airways A319 flight from London Heathrow Airport to Budapest, Hungary, suffered a similar problem:* See UK Air Accidents Investigation Branch, "Report on the Serious Incident to Airbus 319-11, Registration G-EXAC, Near Nantes, France, on September 15, 2006," *Aircraft Accident Report* 4/2009, July 2009.

    a United Airlines flight from Newark to Denver suffered a nearly identical failure: National Transportation Safety Board (NTSA), "Safety Recommendations A-08-53 through 55," July 22, 2008.

    At least four such incidents had occurred in the United States after the FAA directive was issued in 2010: David Porter, "Airbuses Suffer Cockpit Power Failure, Await Fixes," Associated Press, August 11, 2012.

8   *a Reagan-era program of psychological operations initiated to strengthen deterrence against Moscow:* The Reagan-era PSYOP program and its contribution to the "War Scare" of 1983 are described by Benjamin B. Fischer in "A Cold War Conundrum: The 1983 Soviet War Scare," intelligence monograph, Central Intelligence Agency, September 1997.

    "They had no idea what it all meant": William Schneider, a former US State Department official who reviewed classified after-action reports, as quoted in Peter Schweizer, *Victory: The Reagan Administration's Secret Strategy That Hastened the Collapse of the Soviet Union* (New York: Atlantic Monthly Press, 1994).

*This conclusion reflected a broader consensus within the US intel-
ligence community that Kim Jong Un was rational and could be deterred:* This belief is discussed at length in a classified assessment—a
2017 National Intelligence Estimate (NIE)—described in Nancy
A. Youssef, "Why the US Considers North Korea's Kim a 'Rational
Actor,'" *Wall Street Journal,* December 5, 2017.

9 *"The phrase has never, ever been uttered by anyone in the White
House":* An anonymous senior official, as quoted in David Na-
kamura and Greg Jaffe, "The White House's 'Bloody Nose' Strategy
on North Korea Sounds Trumpian. So Why Do His Aides Hate It?"
Washington Post, February 26, 2018.

14 *The US Air Force had established a "continuous bomber presence"
mission at Andersen Air Force Base on Guam:* The "continuous
bomber presence" mission is described in Amy McCullough,
"Bombers on Guam," *Air Force Magazine* 98: 8, August 2015,
20–25.

15 *This work fell to the Joint Information Operations Warfare Center
(JIOWC) at Lackland Air Force Base near San Antonio:* JIOWC's
activities are highly classified, but one area of responsibility is developing approaches to messaging about US capabilities to strengthen
deterrence. See [author redacted], "Cybersecurity: Capabilities and
Related Policy Issues," RL31787, Congressional Research Service,
March 17, 2009.

16 *Pentagon officials highlighted a series of three flights involving B-1
and B-52 bombers in March 2013:* Thom Shanker and Choe Sang-
hun, "US Runs Practice Sortie in South Korea," *New York Times,*
March 28, 2013.
    *Again, in 2016, the Obama administration publicized three more
flights:* Yoo Han-bin, "US Bombers Fly over South Korea for Second Time since North's Nuclear Test," *Reuters,* September 20,
2016.
    with twelve publicly announced flights taking place in 2017: The
estimate of twelve publicly announced bomber flights in 2017 is
based on Department of Defense press releases.
    *Starting in 2017, operations were in some cases conducted at night
and much farther north:* "Air Force B-1B Lancer bombers from
Guam, along with Air Force F-15C Eagle fighter escorts from Okinawa, Japan, flew in international airspace over waters east of North
Korea today, chief Pentagon spokesperson Dana W. White said in a
statement announcing the mission. This is the farthest north of the
Demilitarized Zone any US fighter or bomber aircraft have flown
off North Korea's coast in the 21st century, White said. The mis-

sion underscores the seriousness with which the United States takes North Korea's 'reckless behavior,' she added." US Department of Defense, "US Bombers, Fighter Escorts Fly over Waters East of North Korea," press release, September 23, 2017.

20 *a brand-new system, which the North Koreans called the Pongae-5 surface-to-air missile:* Joost Oliemans and Stijn Mitzer, "North Korea's Pongae-5 Anti-Air Missile: What Do We Know?" *NK News,* June 2, 2017.

21 *North Korean state media openly referenced the "defects" that had slowed its development:* "Kim Jong Un Watches Test of New-Type Anti-Aircraft Guided Weapon System," KCNA, May 28, 2017.

23 *"We received an order that an American bomber was violating our airspace":* Roh's remarks are based loosely on comments by Gennadi Osipovich, the Soviet pilot who in 1983 shot down KAL 007, a civilian airliner that strayed into Soviet airspace—an event widely attributed to the tension that arose from the Reagan-era PSYOPS program. "I saw two rows of windows and knew that this was a Boeing," Osipovich told the *New York Times*'s Michael Gordon. "I knew this was a civilian plane. But for me this meant nothing. It is easy to turn a civilian type of plane into one for military use." He also told Gordon that even "those who did not take part in this operation received double their monthly pay. At that time, monthly pay was 230 rubles. So I expected to be paid at least 400 rubles." Michael R. Gordon, "Ex-Soviet Pilot Still Insists KAL 007 Was Spying," *New York Times,* December 9, 1996.

2. SOUTH KOREA HITS BACK

29 *"It is retrogression of sorts that the President's office exists as a small* Cheong Wa Dae *within* Cheong Wa Dae*":* Choi Sung-jin, "Blue House's Building Layout Ineffective in Emergency," *Korea Times,* November 7, 2015.
the Cheong Wa Dae complex retained two very important government functions: "No Blue House for South Korea's New President," *Associated Press,* May 10, 2017.

30 *Many of her political opponents . . . had demanded to know what became of the "seven missing hours":* Kim Bo-eun, "President's '7 Missing Hours' Still Shrouded in Mystery," *Korea Times,* November 26, 2016.

31 *while another reported that she was having plastic surgery:* James Pearson and Yun Hwan Chae, "South Korea Lawmakers to Quiz

Doctors, Nurses about Park's 'Missing' Seven Hours," *Reuters*, December 13, 2016.

They turned the documents over to investigators and filed a complaint: "Former President Park's Four Aides Indicted for Doctoring Time Log of Sewol Sinking Report," *Yonhap*, March 28, 2018.

33   *"Neither South-North relations nor US-North relations will go far if the other fails":* Kang In-sun, "Interview with Suh Hoon" (in Korean), *Chosun Ilbo*, March 10, 2018, translated by Grace Liu.

"Dialogue is impossible in a situation like this": "Moon Says Dialogue with N. Korea 'Impossible,'" *Yonhap News Agency*, September 15, 2017.

37   *North Korea's relentless "strategic and tactical provocations":* "JCS Chief Nominee Vows to Build Military 'Feared by Enemies, Trusted by Citizens,'" *Yonhap*, August 18, 2017.

"President Moon seems to have meant that we ought to be doing everything we can to prevent a crisis situation": Park Byong-su, "New Chairman of Joint Chiefs of Staff Claims South Korea Can Achieve Air Superiority within Three Days of Conflict," *Hankyoreh*, August 19, 2017.

38   *Lee wanted a big and bold response, but military officials pushed him to consult with the United States:* "Ex-President Lee Ordered All-Out Retaliation after North's Yeonpyeong Bombardment in 2010," *Yonhap*, December 13, 2015.

"South Korea's original plans for retaliation were, we thought, disproportionately aggressive": Robert Gates, *Duty: Memoirs of a Secretary at War* (New York: Alfred A. Knopf, 2015), 497.

satellite images later showed that its retaliation had done little or no damage: Joseph S. Bermudez Jr., *The Yonp'yong-do Incident, November 23, 2010*, Special Report 11-1, January 11, 2011.

39   *"Korea Massive Punishment and Retaliation" . . . had been publicly described in some detail after 2016*: "South Korea Announces 'Massive Punishment and Retaliation' in Response to Fifth Nuke Test," *Hankyoreh*, September 13, 2016.

"wiping a certain section of Pyongyang completely off the map": "S. Korea Unveils Plan to Raze Pyongyang in Case of Signs of Nuclear Attack," *Yonhap*, September 11, 2016.

Pyongyang . . . would "be reduced to ashes": "S. Korea Unveils Plan to Raze Pyongyang."

40   *striking ninety-seven targets over four days, including three presidential palaces and the headquarters of the Iraqi Ba'ath Party:* Anthony H. Cordesman, *The Lessons of Desert Fox: A Preliminary*

Analysis (Washington, DC: Center for Strategic and International Studies, February 16, 1999).

43   *US and South Korean officials did, of course, visit the headquarters:* The US Department of Defense released a pair of images from Admiral Cecil Haney's visit to the ROK Army Missile Command headquarters on June 23, 2015.

45   *"The issues on the rules of engagement . . . should be discussed":* Yi Whan-woo, "Rules of Engagement at JSA in Dispute," *Korea Times,* November 16, 2017.

3. HURRICANE DONALD

56   *Sometimes surprised wedding-goers even had an unscheduled appearance by the president:* Jaime A. Cardenas, "Trump Crashes Nashville Socialite's Wedding at Mar-a-Lago," *USA Today,* February 13, 2017.

Over the years, these shelters had been repurposed to serve as storage and, for a time, as an office for Trump's butler: Alex Leary, "Greeting from Mar-a-Lago: Donald Trump's Presidential Paradise," *Tampa Bay Times,* November 25, 2016.

60   *"Pompeo kept feeding Trump assessments":* This quotation is based on the assessment of "several officials familiar with [White House] discussions" as described by Matt Spetalnick, Arshad Mohammed, and Hyonhee Shin, "'He's Such a Dreamer': Skepticism Dogs US Envoy's North Korean Peace Efforts," *Reuters,* November 3, 2017.

61   *"spends that time in his [executive] residence, watching TV, making phone calls and tweeting":* Anonymous "officials," as described by Jonathan Swan, "Trump's Secret, Shrinking Schedule," *Axios,* January 7, 2018.

62   *"Once he goes upstairs [to the residence], there's no managing him":* An anonymous "adviser," as quoted in Ashley Parker and Robert Costa, "'Everyone Tunes In': Inside Trump's Obsession with Cable TV," *Washington Post,* April 23, 2017.

"But if he wants to watch [television], it's not like we can say, 'Oh, the TV doesn't work'": Anonymous official, as quoted in Matthew Nussbaum, Josh Dawsey, Darren Samuelsohn, and Tara Palmeri, "West Wing Aides Fearful of Directly Attacking Comey," *Politico,* June 7, 2017.

63   *In one case, a golf club member invited a* New York Times *reporter:* Michael S. Schmidt, "Our Reporter Mike Schmidt on His

Golf Club Interview with President Trump," *New York Times*, December 29, 2017.

67 *Of particular interest was a list of late-night phone calls:* Dan Amira, "Blogger Who Allegedly Slept with Female Candidate Releases the Texts," *New York*, May 26, 2010.

68 *Once in office, even uglier rumors about Haley began to spread:* Wolff only hints at the possibility of an affair in *Fire and Fury* (New York: Henry Holt and Co., 2018, 305–306), although he drew attention to suggestive passages in a 2018 television interview with Bill Maher.

Trump had famously posed as his own publicist to spread rumors to gossip columnists: Marc Fisher and Will Hobson, "Donald Trump Masqueraded as Publicist to Brag about Himself," *Washington Post*, May 13, 2016.

70 *Haley called him "Lemon":* This detail and others are drawn from a profile of Lerner by Kambiz Foroohar, "Haley's UN Brinkmanship Comes with Advice by Long-Time Pollster," *Bloomberg*, September 11, 2017.

71 *"there are no dissidents in China":* Shi Jiangtao, "Why Ma Zhaoxu, China's New Man at the United Nations, Signals Greater Ambition on Global Stage," *South China Morning Post*, January 21, 2018.

74 *For instance, Hillary Clinton has often told a story:* Laura Blumenfeld, "For State Department Officers Directing Calls, Adrenaline Always on the Line," *Washington Post*, July 14, 2010.

Madeleine Albright needed to reach a diplomat who was out of contact at a football game: Daniel Stone, "Hillary Clinton's State Department Nerve Center: Inside the Other Situation Room," *Daily Beast*, May 19, 2011.

the State Department had used the New York channel before: Josh Rogin, "Inside the 'New York Channel' between the United States and North Korea," *Washington Post*, August 11, 2017.

75 *"pressure, compete with, and outmaneuver" US adversaries:* Nahal Toosi, "Leaked Memo Schooled Tillerson on Human Rights," *Politico*, December 19, 2017.

Hook had stayed on: "For now, however, another top Tillerson aide, Brian Hook, appears to be staying in place. Hook has also spurred resentment in Foggy Bottom for using the division under his control, the Policy Planning Staff, to effectively take over many decisions and tasks traditionally left to the department's regional and functional bureaus." Nahal Toosi, "Top Tillerson Aides Resign amid State Department Shuffle," *Politico*, March 14, 2018.

77   *"Believe it or not, I do not follow the tweets":* Noah Bierman, "Trump's Chief of Staff: 'I Do Not Follow the Tweets,'" *Los Angeles Times*, November 12, 2017.
     "pushing the tweets in the right direction": Josh Dawsey, "John Kelly's Big Challenge: Controlling the Tweeter in Chief," *Politico*, August 4, 2017.

4. THE NOISE OF RUMORS

85   *In fact, she had merely extinguished a trash fire:* Max Fisher, "North Korean 'Traffic Girl' May Have Won Military Award for Saving Kim Jong Un Poster," *Washington Post*, May 9, 2013.

86   *the US Department of Defense took more than an hour to activate its alternate command center at Site R:* Rick Newman and Patrick Creed, *Firefight: Inside the Battle to Save the Pentagon on 9/11* (Novato, CA: Presidio Press, 2008), 174.

89   *According to Ahmed El-Noamany:* Chad O'Carroll, "Inside North Korea's Cell Network: Ex-Koryolink Technical Director Reveals All," *NK News*, August 20, 2015.

91   *US and United Nations forces captured thousands of hours of secret recordings of meetings, phone calls, and conferences:* This section is modeled on the discussion found in David D. Palkki, Kevin M. Woods, and Mark Stout, *The Saddam Tapes: The Inner Workings of a Tyrant's Regime, 1978–2001* (New York: Cambridge University Press, 2011).

92   *"plotting bastards":* I have chosen a Korean equivalent of "conspiring bastards"—the term that Saddam used to describe the United States. See Hal Brands and David Palkki, "'Conspiring Bastards': Saddam Hussein's Strategic View of the United States," *Diplomatic History* 36, no. 3 (June 2012): 625–659.
     Images of Jang being led away: "Traitor Jang Song Thaek Executed," *Korean Central News Agency*, December 13, 2013.

93   *The North Koreans simply said that Jang had been shot:* Alistair Bunkall, "North Korea: Kim Jong-Un Official Speaks," *Sky News*, January 30, 2014.
     when North Korean agents rubbed a nerve agent in his face at the Kuala Lumpur airport: Kyle Swenson, "A Gruesome North Korean Murder Plot: Trial Sheds New Light on Assassination of Kim Jong Un's Brother," *Washington Post*, October 17, 2017.
     North Korean agents continued to make attempts on the lives of his children: Lee Young-Jong and Lee Sung-Eun, "China Arrests

Would-be Assassins of Kim Han-sol," *JoongAng Ilbo*, November 1, 2017.

94 *"There's a clarity of purpose in what Kim Jong Un has done"*: Zachary Cohen, "CIA: North Korean Leader Kim Jong Un Isn't Crazy," *CNN*, October 6, 2017.
In October 2017, for example, North Korea alleged that it had discovered a plot to assassinate Kim Jong Un: "In May this year, a group of heinous terrorists who infiltrated into our country on the orders of the Central Intelligence Agency (CIA) of the US and the South Korean puppet Intelligence Service with the purpose of carrying out a state-sponsored terrorism against our supreme headquarters using biological and chemical substance were caught and exposed." "DPRK Representative on Principled Stand of DPRK on Terrorism," *Korean Central News Agency*, October 6, 2017.
"get China to make that guy disappear in one form or another very quickly": "Trump on Assassinating Kim Jong Un: 'I've Heard of Worse Things,'" *CBS News*, February 10, 2016.

97 *In December 2014, North Korea suffered a massive distributed denial-of-service attack:* Ashley Feinberg, "So Who Shut Down North Korea's Internet?" *Gizmodo*, December 23, 2014.
And in late 2017, the United States accused North Korea of conducting another large-scale cyber-attack called Wanna Cry: "US Blames North Korea for 'WannaCry' Cyber Attack," *Reuters*, December 18, 2017.

101 *The day before the invasion was set to begin:* The attack on Dora Farm is described in detail by Michael R. Gordon and Bernard E. Trainor in *Cobra II: The Inside Story of the Invasion and Occupation of Iraq* (New York: Random House, 2007), 188–204.

103 *"Right now we present ideal targets for atomic weapons in Pusan and Inchon"*: "Substance of Discussions of State–Joint Chiefs of Staff Meeting Held in Room 2C-923, the Pentagon Building, on Friday, March 27, 1953, at 11:30 AM, Top Secret, Minutes, c. March 27, 1953."
"As early as 1965, Kim Il-sung had said that North Korea should develop rockets and missiles to hit US forces inside Japan": Ko Young-hwan, in "North Korean Missile Proliferation," hearing before the Subcommittee on International Security, Proliferation, and Federal Services of the Senate Committee on Governmental Affairs, S. Hrg. 105–241, October 21, 1997, 18.

104 *"Kim Jong Il believes that if North Korea creates more than 20,000 American casualties in the region"*: Ko Young-hwan, "North Korean Missile Proliferation," 5.

North Korea was *"well aware of [the] foolishness of Saddam Hussein"*: "US Slightest Misjudgment of DPRK Will Lead It to Final Doom: KCNA Commentary," *KCNA*, March 13, 2017.

108 *Iran had, for many years, trained its proxies to attack American-made Patriot defenses:* Conflict Armament Research, "Iranian Technology Transfers to Yemen: 'Kamikaze' Drones Used by Houthi Forces to Attack Coalition Missile Defence Systems," March 2017.

109 *After an Israeli battery shot down a $200 quadcopter with a $3 million Patriot missile:* "Israel Uses Patriot Missile to Shoot Down Drone," *Associated Press*, November 13, 2017.

North Korea released images of drones being used in combat and paraded them through Pyongyang: Joseph S. Bermudez Jr., "North Korea Drones On, Redux," *38North*, January 19, 2016.

Soldiers on runs would log their route: Liz Sly, "US Soldiers Are Revealing Sensitive and Dangerous Information by Jogging," *Washington Post*, January 29, 2018.

a North Korean drone had crashed while taking pictures of the site: Thomas Gibbons-Neff, "Suspected North Korean Drone Photographed Advanced US Missile Defense Site, Report Says," *Washington Post*, June 13, 2017.

111 *They trained to reduce that launch time to about twenty minutes:* The estimate of twenty minutes is provided in an account of Iraqi Scud operations and the challenges associated with hunting them. See Peter de la Billière, *Storm Command: A Personal Account of the Gulf War* (New York: HarperCollins, 2008).

112 *within fifteen minutes, the unit needed to move 15 kilometers away:* The Iraqis trained to be within nine miles of the launch point within fifteen minutes. See Jeffrey D. Isaacson and David R. Vaughan, *Estimation and Prediction of Ballistic Missile Trajectories*, RAND/MR-737-AF (Washington, DC: RAND, 1996).

5. SUNSHINE STATE

115 *Because it was Saturday morning, his son-in-law and daughter were out of contact:* The Kushners discussed turning off their cell phones in a profile for *Vogue*. Jonathan van Meter, "Ivanka Trump Knows What It Means to Be a Modern Millennial," *Vanity Fair*, February 24, 2015.

116 *The secure video conference hardware in the Mar-a-Lago Situa-*

tion Room was made by CISCO: "It's possible the black box to the left of the photo is a Cisco Telepresence Touch, according to Brian Roemmele." Sarah Emerson, "What the Heck Are These Electronic Devices in Trump's Situation Room?" *Motherboard,* April 7, 2017. *Chuck Robbins, had been critical of a number of Trump initiatives:* Berkeley Lovelace Jr., "Cisco's Chuck Robbins: CEOs on Trump Panels Followed Their Conscience and Now It's Time to Move On," *CNBC,* August 17, 2017.

117 *But when the president did not forget, he grew increasingly angry with Tillerson for slow-rolling him:* David E. Sanger, "Trump Seeks Way to Declare Iran in Violation of Nuclear Deal," *New York Times,* July 27, 2017.
When Trump suggested something crazy, Mattis would compliment the president on his strong instincts: This strategy is attributed to Mattis in Peter Nicholas and Rebecca Ballhaus, "Talking to Trump: A How-To Guide," *Wall Street Journal,* January 18, 2018.

121 *The White House would often simply refuse to confirm whether the president was playing golf:* "Officials often don't release details about whether Trump is golfing, and with whom, and reporters have a tough time confirming what he's doing." Amanda Terkel, "White House Says Secret Rounds of Golf Make Donald Trump a Better President," *Huffington Post,* January 2, 2018.
In one case, a white panel truck just happened to appear: Elizabeth Preza, "'We Can See You, Mister!': CNN's Keilar Mocks Truck Driver Who Obscured His Face While Blocking Trump Golfing," *Raw Story,* December 27, 2017. The Secret Service and the Palm Beach County Sheriff's Office both denied placing the truck. See Brett Samuels, "Secret Service Denies Hiding Trump's Golfing from Media," *The Hill,* December 27, 2017.
was parked in a spot reserved for the Palm Beach County sheriff: "CNN Learns Whose Truck Blocked View of Trump," *Anderson Cooper 360,* December 30, 2017.

129 *This is what the historian Roberta Wohlstetter called the "background of expectation":* Roberta Wohlstetter, *Pearl Harbor: Warning and Decision* (Stanford, CA: Stanford University Press, 1962).

130 *Both the Roberts Commission . . . and the 9/11 Commission observed:* See *Report of the Commission Appointed by the President of the United States to Investigate and Report the Facts Relating to the Attack Made by Japanese Armed Forces upon Pearl Harbor in the Territory of Hawaii on December 7, 1941,* Senate Document 77-2, 1942; *Final Report of the National Commission on Terrorist Attacks upon*

the United States (*9/11 Commission Report*) (Washington, DC: US Government Printing Office, 2004).

131 *Former president Trump was emphatic that the commission note his score:* This quote is adapted from a remark Trump reportedly made in 2007 to reporter David Owen, who wrote: "He was upset that I hadn't written that he'd shot 71—a very good golf score, one stroke under par. He wanted the number, and the fact that I hadn't published the number proved that I was just like all the other biased reporters, who, because we're all part of the anti-Trump media conspiracy, never give him as much credit as he deserves." Owen, "Lessons from Playing Golf with Trump," *New Yorker*, January 14, 2007.

6. A FALSE DAWN BREAKS

141 *Kenichi Murakami was the chief of the Tokyo Fire Department:* Kenichi Murakami is, in fact, the name of the chief of the Tokyo Fire Department, although the character depicted here is completely fictional.

142 *The traditional ladder-wielding fireman depicted in Kabuki theater or in a woodblock print:* The description of Edo firefighters is drawn from William W. Kelly, "Incendiary Actions: Fires and Firefighting in the Shogun's Capital and the People's City," in *Edo and Paris: Urban Life and the State in the Early Modern Era,* eds. James L. McClain, John M. Merriman, and Kaoru Ugawa (Ithaca, NY: Cornell University Press, 1994).

145 *The Olympic Security Command Center (OSCC) was now largely functional and outside of central Tokyo:* Tokyo's Olympic Security Command Center is described in Eva Kassens-Noor and Tatsuya Fukushige, "Tokyo 2020 and Beyond: The Urban Technology Metropolis," *Journal of Urban Technology,* published online July 1, 2016, https://doi.org/10.1080/10630732.2016.1157949.

150 *Oh Soo-hyun shared a name with a doctor in a Korean soap opera:* There really is a South Korean television drama with a doctor named Oh Soo Hyun. The Dr. Oh depicted here, however, is a fictional homage to the real Dr. Terafumi Sasaki, who was profiled in John Hersey's *Hiroshima* (New York: Alfred A. Knopf, 1946).

152 *With more than 72,000 hospital beds:* The statistics in this section are drawn from Oh Youngho, "Optimal Supply and the Efficient Use of Hospital Bed Resources in Korea," Working Paper 2015-21, Korea Institute of Health and Social Affairs, 2015.

7. FUMBLE

164 *After reassessing the status of North Korea's nuclear development:*
The 2017 reassessment of the size of North Korea's nuclear arsenal is detailed in two news reports from August of that year.
"The analysis, completed last month by the Defense Intelligence Agency, comes on the heels of another intelligence assessment that sharply raises the official estimate for the total number of bombs in the communist country's atomic arsenal. The United States calculated last month that up to 60 nuclear weapons are now controlled by North Korean leader Kim Jong Un." Joby Warrick, Ellen Nakashima, and Anna Fifield, "North Korea Now Making Missile-Ready Nuclear Weapons, US Analysts Say," *Washington Post,* August 8, 2017.
The low end remained at thirty: "Some US assessments conclude North Korea has produced or can make around 30 to 60 nuclear weapons, said two US officials who weren't authorized to discuss sensitive intelligence matters and demanded anonymity." "Estimates of North Korea's Nuclear Weapons Are Difficult to Nail Down," *Associated Press,* August 18, 2017.
North Korea could be adding as many as twelve nuclear weapons a year to its arsenal: "Sources have told *The Diplomat* that the DIA assesses North Korea, given its current uranium enrichment activities, is likely capable of generating an additional 12 weapons worth of fissile material a year. The DIA assessment of 60 weapons assumes the use of composite pit core designs for nuclear bombs by North Korea; composite pits combine plutonium-239 and uranium highly enriched in uranium-235, the two fissile material isotopes suitable for nuclear bombs, to more efficiently design bombs." Ankit Panda, "US Intelligence: North Korea May Already Be Annually Accruing Enough Fissile Material for 12 Nuclear Weapons," *Diplomat,* August 9, 2017.

165 *The estimate that increased the number of North Korean nuclear weapons . . . had even been leaked to the* Washington Post *in the summer of 2017:* Warrick, Nakashima, and Fifield, "North Korea Now Making Missile-Ready Nuclear Weapons."

167 *"It was built of four and a half feet of steel and concrete":* Donald Trump, as quoted in Tom Junod, "Trump," *Esquire,* January 29, 2007.

170 *"Kim's missiles keep crashing":* Jeremy Scahill, Alex Emmons, and Ryan Grim, "Read the Full Transcript of Trump's Call with Philippine President Rodrigo Duterte," *Intercept,* May 23, 2017.

Mike Pompeo . . . had figured out . . . how to carefully move the goalposts by referring to North Korea's ability to build a reliable ICBM: See, for example, Pompeo's remarks at the Foundation for the Defense of Democracies 2017 National Security Summit, held on October 19, 2017.

171 *"We have missiles that can knock out a missile in the air 97 percent of the time":* Glenn Kessler, "Trump's Claim That a US Interceptor Can Knock out ICBMs '97 Percent of the Time,'" *Washington Post,* October 13, 2017.

176 *The current plan, OPLAN 5015, was a preemptive attack:* Park Byong-su, "S. Korean and US Militaries Draw up a New Operation Plan," *Hankyoreh,* August 28, 2015.

"The nuclear weapon's only good against cities": Interview with General Charles Horner, commander of the US Ninth Air Force, conducted by *Frontline/BBC,* c. 1995.

177 *"No one advanced the notion of using nuclear weapons":* George H. W. Bush and Brent Scowcroft, *A World Transformed: The Collapse of the Soviet Empire, the Unification of Germany, Tiananmen Square, the Gulf War* (New York: Alfred A. Knopf, 1998), 463.

When Mattis was out of government, he worked closely at Stanford with George Shultz: Paul Sonne, "How Mattis Changed His Mind on Nuclear Weapons," *Washington Post,* February 5, 2018.

178 *"I don't think there's any such thing as a tactical nuclear weapon":* Aaron Mehta, "Mattis: No Such Thing as a 'Tactical' Nuclear Weapon, but New Cruise Missile Needed," *Defense News,* February 6, 2018.

8. A WORLD WITHOUT NORTH KOREA

189 *Kim Jong Un . . . knocked it down:* Curtis Melvin, "Kim Il Sung's Hyangsan Palace Demolished: Building Kim Il Sung Reported to Have Died in Razed, Replaced with Young Trees," *NK News,* April 24, 2014.

In 2019, Kim ordered the construction of a magnificent new palace: The construction of the palace is a fiction, but the construction of the airstrip is real. James Pearson, "The Flying Marshal: North Korea Builds Private Runways for Plane-Loving Kim," *Reuters,* August 19, 2015.

190 *Admiral Philip Davidson was the commander of US Pacific Command:* The depiction of Davidson is based on Gordon Lubold and

Nancy A. Youssef, "Likely US Pacific Commander Has Spent Little Time in Asia," *Wall Street Journal,* March 2, 2018.

191 *popular with the press and fawning politicians for his blunt remarks:* Jane Perlez, "A US Admiral's Bluntness Rattles China, and Washington," *New York Times,* May 6, 2016.

The Chinese government in particular reportedly had sought Harris's removal: "China Urged US to Fire Pacific Command Chief Harris in Return for Pressure on North Korea," *Kyodo,* May 6, 2017.

Although some found Harris undiplomatic, Trump did not: Gerry Mullany and Jacqueline Williams, "Trump's Pick for US Ambassador to Australia Heads to Seoul Instead," *New York Times,* April 24, 2018.

In one case, the phrase caused a minor panic: Dan Lamothe, "'Fight Tonight'? Explaining Trump's Retweet That Says US Bombers Are Ready to Strike North Korea," *Washington Post,* August 11, 2017.

193 *It turned out that Iraqi units, facing heavy bombardment, had simply deserted their equipment:* Perry D. Jamieson, *Lucrative Targets: The US Air Force in the Kuwaiti Theater of Operations* (Washington, DC: US Air Force, Air Force History and Museums Program, 2001), 90–91.

194 *"reduce the US mainland into ashes and darkness":* "KAPPC Spokesman on DPRK Stand toward UNSC 'Sanctions Resolution,'" KCNA, September 13, 2017.

203 *The phrase came up again and again in interrogations:* The quotation and a story about its meaning told by a North Korean defector named Kim Hyun Sik appear in "The Secret History of Kim Jong Il," *Foreign Policy,* October 6, 2009.

209 *the United States could not confirm that even a single one of Saddam's Scuds had been destroyed:* According to an official postwar assessment, "there is no indisputable proof that Scud mobile launchers—as opposed to high-fidelity decoys, trucks, or other objects with Scud-like signatures—were destroyed by fixed-wing aircraft." Thomas A. Kearney and Eliot A. Cohen, *Gulf War Air Power Survey: Summary Report* (Washington, DC: US Government Printing Office, 1993), 89–90.

210 *"In the end . . . the best one can say is that some mobile launchers may have been destroyed":* This sentence is from an official post–1991 Gulf War assessment cited earlier also asks: "How effective were such efforts? It is hard to say in a tactical sense; the evidence of how many mobile Scuds and their launchers Coalition air attacks destroyed or damaged remains spotty. It does appear that a number

of tanker trucks on the way to Jordan or Basra paid a severe price for having infrared signatures resembling mobile launchers; some Bedouins also may have paid a similar price for having elongated, heated tents in the desert blackness that looked like canvas-draped Scuds. *In the end, the best one can say is that some mobile launchers may have been destroyed.* Although Iraqi launch rates of modified Scuds —particularly of coordinated salvos—dropped over the course of the campaign, and while mobile Scud operations were subjected to increasing pressures and disruption, most (and possibly all) of the roughly 100 mobile launchers reported destroyed by Coalition aircraft and special operation forces now appear to have been either decoys, other vehicles[, or] objects unfortunate enough to provide Scud-like signatures" (emphasis added). Thomas A. Kearney and Eliot A. Cohen, *Gulf War Air Power Survey: Operations Effects and Effectiveness,* vol. 2 (Washington, DC: US Government Printing Office, 1993), 189.

211 *"Those guys were like cockroaches":* Tom McIntyre, as quoted in William L. Smallwood, *Strike Eagle: Flying the F-15E in the Gulf War* (Sterling, VA: Brassey's, 1997), 138.
"It's a huge flame and your first reaction is that it's a SAM": McIntyre, as quoted in Smallwood, *Strike Eagle,* 138.

9. WHEELS UP

214 *For the invasion of Iraq, the Navy moved more than 56 million square feet of cargo:* The statistics and comparison are to be found in D. L. Brewer III, "Operation Iraqi Freedom—Clearing the Hurdles," *SEALIFT,* June 2004.

215 *North Korea was targeting Texas because of its excellent business climate:* Katie Glueck, "Perry on Why N. Korea Targets Texas," *Politico,* April 3, 2013.

219 *We did tests, the foundation is anchored into the coral reef:* Donald Trump, as quoted in Tom Junod, "Trump," *Esquire,* January 29, 2007.

221 *"There's no big red button to put that [interceptor] in play":* Colonel Kevin Kick, as quoted in "Inside the Gates: Alaska's 49th Missile Battalion," *KTVA,* January 18, 2018.

<?> *The panel proposed replacing the system in Alaska entirely, calling the defense it offered "fragile":* "The ground-based interceptors (GBIs), as part of the GMD system deployed at Fort Greely, Alaska (FGA), and Vandenberg Air Force Base, California (VAFB), evolved to their current configuration through a series of decisions

and constraints. They provide an early, but fragile, US homeland defense capability in response primarily to a potential North Korean threat." Committee on an Assessment of Concepts and Systems for US Boost-Phase Missile Defense in Comparison to Other Alternatives, *Making Sense of Ballistic Missile Defense: An Assessment of Concepts and Systems for US Boost-Phase Missile Defense in Comparison to Other Alternatives* (Washington, DC: National Academies Press, 2012), 130–131.

mocking the "hobby shop" approach of the people who built it: "MDA's [Missile Defense Agency] efforts have spawned an almost 'hobby shop' approach, with many false starts on poorly analyzed concepts. For example, analysis of successful programs with missiles of comparable complexity—that is, with the comparison costs at a similar point of development maturity and at 2010 dollars—suggests that the current GMD interceptors are approximately 30 to 50 percent more expensive than they should be at this point in the program." Committee on an Assessment of Concepts and Systems, *Making Sense of Ballistic Missile Defense,* 11.

In nearly twenty years of testing, the system had worked only nine out of eighteen times: Sydney Freedberg, "GMD Missile Defense Hits ICBM Target, Finally," *Breaking Defense,* May 30, 2017.

223 *"It's stupid":* David Willman, "Trump Administration Moves to Boost Homeland Missile Defense System Despite Multiple Flaws," *Los Angeles Times,* December 24, 2017.

But tests were expensive, costing nearly $300 million each: George Lewis, "How Much Do GMD Tests Cost?" *Mostly Missile Defense,* December 28, 2012.

One document plainly admitted that the "deterrence value" of the system was "decreased by unsuccessful flights": US Department of Defense, Missile Defense Agency, *Final Report of the Missile Defense Agency's Independent Review Team (IRT),* 2005.

224 *"It assumes that the failure modes of the interceptors are* independent *of one another":* James Acton, as quoted in Kessler, "Trump's Claim That a US Interceptor Can Knock out ICBMs '97 Percent of the Time.'"

"If there's a foreign object in one unit, it's sort of whistling past the graveyard": David Willman, "There's a Flaw in the Homeland Missile Defense System. The Pentagon Sees No Need to Fix It," *Los Angeles Times,* February 26, 2017.

226 *"give us a limited capability to deal with a relatively small number of incoming ballistic missiles":* The quote is from actual secretary of

defense Donald Rumsfeld during a December 17, 2002, briefing at the Department of Defense.

"The method used by the Army to assess warhead kills": This quote is a passage from actual testimony by Steven Hildreth, a researcher at the Congressional Research Service, who independently reviewed the data provided by the Army on the performance of the Patriot missile defense system in the 1991 Gulf War. Congressional Research Service, "Evaluation of US Army Assessment of Patriot Antitactical Missile Effectiveness in the War against Iraq," testimony prepared for the House Government Operations Subcommittee on Legislation and National Security, April 7, 1992.

227 *"normally a protocol no-no"*: Andrew Card, speaking about September 11, 2001, as quoted in Garrett M. Graff, "'We're the Only Plane in the Sky,'" *Politico*, September 9, 2016. Many of the following quotations about Air Force One, as cited, are in fact real recollections of real people from September 11, 2001. Notable as source material in this regard is Graff's excellent oral history of the day, as published by *Politico*, as well as an account by Mark Tillman, the pilot of Air Force One that day, that appeared in Dennis Wagner, "On 9/11, Air Force One Pilot's Only Concern Was President Bush's Safety," *Arizona Republic*, September 11, 2011.

"My boss ... called and told me to depart as soon as the president got on board": Tillman, as told to Wagner, "On 9/11, Air Force One Pilot's Only Concern Was President Bush's Safety."

"They were drooling all [over] the luggage": Sonya Ross, speaking about September 11, 2001, as quoted in Graff, "'We're the Only Plane in the Sky.'"

228 *"It was a full-thrust departure ... up like a rocket"*: Tillman, as quoted in Wagner, "On 9/11, Air Force One Pilot's Only Concern Was President Bush's Safety."

"We were climbing so high and so fast": Ellen Eckert, speaking about September 11, 2001, as quoted in Graff, "'We're the Only Plane in the Sky.'"

10. BLACK RAIN

230 *Their voices can convey what our words cannot*: The survivor stories are, in fact, accounts from the Hibukasha-Japanese people who survived the bombing of Hiroshima and Nagasaki in 1945. The translations have been lightly edited in this text. The testimonies presented in this chapter are largely drawn from interviews pre-

sented in the television program *Hiroshima Witness,* produced by the Hiroshima Peace Cultural Center and NHK, Japan's national public broadcaster. These interviews were translated into English by the college students Yumi Kodama, Junko Kato, Junko Kawamoto, Masako Kubota, Chiharu Kimura, and Kumi Komatsu, who were advised by Laurence Wiig, and they are now posted at the Atomic Archive. Condensed versions are also available on the website of the Hiroshima Peace Memorial Museum: http://www.pcf.city.hiroshima.jp/.

234 *"There was the flash and darkness":* Testimony of Tomiko Sasaki, one of the Hatchobori Streetcar Survivors, *Hiroshima Witness.*

"It was like a white magnesium flash": Testimony of Akiko Takakura, *Hiroshima Witness.*

"When the blast came, my friend and I were blown into another room": Testimony of Akira Onogi, *Hiroshima Witness.*

"I was at the window when the flash went off": Testimony of Kinue Tomoyasu, *Hiroshima Witness.*

235 *"I cried out, and as soon as I did I felt weightless, as if I were an astronaut":* Testimony of Hiroshi Sawachika, *Hiroshima Witness.*

"I'd never heard the word 'decapitation attack' before": Ari Fleischer, speaking about September 11, 2001, as quoted in Graff, "'We're the Only Plane in the Sky.'"

236 *"That was our Pearl Harbor":* Paul Germain, speaking about September 11, 2001, as quoted in Graff, "'We're the Only Plane in the Sky.'"

"They broke for commercial. I couldn't believe it": Fleischer, as quoted in Graff, "'We're the Only Plane in the Sky.'"

237 *"I saw a young boy coming my way":* Testimony of Kinue Tomoyasu, *Hiroshima Witness.*

239 *"I looked next door and I saw the father of a neighboring family standing almost naked":* Testimony of Akira Onogi, *Hiroshima Witness.*

"I really thought I was dying because I drank so much water": Testimony of Hiroko Fukada, *Hiroshima Witness.*

241 *"Communications systems were overwhelmed with traffic":* Tillman, as quoted in Wagner, "On 9/11, Air Force One Pilot's Only Concern Was President Bush's Safety."

242 *"We felt terribly hot and could not breathe well at all":* Testimony of Hiroko Fukada, *Hiroshima Witness.*

243 *"I still felt very thirsty, and there was nothing I could do about it":* Testimony of Akiko Takakura, *Hiroshima Witness.*

"The houses on both sides of the railroad were burning": Testimony of Akira Onogi, *Hiroshima Witness*.

"I could see people running in the dark": Testimony of Takehiko Sakai, *Hiroshima Witness*.

244 *"The fire and the smoke made us so thirsty"*: Testimony of Akiko Takakura, *Hiroshima Witness*.

246 *"It was all quiet and the city was wrapped, enveloped in red flames"*: Testimony of Takeo Teramae, *Hiroshima Witness*.

"I was pushed into the river with many other people": Testimony of Hiroko Fukada, *Hiroshima Witness*.

"An awful thing happened when I reached the other side, and was relieved": Testimony of Hiroko Fukada, *Hiroshima Witness*.

"The water was swirling around me, and later I learned that was a tornado": Testimony of Hiroko Fukada, *Hiroshima Witness*.

247 *"Later on in the evening, when we were sitting around without having much to do"*: Testimony of Takehiko Sakai, *Hiroshima Witness*.

"When controllers asked if we were aware of an unidentified plane bearing down on us": Tillman, as quoted in Wagner, "On 9/11, Air Force One Pilot's Only Concern Was President Bush's Safety."

"Air Force One has defenses to protect against attack": Tillman, as quoted in Wagner, "On 9/11, Air Force One Pilot's Only Concern Was President Bush's Safety."

249 *"It was very, very hot"*: Testimony of Keiko Matsuda, *Hiroshima Witness*.

"There was a sticky yellowish pus, a white watery liquid coming out of my daughter's wounds": Testimony of Kinue Tomoyasu, *Hiroshima Witness*.

250 *"There were too many people"*: Testimony of Akira Onogi, *Hiroshima Witness*.

251 *"I felt someone touch my leg. It was a pregnant woman"*: Testimony of Hiroshi Sawachika, *Hiroshima Witness*.

"It was on television. I saw it": Donald Trump, defending the false claim that "thousands" of Muslims cheered on September 11, 2001, as quoted in Glenn Kessler, "Trump's Outrageous Claim That 'Thousands' of New Jersey Muslims Celebrated the 9/11 attacks," *Washington Post*, November 22, 2015.

252 *"As military trucks came into the city, they started loading bodies into truck beds"*: This quote is adapted from a poem, "The Remains of Uncle Yataro," by Kikuko Otake, who was five years old at the time of the Hiroshima explosion in 1945 and who later wrote a book of poetry that retells the recollections of her mother Ma-

sako (*Masako's Story: Surviving the Atomic Bombing of Hiroshima* [Tokyo: Ahadada Books, 2007]):

> *As military trucks came into the city,*
> *[they] started loading bodies into a truck bed.*
> *First, three soldiers tried to lift a burned body,*
> *but they dropped it to the ground, losing their grip,*
> *when the skin sloughed off.*

"*When I came to, it was about seven in the evening*": Testimony of Yoshitaka Kawamoto, *Hiroshima Witness*.

253 "*ordinary people saved each other*": The quotation is, in fact, by a survivor of the September 11, 2001, terrorist attacks, Robert Snyder, as quoted in Michael Keller, "New York Stories: An Oral Historian Takes on 9/11," *Atlantic*, September 7, 2011.

254 *The construction of a new command center at Offut alone had cost $1.2 billion:* Steve Liewer, "Work on New $1.2 Billion Strat-Com HQ Will Soon Enter Phase 'Fraught with Risk,'" *Omaha World-Herald*, February 14, 2017.

255 "*One of the awkward questions we faced . . . was whether to reconstitute Congress after a nuclear attack*": This quote describing the decision-making is from an actual "continuity of government" exercise during the Reagan administration. James Mann, *Rise of the Vulcans: The History of Bush's War Cabinet* (New York: Penguin, 2004), 141–142.

257 *Staff had sometimes joked that Hicks was the "real daughter*": Michael Wolff, "'You Can't Make This S—— Up': My Year inside Trump's Insane White House," *Hollywood Reporter*, January 4, 2018.

"*When a bad story would come up, she would volunteer*": Former Trump campaign senior communications adviser Jason Miller, as quoted in Eleanor Clift, "How Hope Hicks Became the Ultimate Trump Insider," *Town & Country*, February 2, 2018.

"*She's like a security blanket for the boss*": An anonymous "person who speaks to the president," as quoted in Emily Jane Fox, "'She Is Like a Security Blanket': Hope Hicks, the Linus of the West Wing, Delivers a Devastating Blow to Trump," *Vanity Fair*, February 28, 2018.

258 "*There was nothing in the world like her*": "Donald Trump singled out a 'young socialite' at his club at Mar-a-Lago by telling a reporter [Michael Corcoran with the now-defunct magazine *Maximum Golf*], 'there is nothing in the world like first-rate pussy.' . . . Corcoran used the quote as the kicker in his piece, but says it was changed by the editor in chief, who replaced the obscenity with the

word 'talent.' Joe Bargmann, Corcoran's editor at *Maximum Golf*, confirmed Corcoran's account. 'I was asked to change the last word of the story from 'pussy.' When I refused, my top editor changed the quote,' Bargmann told The Daily Beast." Brandy Zadrozny, "Trump Bragged: 'Nothing in the World Like First-Rate P**sy,'" *Daily Beast*, November 29, 2017.

CONCLUSION

259 *All told, nearly three million people died in the span of about for-ty-eight hours:* All casualty estimates were created using Alex Weller-stein's "Nukemap" website: https://nuclearsecrecy.com/nuke-map/.

260 *The public health implications of entire populations with com-promised immunity are wide-ranging and severe:* Jennifer Leaning, "Public Health Aspects of Nuclear War," *Annual Review of Public Health 7* (1986): 411–439.

262 *more than 80,000 federal jobs were located in northern Virginia and the area was home to more than 100,000 federal workers:* The statistics are from the FRED data provided by the Federal Reserve Bank of St. Louis and the US Office of Management and Budget (OMB).

263 *which in turn is believed to be responsible for the famines that have struck Africa, South Asia, and China over the past few years:* All sta-tistics are derived from Ira Helfand, *Nuclear Famine: 2 Billion Peo-ple at Risk?* (Washington, DC: Physicians for Social Responsibility, 2013).

264 *with the costs associated with rebuilding Manhattan alone esti-mated at between $15 trillion and $20 trillion:* Estimates are derived (and adjusted for inflation) from Barbara Reichmuth, Steve Short, Tom Wood, Fred Rutz, and Debbie Schwartz, "Economic Con-sequences of a Radiological/Nuclear Attack: Cleanup Standards Significantly Affect Cost," Pacific Northwest National Laboratory, 2005.